WINDS OF LIFE
THE BENEDICTION OF PAUL
BOOK ONE

PATRICIA MCCLURE

WAYZGOOSE PRESS

Cover Design by Getcovers

Edited by Maggie Sokolik

ISBN: 978-1-961953-15-4

V5312024

We learn from stories.
To the greatest storyteller I know, my husband, Wally.

CONTENTS

CHAPTER 1
SAINT ALBERIC'S MONASTERY

Psalm 64: 3
To you we pay our vows.
You who hear our prayers.

On a crisp March morning, in the darkness before sunrise when nature alone stirs, Father Joannicus Brookes rose after a fitful sleep. His black habit was chilly, waking his sleepy body as he quietly crept from the monastery to the church. He chose the connecting hall rather than suffer the wind with its hint of snow. Moving swiftly and silently, he prepared for the best hour of his day, where not even heavy thoughts of the night could reach him. Morning prayers would begin soon, with the ringing of the bells. He and his confreres would gather to recite the psalms. This Benedictine ritual would continue even after his death.

As he stepped into the sanctuary, his nose filled with the scent of wax and incense, reminding him of the first day he entered the Catholic church. He had been a Baptist then. Peace embraced him like a lover. The flicker of candlelight guided his way from the atrium into the church proper. In the dimness, he glided to his assigned monastic seat, a haven away from the worldly woes that haunted him. He breathed deeply, releasing the rumbles of his mind. Although plain and sturdy, the cushioned chair was as comfortable as a feather bed. The large room caressed him in warmth. He tucked his hands under his scapular, the long piece of cloth hanging from his shoulders to the floor like a tapestry covering his chest and back. He closed his eyes and relaxed as if sinking into a hot tub. His heart and soul swelled with God's touch.

An earthshaking thud ripped Joannicus from his cocoon. He whipped around to see if the walls still surrounded him.

Two novices ran into the church and skidded to a stop.

"Oh my God, did you see that? I'm going down there."

Joannicus made a soft noise of displeasure. They were talking before the nightly silence officially broke.

The shorter one took a step closer in the dim light.

"Father Joannicus, the barn just collapsed. We're going there to help."

The taller one elbowed and hissed, "May we?"

Joannicus nodded as they hurried away. The taller one stopped and turned. "Aren't you coming?"

"Be right there," Joannicus responded.

He waited. The wind howled, causing him to shudder. Joannicus despised the cold, so he would stay and pray instead of running to help.

The bells did not ring that morning, for the novices had forgotten their duty in their excitement. That word had haunted him all night. What was his duty? As a professor of theology, he had a teaching job, but his responsibility was to God. He marveled. How easy it was for some to forget why they gathered in the dark. He rose, made his way to the atrium, and stood at the large window, viewing the farm and graveyard—a blending of life and death. The pre-dawn snow blew sideways as he bit his lower lip.

When he entered the monastery of Saint Alberic's at age 18, he knew the will of God. He would dedicate his existence to prayer, and God would take care of the rest. From the window, he watched the glow of lights and the black dots of monks, moving like ants on ice cream. He worried that the world, like the weather, would refuse to keep its distance. He said softly, "Don't concern yourself about money, what to eat, or where to sleep."

Worry would not step away. The college's financial troubles had crept into his office on official letterhead, requesting him to teach without salary. The Dean of Theology teaching for free rankled him. He had no problem with doing charity or the work of God.

What bothered him was the double standard, the presumption that monks didn't need cash. That stung like the winter wind. Monks had expenses, too. They may follow a Rule written in the Middle Ages, but they had bills like everyone else. He didn't take a vow of poverty, but he lived frugally. Benedictines took vows of obedience, conversion, and stability. The Catholic Church did not subsidize monasteries. They stood alone. The monks had to support themselves by earning money.

Monks survived by teaching. One less paycheck put a chink in the monastic budget. Older monks needed hip replacements, ancient tractor parts broke, and now, apparently, a barn was without walls. There were no answers in the freshly fallen snow.

Have faith; God will provide.

He stared at his reflection in the window. The sound of footsteps alerted him that the other monks were arriving. The outside doors opened, and winter rushed in, bringing in two snow-haloed co-eds. The hike from the dorms put a rose color on their cheeks. They looked very alert for this early hour, a look they lacked in the afternoon during his class. As the monastery's Guest Master, he knew it was his responsibility to sit with them. They would take this simple act of hospitality and turn it into favoritism. *Why were they here?* Joannicus consoled himself, knowing that next week, they would pursue a different activity.

Hopefully, one that didn't involve him.

The girls glowed and giggled.

They are not here to pray. These same students twittered during class about how handsome he was. Father Dimples with the curly hair. He frowned. If only he could not blush when he heard them outside his office discussing the curls on his head that refused to stay put, no matter how short he kept it. He couldn't wait until he was gray and bald.

"The barn collapsed," spoke one girl.

He reconsidered his decision to stay warm, thinking that if he'd gone to help, he wouldn't have had to endure this.

He couldn't call them women. They were babies in a woman's body.

"It is time to pray. Please take a seat behind the left choir," Joannicus said.

"Where's the choir?"

He glanced at the monks sitting opposite each other in three rows. Wasn't it obvious? Hadn't they been listening in class when they talked about monastic life? Joannicus slipped his hand into his pocket and gripped his rosary. "Two rows behind the monks."

They stood smiling like sheep waiting for grain. He led the girls inside, knowing that their presence would be a challenge because of the distraction. Prayer began with the acolyte's voice speaking the first words of the day: "Oh Lord, open my lips." The monks responded, "And my mouth shall sing your praise."

Attendance was sparse. Joannicus surmised that the unusual events caused monks to skip morning prayers.

Nothing is more important than praying. Thank God we are all alive.

Midway through prayers, most of the community had arrived, some wet, others disheveled from sleep. Brother Ambrose lumbered into the church, last and late. His presence gave Father Joannicus hope. The farm was this man's life, and seeing him arriving at morning prayers spoke volumes about the importance of praying. The giant monk's shoes squeaked loudly, adding a counterpoint to his heavy breathing. Snowflakes clung to his massive beard as he sat two chairs away from Joannicus and the girls, leaving his usual place empty.

The smell of wet wool and tobacco drifted towards them. The girls covered their noses.

Thank you, Lord, thought Joannicus. The odor of Ambrose as he unthawed would cause these hyper-hormonal women to think twice about coming tomorrow.

After prayers, Joannicus left the students in the atrium, drawing his hood over his head. He hunched against the cold and hurried to catch the community as they walked from the church to the refectory. A small group stood bundled tightly together, watching the monks file past them as if counting train cars. Joannicus assumed they were lawyers or bankers from their formal attire and briefcases. He hoped they were just lost and missed the signs to the town. The business offices did not open for another hour. Worrying about the college's financial future made his stomach squelch the hunger he had felt moments before. He did a reverse turn, jogged to his cell, gathered his leather satchel, and headed down the hill to his office. What could he do to produce money? The darkness of the question dulled his heart.

His hands were too soft for farm work, his mind too active to tailor. They could open a hotel or a restaurant. Perhaps he could make beds and serve food.

The sturdy brick building of the college glowed with brightness in the pre-spring morning. The wooden floors groaned and creaked as he walked to his office on the third floor. Soon, the halls would echo with student voices, reminding him of the other world, the one that he had successfully escaped.

He had only two skills–teaching and praying. Who would pay him to pray professionally? Today, he did not want to be instructing the hungry youth. He wanted to wail like the wind into God's ear.

After teaching, he returned to his office, a long, narrow room much larger than his monastic cell. An oaken desk midway separated the space. He had placed a sturdy wooden chair in front of the desk for those times that students insisted on speaking with him. Unfortunately, the pupils were more like starfish than hummingbirds. They clung to him after class.

I am only here to lead you to God, thought Joannicus. The hungry minds did not understand. That was how an old greenish sofa, worn-out chairs, and coffee-ringed end tables brought on the backs of healthy young men ended up in this space. The faded cushions begged 'to come, relax,' and yet, Joannicus knew no rest. The struggle for salvation required constant vigilance. As cliché as it was, the devil did not sleep. Therefore, he daily fretted over the souls of his pupils.

Toward the back of the office stood two eight-foot bookshelves, sagging with volumes of words. They needed a good dusting and purging. Even uplifting phrases could block God's soft, intimate voice that caressed his heart.

The vast arched window complimented the tall ceiling and gave the room a sense of grandeur. Joannicus stood looking out at the snowy hilltop. He'd removed the blinds the day he moved in so nothing would obscure his view of the monastery.

The clock inched as he glanced from his essays to the window. A frozen plant on the sill reminded him that his other plants needed water. He pulled his woolen sweater sleeve down to cover his icy fingers. The radiator hissed in protest as he fiddled with the knob. He climbed onto the arm of the sofa and stretched to turn on the fan that perched atop the bookshelf. That would move the air from the high ceiling to the earthly space where he sat. His hands refused to warm.

Today, he wondered why he had picked a monastery in Montana when there were many Benedictine houses in southern climates. Next winter, he would ask for retreat work in the south. The papers on his desk fluttered, calling for his attention, insisting on his guidance to correct and give hope and insight. He admired the floral handwriting but could not bring himself to read the words. Something was lacking in him, making him hollower than hallow inside.

He needed to reconcile preaching and teaching. Nobody pays a man to preach, so maybe teaching could be the same as saving souls.

His classes were the first to fill, and often, he had students in attendance who had neither paid nor registered.

When three o'clock arrived, Joannicus hurried up the hill to the monastery. The walk didn't take long, but he shivered with cold. He stopped in the community room for a moment to check his mailbox. He glanced at the chalkboard that had reminders of changes to the routine of monastic living, grateful that nothing had changed. He gathered his memos, hoping for a quick exit, his joy tangible as he thought about the upcoming hour of solitude.

This place looked like any institutional gathering space, with several sofas and overstuffed chairs, tables with puzzles, and shelves with games, missing only a droning television. But today, the area was a labyrinth of distractions. As he walked through the room, the kitchenette, with its tiled counter and large coffee urn, beckoned him to have a cup of warmth on this dreary day. The stone fireplace blazed as a reminder that spring was still sleeping. He moved closer to it for a few minutes of comfort.

"Oh, Father Joannicus," Brother Mellitus called, eyes twinkling with excitement. "This is our Guest Master. He's the one who'll see to all your needs, wants, and desires. Even tuck you in and read you a bedtime story. The man is full of stories, a parable teller like his Savior."

Joannicus gave him a quizzical look. Besides Mellitus, only Brother Moses stood nearby.

"Brother Mellitus, have you been sniffing the wine? Seriously, I'm sure Brother Moses knows who I am. Thank you for the compliment." However, he knew it to be a slur.

"I was talking to our guest. Apparently, you've been once again pretending you're a hermit rather than taking hospitality to its fullest. The Abbot's been looking for you all afternoon."

Joe's patience waned, and the clock continued to tick. He took several steps toward the exit. "The Abbot knows my schedule. Since when is Brother Moses a guest?"

Brother Moses lifted his scapular to reveal a curly-haired boy who looked as if he'd stepped out of the pages of Sears and Roebucks: polished shoes, pressed slacks, and a tie complete with a tie tack.

"So, Holy One, what do you think, a miniature of you? I thought you were alone all those late nights in your office. Guess you've got some explaining to do."

Father Joannicus drew a sharp breath. The accusation of sin

reddened his cheeks, though he was innocent of the crime. Brother Mellitus always liked to point out one's humanity and the potential for failure as a monastic.

Years of contemplative living curbed the defense forming on his lips. He frowned. The child stuck a thumb in his mouth and slid back under the scapular.

"Come on. Even Brother Moses thinks there's a familial resemblance. We were wondering who the mother was and didn't say Mary. That story has already been told. Admit it, the boy looks like a little Joe."

The boy had curls and brown eyes. The comparison was a cruel joke. Mellitus would not ruin his day.

"I'm not Joe. My name is Paul," a muffled voice said from under the thick black cloth. "Paul Warner."

"Seriously," Joannicus said. "Let's go find your parents and get you settled in."

"I think you're it," Mellitus said, still amused by his observations.

Father Joannicus's shoulders dropped. Like a bear thwarted from nocturnal rest, he hugged the crumpled mass of papers in his arms.

"Father," Moses said. "Perhaps you need to read the Abbot's memo about Paul."

"Memo?" Joannicus said, his heart pleading that he didn't have time for this.

Brother Moses pulled out the message from the notes that Father Joannicus held.

"Alone? All week?" Joe's voice dipped, and the child eyed him from the folds of black cloth.

"I'm sure Abbot Gordon has a plan," Moses said. Mellitus laughed.

What was the Abbot thinking? Oh, dear God, it seemed too simple, too obvious.

His mind whirled.

"If you will come with me, please," Joannicus said, wanting to run away. "I'll show you to your room."

Joannicus picked up the small green suitcase and hurried out the door. Paul ran to keep up with him. The three-story guest-house stood dark and empty across the courtyard.

They entered, and Joannicus murmured a prayer, "I'm coming, God," feeling the pain of a young lover missing the sight of his beloved between classes.

"Who are you talking to?" Paul asked.

"God."

"God is here? The man with the necklace is looking for him."

"That's called a pectoral cross. The Abbot is not searching for God. He has found Him."

"Oh," Paul said. "Is that why I am here? To find God? Does he like to play hide and seek?"

The child had misunderstood. Was there any point in explaining? Joannicus knew nothing about children, and this one would go soon enough. He unlocked a door with the plaque that read Saint Placid. "Here's your room." *Placid.* Perhaps this space would instill calmness into the boy.

The modest space held two single beds, each with a handmade quilt, a sink, a writing desk, and an oversized reading chair with a colorful woolen wrap draped across the back. Father Joannicus placed the suitcase on the chair.

The child lingered in the doorway and asked, "Is that your bed?"

"No."

"Mama and I share a bed. She's very sick. She sleeps a lot. I was very sad. Now she's awake. The lady sometimes lets me see her, but not today. Today, she brought me here. She was very, very mad." Paul ran to the window. "I like your house. How come you wear a dress?"

The child was not Catholic-born. Not knowing how much to explain, Joannicus said, "This is my uniform. It's called a habit."

"The lady said habits are bad, like picking your nose. Where are your toys?"

"No toys, but here's some paper," Joannicus said, pulling the desk drawer open. "You can draw a picture."

Paul looked at the pencil. "Don't you have colors?"

Joannicus glanced at the clock, forty-five minutes until Mass. "Colors? What's wrong with black and white?"

"This is just gray," Paul said.

Joannicus's jaw clenched as he felt a surge of anger. *Remember, he is a child.*

The expectant big brown eyes stared at him.

Joannicus searched for a pen. The memo on the top of his papers caught his attention again: *"Everyone should spend time with Paul, for this may be the answer to our prayers..."*. He shook his head.

"I want to play hide and seek." Paul raced past Joannicus and tapped him. "You're it."

"Hold on," Joannicus said, finishing the memo. Paul's mother, Sarah, was offering him to the monastery. People didn't do that anymore. That happened in the Middle Ages when the nobles would send their children to become serious scholars. Now, only eastern monasteries took in minors, and not just one–hordes of them.

Joannicus shook his head. She would give them $1.5 million to raise her son. The arrangement involved the monks alone, with no nanny and no boarding school.

What a frightening concept.

Why didn't she make this offer to a convent? Women were

better with children. They had a week to decide. The desperation of the deal frightened Joannicus.

"Paul?" Joannicus called, his voice trailing down the silent hall. After checking both bathrooms, he headed to the kitchen and refectory.

The bells for Mass beckoned. Joannicus felt the tug to turn and dash to the church. His heart ached. His hour had evaporated. On the lower level, the smells of dinner filled the hallway. Although Lent meant meager and meatless meals, the aroma appeared sinful. His mouth watered. *Is it a sacrifice to eat gourmet meals during Lent?* He pondered this as he entered the kitchen.

A balding man smiled, and his face wrinkled in pleasure in the nearly spotless space.

"Missing something, Father?"

"Did you see our young guest?" Joannicus asked as his stomach growled in anticipation of a second meal.

Brother Barnabas tossed his head and pointed to the end of the counter. There Paul sat, nibbling a slice of freshly baked bread.

"Mark this day, the first time the Guest Master lost our visitor."

"I didn't lose him. Technically, he didn't stay put," Joannicus said, attempting a harsh look at the child.

"Children usually don't, Father."

"I got hungry," Paul said. "I came to what smells so good. Mama said mammasteries are closer to heaven, and we both agreed that heaven has the goodest food."

"This is a monastery, and we have the best food. Thank you, Brother Barnabas. Mr. Warner, it is time for Mass. Please follow me."

Paul laughed. "Nobody calls me that. You're silly."

After placing Paul in a chair inside the church, Joannicus hurried to the vestment room and glanced at the words over the door:

As for me and my house, I will serve the Lord.

Once vested for Mass, Father Joannicus peeked into the church and noticed that the seat assigned to Paul lacked his presence. Joannicus walked slowly to take his place in line as the community assembled for Mass, debating if he should search for the child.

Serving wasn't hard, just all the other stuff.

CHAPTER 2
GUEST MASTER

Psalm 100: 6
*I look to the faithful in the land,
that they may dwell with me.*

"Son of a bitch," Paul said.

Father Joannicus felt his ears turning red. He feared the people waiting for Mass to begin would overhear the conversation. He took the child back to his seat twice with instructions to sit and stay. His childhood puppy was more obedient than Paul. Joannicus made his way through his confreres as they stood preparing to process into the church for Mass.

"Child," Brother Ambrose said, shaking a massive, calloused, stained finger. "We don't talk like that."

Father Joannicus paused momentarily, wondering if he should pretend he missed what Paul said. He watched Brother Mellitus wipe a tear of laughter from his cheek with his sleeve and hand Paul a piece of candy.

"Seriously, Brother Mellitus," Joannicus scolded, suspicious of how much coaxing had gone on.

"Don't oppose the will of God, Father," the white-haired monk said. "Remember what happened to those who did. Jonah, Pharaoh, and Saul, they all got theirs."

Joannicus placed a firm hand on Paul's shoulder, herding him away. "How do you know this is God's will?"

"How do you know it isn't?"

The organ music started. Father Joannicus waited as his confreres in liturgical robes filed past him in procession to begin Mass. Impatience trickled into his heart.

"He wanted to know a bad word. I was..." Paul said.

"Shush, you need to be quiet now. Behave and don't leave the church."

Paul's lower lip quivered as he melted onto the floor. Even Joannicus guessed what would happen next.

Father Jacob Mackenzie Knows the Song stood behind Joannicus, giving him finger horns. Paul's tears evaporated. Was Jacob losing his mind, or was this the man's first miracle? Father Jacob stood out even in a crowd of black robes. He was tall, native, and the only monk with a braid. Paul rose from the floor and ran after him. The principal celebrant cleared his throat a few feet from the entrance to the sanctuary. Jacob stopped and tiptoed into the church. Mesmerized, Paul followed his lead.

Dear God in heaven, give me patience, Father Joannicus prayed as he entered the church, slightly embarrassed but thankful that the child was not wailing in competition with the organ.

They placed the child in a chair behind the community. Tuesday afternoons brought only a few devoted people to the church for services. Before the homily began, Paul had moved from the third row of chairs to the fifth. Joannicus watched the child making his way counterclockwise in the octagonal space.

Normally, his focus was on the altar. Did all children misbehave at Mass? He was the guest master, not a babysitter.

A novice returned to his seat as Joannicus realized he had missed the reading for the day. Paul moved from the seats to the windows framed in rich dark wood. In between the panes were rectangles of stained glass. The child giggled as he peered outside.

Paul continued to tiptoe around the octagonal church. He stopped and looked at the child-size statue of Saint Alberic, which stood next to the tabernacle chapel. Father Joannicus held his breath as Paul fingered the wooden saint's scroll, hoping the figure would not topple over.

Finally, the action at the center of the room attracted the child's attention. The principal celebrant stood before the wooden altar, and the priests co-celebrating with him formed a semi-circle around him.

Why weren't they distracted? He certainly was.

The altar was so large that it took four monks to move it. Thankfully, they only did that with the change of each liturgical season. It was the season of Lent, and the church lacked flowers, but a blue cloth fell softly to the floor, covering the altar and making it the focal point of the room and season. Joannicus followed the movement of his confrere and struggled to find his place in the Eucharistic prayer. He scanned the room for Paul. His anxiety rose.

He's not my responsibility, Joannicus chanted to himself. The voices and rhythms of prayer drew him to concentrate on the consecration at the altar until he saw green socks peeking under the tablecloth. He glanced at Jacob, who instantly avoided his gaze. Someone needs to get the child. *It should be Abbot Gordon,* thought Joannicus, panic growing. He feared Paul would pull the cloth, sending Jesus tumbling to the floor.

Paul crawled out from under the table and stood next to the celebrant. The boy's eyes barely peeking over the top of the altar.

"Whatcha doing?"

"Celebrating," the priest said. Amusement wrinkled his face as he poured the wine from the glass curette to the silver chalice.

"Is that Kool-Aid?"

Someone snickered. Father Jacob spoke part of the Eucharistic prayer, and Paul ran up to him.

"Who you talking to?"

"God," Jacob answered, but to Joannicus's ears, it sounded like a question rather than a firm belief.

"Which one is he?" Paul asked, looking at the semi-circle of robed priests.

Father Jacob's weight shifted from one foot to the other.

Brother Mellitus laughed and spoke up in the silence. "He isn't one of them."

At least nobody said He isn't here.

As the monks moved one by one to receive communion, Joannicus kept one eye on the wandering child and watched him crawl back under the altar. After receiving the body and blood, Father Joannicus quickly bent down and lifted the blue cloth. The child sat bathed in indigo light.

"You found me. You're good at playing hide and seek."

"Child, come with me, please." His words clipped as he controlled his growing rage.

"Are we done? Hey, I can do some *karot-tee*. Wanna see?" Paul jumped in the air and swung his arms in a chopping motion. "Hi ya." Then he stood facing Joannicus and angelically poised. He bowed.

Brother Mellitus clapped. "Jesus and a show, bravo."

Father Joannicus felt as if he was living in a circus tent. He frowned as he changed his robes, robbed of the invitation to love and serve the Lord, and miffed that someone hadn't stopped the boy from interrupting Mass. Making a guest behave was not the Guest Master's duty.

If he stays, he will be someone else's responsibility. No, he can't stay. We have important things to do, like teaching and praying. A child would disrupt that.

Father Joannicus left the church, walking across the courtyard to the refectory, as Paul darted past him. This child was a pagan and in constant motion. One problem was utterly treatable, but the other, slowing a child down, he knew nothing about.

"You're it," Paul said, tagging a random black robe and disappearing into the building.

Father Joannicus saw Father Jacob sitting on the bench outside the refectory's hallway. The monks stood waiting for Abbot Gordon to lead them to dinner.

"What are you doing this evening?"

Father Jacob shook his head. His long black braid snaked its way out of his cowl.

"You are the Guest Master. It is just a child."

"What do I do with him?"

"Turn him loose in the community room after dinner. It is the will of God," Jacob said, pointing upward.

Father Joannicus watched Paul weave his way through the sea of black robes.

"We gonna eat? I..." Paul stopped and looked up at Father Jacob. "You're an Indian. You look different from other Indians. You got pretty blue eyes, but that's not right."

It amazed Joannicus how much Paul learned, heard, recorded, and reported. The talent was remarkable but dangerous. This child among them could upset the balance of silence and discretion.

"I am Apsáalooke. I like blue, so I stole them. Want them back?" Jacob said, opening his eyes wide.

The child backed away. "*Eww*, no, thank you."

Father Joannicus whispered to Father Jacob as they entered the refectory. "Come to the guest dining room and eat with me, please?"

"It is Lent. I need the penance." An impish smile appeared on his face.

Father Joannicus shoved his hand into his habit pocket and fingered his rosary. Penance? As a parish monk, the man ate alone. Then it became clear. The penance came by eating with a group of monks who ate in silence.

The guest dining room held two tables set for four people, with tablecloths and linen napkins. The dishes matched, and the silverware had 925 on the underside. Joannicus liked the little rose patterns that reminded him of the flatware he grew up with as a child. Joannicus lost his appetite as Paul fingered and played with his food.

He doesn't even know that the cloth napkin has a purpose. Six days, it's only for six days. This is ridiculous. We shouldn't be considering purchasing a child for our financial gain. It's not even worth—he could not finish the thought because Christ's words came to him. "Suffer the children to come to me."

After dinner, Joannicus took Paul to the community room. This space was like a large living room with comfortable sofas and chairs. A fireplace and kitchenette sat on opposite walls of the room, and several tables held jigsaw puzzles and shelves filled with books and games. Tonight, all the monks gathered to see the boy and assess the proposal. Paul seemed reluctant to leave his side and tried to disappear into the folds of his habit. Joannicus tried to extract Paul, but the child clung to the black cloth like a tether. Joannicus towed the boy towards a table.

"Well, well, look who blesses us with his presence," Brother Mellitus said from his wheelchair. "And he has brought little Joe."

"My name is Paul." Quickly, the child tried to hide under Joe's scapular. They wrestled for a moment with the length of the material, and Paul finally settled, peeking around the voluminous black skirt.

"Shoo," Mellitus said to Joannicus with a wave of his bony, pale hand. "Isn't someone's mortal soul in need of redemption?"

"Want to play?" Brother Moses asked, his cherub face lighting up as he handed Paul a red checker.

Paul shrugged his shoulders and put a thumb in his mouth. Joannicus moved away from the clinging child to an empty chair.

"It's easy. You distract Moses," Mellitus said, pointing to the outside. "Whoa, is that a burning bush? Then you jump his pieces." He moved two red pieces off the board.

Moses turned back to the game, unaware of the cheating. "No, you don't do that."

Mellitus winked at Paul. "Do you want a cookie?"

Paul smiled and nodded. Jacob leaned over Moses and moved a red checker, ridding Mellitus of one of his newly crowned kings. Mellitus slapped Jacob's hand.

"Get the boy a cookie, Moses," Mellitus ordered.

Brother Moses frowned. "Oh, Brother Mellitus, it's Lent. There are no cookies."

"Lent, shment. Look in the big red pot. There is a complete box of Oreos. Besides, Lent doesn't apply to children. The Rule says to let them eat."

"Before the regular meal," Jacob said. "Not after. Besides, he just ate dinner."

"He's our guest," Mellitus said, taking two more pieces and

crowning several of his black pieces. "You should read the part of the Rule on hospitality."

Joannicus sat at the table and pulled his briefcase in front of him. "And you, Brother, should re-read Chapter 4, The Instruments of Good Works."

"Oh, gang up on an old man. Thank you very much," Mellitus said. "My day is complete. I've heard from the good and the bad. Now, where's the ugly?"

Joannicus scanned the room for Brother Ambrose, who usually played checkers with Moses. Perhaps with the barn trouble, he had more work. A tinge of guilt ran through him. Farm work sounded better than babysitting.

Father Jacob came over to the table with the proposal. "Do you think the Abbot is serious?"

"And why the hell not?" Mellitus said, banging his fist on the table.

The sound caused Paul to jump and run over to Joannicus.

Moses flushed pink. "The Abbot said to keep an open heart."

"We aren't set up for children," Jacob said gently, folding the paper into an airplane.

Paul awkwardly tried to climb into Joe's lap, who instantly became uncomfortable with the familiarity. This child could not stay with them. Who'd care for him? The Abbot? The Novice Master? He shot a quick prayer to God, not the Guest Master.

"I'd enjoy a little brother to share my wisdom with," Moses said.

Mellitus shook his head and said, "If you had any wisdom to spare. Besides, we're set up with a farm. It's sufficient for most of our members."

Why was this man so caustic—and to Moses, of all people?

Mellitus looked like a harmless old man, with soft white hair, but he was not. Joannicus winced as he recalled how Mellitus made his novitiate a living hell. The old monk apologized. "I was just preparing him for his afterlife." The man's wit had more barbs than a porcupine.

Joannicus pulled a stack of student papers in need of grading from his leather satchel. "You seriously can't all think this is a viable solution."

Paul sat perched on Joe's knee and reached for the glass vase in the center of the table. His fingers barely touched the edge. Joannicus pulled him back and placed a blank sheet of paper in front of him.

"I think we should suggest that the Abbot get a puppy. Shorter life span and more easily trained," Father Jacob said, sailing the proposal transformed into a paper plane across the room.

Brother Mellitus laughed.

Paul rummaged through the satchel, pulled out a pair of scissors, and cut the papers in front of him.

"Those are my papers, and that's not safe," Father Joannicus said, taking the scissors away.

Paul reached for the sharp ends. "I know how to cut."

"Not with those. You could cut your finger off, bleed all over the floor, and I lost my thread and needle, so I won't be able to sew them back on," Father Joannicus said, hearing his father come out of his mouth.

Paul studied Joe's face and then laughed. "No, I wouldn't. Mama said I could."

Joannicus put the scissors away.

"I suppose we could adjust. This isn't right. We are Benedictine. God has to come first. Nobody is more important. This is all ridiculous."

"I find a child's life far from ridiculous," Moses said in almost a whisper as they watched Paul stamp 'property of Reverend J. Brookes' on his forearm and hand.

22

"His life is for sale," Jacob said as Father Joannicus snatched the stamp from Paul. "What else do you call the offering of money?"

Brother Moses looked at each of them. "They presented it well in the legal proposal. It's not a sale."

The group stared at Brother Moses.

"You read that?" Joannicus said, impressed that Moses even understood the lengthy document. For most of his monastic life, he came across as simple and uneducated.

Paul slid off Joe's lap and retrieved the paper airplane.

"It's her last will and testament. Doesn't that account for something? You pay to adopt kids. It is sort of the same–only she is paying us. He'd be a dorm student, only long-term. We're just guardians. The money's secondary. Where will he go?" Tears glistened in the corner of Moses' eyes.

"Seriously, the same as any other child. There are Catholic couples who'd love to adopt a child."

Jacob shifted in his chair. "We don't get to pick our childhoods. We just survive them."

Brother Mellitus snorted. "Can't you see a miracle when it appears in the flesh?"

Jacob grabbed the remaining cookie on the plate. "I see greed, not very damn miraculous."

Paul made a paper plane from one essay in front of him. Joannicus wrestled it from him, thinking this place was not a proper home for a child.

Brother Mellitus flipped a checker into the air, catching it with one hand. "And at age five, what's the likelihood of his finding a home? It's all about the money. Who better to spend it than us? Think of the good we could do."

Brother Moses sighed. "Do I want to live the rest of my life knowing I sent him away?"

Joannicus pushed the squirming child off his lap. "That's not fair."

Brother Moses smiled. "We're in his life, regardless of if we want to be. It's true–he can spend a week with us, and we can send him on his way. He may never remember a single thing about it. But I will. That's what I have to consider when I make my choice."

The bells rang, inviting them to prayer.

"I miss my mama," Paul blurted out.

Joannicus rose. He had heard enough. A room of monks could take care of one child. Joannicus made his way down the dimly lit hallway, anticipating at least a half hour of solace and bliss.

"Wait for me." Paul's wet hand slipped into his.

"I think you should get ready for bed. I will see you after prayers."

"I want to go with you." Paul's hand tightened on his.

"I'm going to prayers."

"I'm good, it's okay. I want to pray."

Those big brown eyes bothered Joannicus. How could he deny a request to pray?

Paul sat with his thumb in his mouth, leaning heavily against Joannicus for the length of the prayers. Joannicus sat frozen in time, his soul trapped.

CHAPTER 3
BABY SITTING

Psalm 37:18
For I am on the point of falling.
And my pain is always before me.

Father Jacob Mackenzie Knows the Song stomped his feet at the sliding glass doors outside the community room. Brother Ambrose left puddles on the floor, making his way to the coffee urn.

Brother Ambrose handed him a mug. "Thanks for helping me. With only one barn up, things are chaotic and cramped."

"You are welcome. I was up anyway. Dreams. Moose calves born in winter."

"Is that some kind of warning?"

Father Jacob shrugged his shoulders. "It was a dream. A

newborn calf covered in snow. I felt his courage." He could still see the wet, knobby-kneed calf struggling to find its mother.

Jacob turned his head. "Do you hear that noise?"

"What?"

The dream still lingered as Jacob frowned, shaking his head. Was that the wind? He sipped his coffee, holding the mug, allowing it to warm his frozen fingers. The noise, a high-pitched whine like an oil-hungry motor, caused him to put his cup on the counter. The hallway was dark. Jacob looked to the right and left. The doors to the front of the monastery rattled. He went to the iron gates separating the private and public spaces. He moved into the bright entryway, and the cry grew louder. The guest parlors and the Abbot's office lay black. Jacob went to the etched glass front door and opened it. The air burst through, chilling him. A pajama-clad Paul stood there, shivering. Jacob picked up the bare-footed child and hurried to the community room.

Brother Ambrose stood before the fireplace, casting a monstrous shadow across the space. "What'd I tell you about bringing wild things inside?"

"Rose, honestly." Jacob picked up his coffee mug and took a gulp.

"Don't scold me. I'm not the idiot Guest Master or Abbot who knows nothing about children." Ambrose fumbled with the tiny buttons on Paul's frozen spaceman pajamas. "Let's get him warm. They won't give us the millions if we off him before we sign."

Paul's body quaked.

"None of that is funny," Jacob said, wrapping the naked child in a woolen throw and setting him in front of the fire.

"So, do you think what I think about his patronage?"

Jacob chuckled at the malapropism as he thought about Joe hiding behind his office door to avoid female staff and students. "Paternal heritage." The boy looked like a miniature version of Joe, with his curly brown hair and round face. Yet Jacob was sure this was not Joe's son. Joe took his vows more seriously than the Pope.

Paul's teeth stopped chattering. "I closesed the door, and it locked."

Thankfully, the boy remembered where the monastery was, for explaining why a child froze on their doorstep would be difficult.

Brother Ambrose handed the kid his coffee cup.

Jacob snatched it away. What was the man thinking?

The trembling stopped, and the boy grew pink. When he yawned, Ambrose scooped him up and, with great tenderness, tucked him in on the sofa. "Down and under, eyes shut."

Jacob marveled at the magical compliance that occurred. With cups refilled, they both stared at the sleeping child. Jacob's thoughts floated back to the warm little bodies of his children snuggled in sleep next to him. The acid churned in his stomach, threatening to creep up his esophagus. He looked up and saw Ambrose's eyes fixed on him. The bell for prayers cried out in the morning's silence. Ambrose took the mug out of Jacob's hands.

"Come, time to pray."

"What about...?" Jacob nodded toward the placid child.

"He's asleep."

"But what if..."

"Where's he going to go?" Ambrose asked as he lumbered away. Jacob followed, thinking there were many unlocked doors for a small kid to explore, but they would return in thirty minutes after prayers.

Jacob sat, struggling to keep his mind from worrying as the images of children laughing and dying threatened to invade the morning—his offspring. The events of his past seemed like yesterday, and his security felt violated. He breathed deep and slow, letting the smell of incense calm him as he embraced the rhythms of contemplative living. His gaze wandered to the blissful face of Joannicus.

Jacob wished he had that kind of monastic faith.

The monastery was just a Band-Aid, not a blanket, for Jacob. He listened to the click of rosary beads as the demons of melancholy faded.

One of the three novices spoke, "Oh Lord, open my lips..."

Jacob would have preferred the other opening. "Oh God, come to my assistance." He felt a protective salve of routine coat him and hoped it would last until evening. Now he knew why the Abbot summoned him. He could return to Saint Clare's parish, having made a minimal visit. This child was not an answer to a prayer or their financial worries. Jacob's God didn't work like that.

A barley husk plopped onto his psalter, and he turned to his right, watching Brother Ambrose performing his morning ritual of cleaning his beard. Jacob leaned forward and looked to his left. Abbot Gordon appeared normal, but Jacob wondered why the man thought this child solved their problems.

Midway through Psalm 53, Paul entered the church naked. His face flushed with sleep, and he rubbed his eyes in the light's brightness. Father Jacob waited to see if anyone moved. Nobody did. Joannicus had his head bent, and his eyes closed tight. Others appeared frozen.

A whimper echoed in the silence.

"Oh, for pity's sake," Brother Ambrose grumbled as he marched over to Paul.

"There you are," Paul said. "What are you doing?"

"Praying."

"Again? I thought you did that tomorrow."

Ambrose scooped the blanket and child, placing them next to him. Paul's loud sigh filled the silence of the church. Jacob watched the brief struggle between man and boy as the child moved to climb into the big lap.

"I need cuddles," Paul said emphatically. He climbed back onto Ambrose, who shrugged and complied. Paul examined the large man, running a hand over his crewcut and burying his fingers into the massive tangle of beard.

Jacob smiled as the child sat sucking his thumb, calm and content in the huge monk's lap.

At the end of prayers, the monks filed out of the church in pairs. Ambrose carried Paul to the atrium, trying to mummify him with the blanket.

Jacob listened to Abbot Gordon's voice, "Father Joannicus, it's your responsibility to tend to the child while he's in the guest-house. You're the Guest Master."

When Abbot Gordon left, Joannicus turned around and muttered, "Most guests don't require dressing. Where are his clothes?"

Brother Ambrose frowned and headed to the refectory, offering a slight apology, "Sorry, we figured he'd sleep."

Paul ran out the door. The woolen blanket cape flapped in the wind as he went toward the guesthouse, leaving snow prints.

"At least we know he has a healthy constitution," Jacob said. "He got locked out. I guess we are not good with children yet."

"Yet." Joannicus's voice sounded shrill as they headed to the guest house across the quad.

"I cannot wait until Easter is here," Jacob said, knowing the fasting regime that Joannicus had chosen for his private Bona Opera. "You all get so grumpy during Lent. The Abbot discourages excessive fasting."

"Seriously, what have you given up for Lent? And for your information, I'm not fasting." Joannicus opened the door, and Paul ran inside. His wet footprints decorated the hallway floor.

Jacob raised his eyebrows.

Paul knocked on the room door. "Nobody's home."

Joannicus pursed his lips as he unlocked the room. "Sacrificing isn't for the Abbot. It's for the improvement of self."

"It might improve you, but the rest of us suffer."

Paul darted in, and Joannicus stepped back. Jacob stuck his head into the room. The curtains blew frantically through the half-opened window. Both beds showed signs of use, but not for sleeping. The coverlet was draped over the chair and desk, revealing a makeshift cave. The four dresser drawers hung open, with contents neatly shoved to one side.

"Hurricane?" Jacob said.

"Great, this is just great." Joannicus closed the window and turned off the heat. "I don't have time to play Mary Poppins. I'm the Guest Master, not the babysitter. Stop jumping on the bed. Get dressed. How was I supposed to know he needed supervision through the night?"

Paul landed with a thud a few inches from Joannicus.

Jacob smiled. They had a junior Olympian.

"He asks so many questions. How do I explain the difference between a father monk and a brother monk?" Joannicus said as he rifled through the dresser, tossing clothing at Paul.

"A father is ordained, and a brother is not. This is only a visit. We cannot keep him," Jacob said.

Joannicus stood straight. "Seriously, he'll ask what is ordained."

"I will take the child to breakfast. As for the sleeping, my kids slept through the night. Take shifts, as we do with the dying," Jacob said.

The sooner this is over, the better.

Joannicus was unraveling, and it hadn't even been 24 hours. Jacob took the half-dressed Paul by the hand. Shoes are unnecessary, reasoned Jacob, as he wrestled a shirt onto the boy. They headed downstairs, where the monks waited to enter the refectory.

"We will get our food and eat here," Jacob said, opening the guest dining room.

Paul hopped on one foot and then the other.

"Quit."

Paul pointed to the refectory. "I want to eat in there."

Jacob thought for a moment. The monks ate in silence. "You cannot. You are too loud."

"I can be not," Paul said, marching into the refectory. The room was plain, with unadorned wooden tables set for six. The Abbot's table graced one end and the food service at the other. Each monk had his own silverware wrapped up in a personalized napkin holder. The cuisine was always simple, and choices were limited. They never lacked for homemade bread, fresh fruit, and vegetables.

Paul stomped as Jacob scooped scrambled eggs onto his plate. A low growl came from Paul when Jacob placed a slice of melon. Paul slipped into a vacant spot beside Brother Ambrose, daring Father Jacob to stop him. Jacob took the other empty chair. Savoring his coffee, he watched as Paul smashed his muffin. Oatmeal dribbled into Ambrose's beard, and Brother Moses licked his fingers of spilled jam.

Looks like he'll fit in just fine.

Brother Ambrose's chair scraped along the floor as he rose to refill his coffee. With two fingers, Paul wiped the spilled oatmeal from the table, tasted it, and then moved the bowl of oats to his place and ate. Brother Ambrose sat, glanced at Paul, and then glared at Jacob, who suppressed a grin. If Ambrose could speak, Jacob knew he would have said, "You making ME fast, who died and left you, Abbot?"

After the meal, Father Jacob steered Paul to the Abbot's office, but the door remained shut, an unspoken message of do not disturb. Paul rattled the iron gates.

"Who are they?" Paul asked, tracing the edges of the metal angels that adorned the gates.

"Angels," Jacob said, trying to decide what to do with Paul.

"What're their names?"

"Michael and Gabriel."

"What are they doing here?" Paul asked, peering into their hollowed-out eyes.

"Guarding."

"Why?"

"We need protection."

"From who?"

"Elias. Quit already."

"Who's Elias?"

Jacob's chest constricted. The past rushed in—Elias, his dark-haired son, was always full of questions. He blinked, his eyes stinging.

A tug on his scapular brought him back to the present.

"What's wrong?"

"Nothing, just a little lost." People, he needed people. He ushered Paul out the front door into the courtyard. An owl hooted, and Paul whirled around, looking for the sound.

"There it is."

The barn owl blinked from his perch. *You are up past your bedtime, Brother Owl.* Message received, be the silent observer, leave history where it belongs. Jacob breathed easier.

"Phew, what's that smell?" Paul said, spinning like a puppy chasing his tail.

"The brewery. We make beer."

"Mama says beer is bad."

He wouldn't take the child to see the making of Absolution Ale. Too many bottles, and too early for beer samples. Jacob knew he would need redemption in a bottle by sunset. The former Abbot had made a wise choice when allowing the monastery to pursue beer-making. An ale for every sin. Dark ale for mortal sins and pale for venial sins. What could be more marketable? He thought he should tell Abbot Gordon that beer was more profitable than children. They only needed to focus on distribution and move beyond southeastern Montana.

They wandered to the fifth building on the hilltop, which was the tailor's shop. Junior monk Stephen sat at the counter and nodded to Jacob as they entered. The first floor was the gift shop where they sold the weavings they made. Rows of sweaters, vests, hats, and gloves of soft earthen colors, tablecloths, banners, and runners in vibrant, intense reds and oranges contrasted with the dark wooden walls. Bins of rosaries, medals, and holy cards dotted the room. Paul glanced at the displays, then ran up the stairs.

Father Jacob followed. Paul stood with his mouth open, mesmerized by the sights before him. Two monks sat spinning wool. The clicking rhythm reminded Jacob of a tribal drum.

Rows of looms lined the room. Paul looked miniature compared to the large machines. The loom thudded and swooshed with the movement of the shuttle and pedals. Father Cuthbert stopped his weaving and climbed down from his perch.

"This looks like a rainbow room. Mama says rainbows are joy spilling from the clouds."

"Does she now? What else does Mama say?"

"That all is good. She's resting. That's what the lady said. I get to see her soon."

Jacob wondered if that would happen.

"Mama sounds like a smart lady."

Paul pressed his nose against the pristine glass. "Oh, she is.

She teached me everything about stars and rainbows. We're going to see the stars close up. Mama said, when she gets stronger, we can go."

Father Cuthbert handed Paul a mass of tangled yarn.

"How long has she been sick?" Jacob asked. Several working monks paused and glanced tentatively at him, one clearing his throat as if to say, *'Don't go there.'*

Paul shrugged his shoulder. "We play together. I tell her stories and make her laugh and get her water. The visitor lady comes and takes me to the park and brings food."

Jacob guessed a hospice worker. Which meant Mama was not coming back.

Paul wound a loose string of yarn around his arm. "I was in the hospital. You like hospitals?"

Hospitals. Jacob shivered. "No, I dislike hospitals."

"Why?"

"Because people di... because the walls are white," Jacob said. Children didn't need to know everything.

"I was sick, and now I'm better. Mama is just slower." Paul tilted his head to one side. "She was sick before me. She took a nap, but she slept a long time. I got lonely."

The rhythm of weaving stopped. Paul's face sagged, and his shoulders dropped. Jacob bit his lower lip.

"Mama didn't wake up, and the visitor didn't come."

Tears trickled down Paul's cheeks like marbles on a hill. Jacob held his breath.

"I got hungry and ate all the special cookies. I didn't mean to."

Paul cried. Jacob sat on the floor, pulling the child into his lap. His heart ached as he struggled between comforting the boy and flinging him away.

Damn you, God. Do not do this. Do not break my heart again.

He saw it was useless and too late. He knew the ache of love.

34

Paul sobbed. Words could not soothe this sadness. The other monks in the room sat frozen and silent.

Paul breathed more easily, and Jacob wiped the tears with his palm.

"I have some balls of yarn," Father Cuthbert said as he rolled them to Paul.

Paul chased after the balls, finding and tossing them in all directions.

Jacob retrieved several and followed a dozen handprints on the windows to where Paul had stopped. The melting of the fallen snow left brown marks, which made patterns and paths like an etch-a-sketch landscape. The red barns and the collapsed mess became visible in the day's brightness. Jacob could make out the sheep being herded into tents.

"What's down there?"

"The farm."

"Can we go there? I likes animals. Do you got horses?"

"And chickens and pigs, oh my."

The farm was a good idea. Two adults were better than one.

Jacob snatched the moving child just before he darted between the lines of yarn on the loom.

Close call. He was out of practice.

This was more challenging than he remembered. They walked to the guesthouse across the courtyard to retrieve shoes. The hilltop seemed void of monks. Jacob recalled the first day he ventured up the hill from the school below. A step back to a time when life wasn't so hectic. The silence was refreshing. A peaceful purposefulness that rose from the ground like wildflowers. Paul darted fast and then slowed as if racing an invisible friend. Jacob's monastic living was his escape from a life of sadness and loss. Would it be Paul's salvation, too?

CHAPTER 4
DAY IN. DAY OUT.

Psalm 83: 4
The sparrow herself finds a home and
the swallow a nest for her brood.
She lays her young by your altars.

Lunch came, but no Joannicus. Father Jacob took Paul down the hill to the farm. The sun shone brightly, hinting of future days laden with warmth. It was a false promise, for the bitter cold would engulf all as soon as the sun disappeared. Spring arrived in fits on the plains with its snow-blanketed mornings and sunny, hope-filled afternoons. The sunlight uplifted Jacob's otherwise gloomy mood. In one day, the burned wood had disappeared. The place was a buzz of activity, with workers sawing and hammering.

Brother Ambrose moseyed over to Jacob and elbowed him.

"You know, your stepdad has been very helpful in getting this barn erected."

Father Jacob crossed his arms. "Yeah? Well, I am glad he is good to somebody."

"Cute kid, full of life," Brother Ambrose said.

Paul dumped handfuls of grain in the trough as the chickens squawked and fluttered excitedly around him. He then stuffed hay into feeding boxes. The cow snorted, startling Paul, who fell with a thud onto the ground. Father Jacob laughed at the toppled-over boy.

The boy can't stay. The job is exhausting. He remembered parenting and knew he was semi-successful at it. But he was now out of practice.

Paul ran to the yard as the sheep scattered. Scholastica, the Australian Shepherd, circled to keep sheep and child corralled. Ambrose scooped the boy up like a grain sack and slipped a leather harness around Paul's waist. He then hooked one end to the fence post, tethering the youngster.

"Is that legal?" Jacob asked, admiring Ambrose's ingenuity.

"I don't have all day to watch him, and I'm 80% sure the sheep are smarter than him. They'll keep their distance." Paul ran the length of the tether. The ewes kept healthy inches away from him. Scholastica barked warnings at both.

Brother Ambrose walked into the barn and mucked the empty stalls.

"How'd you get stuck with him?"

Jacob stood in the doorway, worried that Paul would somehow escape. "Guess everyone else is afraid of him. There's a new babysitter tomorrow, and I am returning to my parish. Do you think he will get to say goodbye to his mom?"

"I hope so. It's always harder when you don't."

"It hurts either way." Jacob grabbed a shovel.

Ambrose stopped and stood straight, mopping his brow. His eyes narrowed. "Are you doing all right?"

"Yes," Jacob said, avoiding the man's gaze and thankful for the quiet acknowledgment of his suffering.

"Still aches, huh? Okay, dumb question. So, are you voting no?"

"Is there any other vote? I called him Elias this morning. After eight years, I thought I would feel differently, but the emotions spring up like a Fatima miracle."

Both men paused and listened to the lack of commotion. They hurried to the barn entrance. Jacob feared they would find a boy trampled by the sheep–or worse–an empty harness. When they arrived, they found a sleeping child on a bale of hay surrounded by hungry ewes. Jacob worried Paul would get a chill even though he was bundled in a coat and wool cap.

After his nap, Paul stunk like the barn, and Brother Ambrose suggested a bath. They tossed Paul into the truck bed and rumbled up to the hilltop. Jacob watched nervously out the back window as Paul laughed and rolled around.

Brother Ambrose grabbed Jacob's arm as he was about to enter the community room.

"Where are you going? You're doing this with me, like all monastic things. Besides, it's Lent, and you really need to do a little penance," Ambrose said.

"I have not sinned," Jacob said as he followed the man into the bathroom. Jacob filled the tub as Ambrose dumped Paul out of his clothing.

Paul shook his head when he saw the water level. "I gets to have more water than that."

"Really, who says?" Jacob asked, amazed at the child's boldness.

Paul climbed into the tub, pointing to his chest. "Mama lets me full up to here. I want bubbles."

Jacob tapped the top of Paul's head. "Not up to here?"

"Silly, I'm not a fish. I have to have air."

Ambrose laughed and poured a generous amount of soap into the tub.

"What's Lent?" Paul asked, scooping bubbles.

"A time when monks get cranky." Jacob reflected upon Father Joannicus and his zeal. All the monks working to improve themselves made for a sensitive lot. He didn't enjoy visiting during Lent because they tried too hard to be holy.

Suddenly, Paul slid down and ducked his head under the water.

"Child, don't do that," Ambrose said, pulling him up. "I thought you weren't a fish."

Paul laughed. "I'm not, but I can hold my breath."

Ambrose glanced at Jacob. "Did you bring clothes?"

"Me?" Jacob jumped out of the way as a whale-size splash crashed onto the tiled floor. "I told you this job was too hard. I wonder what the woman was thinking."

Ambrose shook himself like a wet St. Bernard. "This is the best place to teach values and morals." The large man stood and wrung out his scapular. "Okay, bath time is over."

Obediently, the child scampered out of the tub and took off running.

"Oh, damn. You better go after him."

Jacob followed the sudsy trail that led into the community room, wondering why he was the one chasing the child. As he stuck his head in the doorway, he heard Mellitus shout, "Run, boy," and saw Paul exiting the other door. The clang of Michael and Gabriel on the iron gates told Jacob that Paul had escaped the building.

Jacob jogged to catch up to Paul, grateful that the youngster was heading toward the guesthouse. Abbot Gordon walked across the courtyard as Paul streaked by. Jacob didn't linger.

Paul ran to the door, pushed the code, and clicked the lock open. With the boy safely inside the building, Jacob waited for Ambrose, holding the door open for the out-of-breath, damp man.

"What'd the Abbot say?"

Jacob grinned and said, "Nothing important, but I bet the child has a monastic schedule tomorrow."

Thump, thump, thud echoed down the hall.

Ambrose headed toward the noise. "I guess, like anything else, there's a learning curve. We'd get the knack. Parents don't have a manual."

"Oh, but they do," Jacob said.

Brother Ambrose looked at him skeptically as Paul bounced on the bed.

"It is just written in a foreign language."

Paul suddenly jumped for Ambrose. Ambrose caught him with remarkable alertness and wrestled him into mismatched clothing.

The child brought joy and a spark of life. Jacob remembered the feeling from when his children were young.

"Rose, do you believe this is the best place for Paul?"

Paul continued to sing and bounce.

"What are we struggling to do here?"

"I do not know," Jacob said sheepishly.

"Oh, for heaven's sake, we're trying to be perfect, good, and saintly. We are all about morals, learning right from wrong."

Committed. They were a mismatched bunch of misfits, except for Joannicus. He embodied the ideal of monastic living. Most barely got beyond the first chapter of the Rule of Saint Benedict.

If he and Faith had died, leaving his children orphans, would he have wanted the monks to care for them? A group of misfit men who accept miracles and relics.

Losing Faith and the children brought a lump to his throat. That wasn't the actual issue. What bothered him was that Sarah Warner had picked Saint Alberic's and dangled money before them.

The bells rang for Mass, calling a timeout from the duties. Jacob sighed. He needed a moment to shore up the cracks in his heart. One day with a child and he had lost ground. His moat of distance was drained.

After Mass and dinner, Paul vanished into the bowels of the community. Jacob savored the peace and soothed himself with Absolution Ale. Paul seemed comfortable and easily distracted with so many to keep him entertained. As he headed to prayers, like a lemming to the cliff's edge, it troubled him, Ambrose's herd-like faith. Who would he have picked to care for his children, given the choice, a choice he would have preferred to the reality he lived with? After prayers, he entered an empty atrium.

Paul ran up to him. "Where'd everyone go?"

"Bed. Monks get up early." Jacob turned, grateful to see Joannicus. "Where were you hiding?"

Joannicus looked down the hall at the dark figures filing silently into the monastery. He ignored Jacob's question. "Where are my confreres?"

"What are *conforevers*?" Paul asked.

"*Confreres*. Fathers and brothers, the community," Joannicus said.

Jacob chuckled at the idea of monks frightened by a four-year-old. He liked Joe's simple answer to the child's curiosity. "Come on, I will help you." He wished he could hide.

Paul ran to the guesthouse. *Where does he get that energy?*

"Are you spending the night with him?" Joannicus asked.

41

Jacob stopped and studied the frantic highway of ants trailing from the wall to the walkway and beyond.

"No, thank you. I am done. Besides, I have ants to count. There's a lot on the sidewalk."

"Seriously?"

Joannicus moved inside as Jacob paused. Animal wisdom was to be heeded. They were a symbol of community, strength, and perseverance. This movement caused Jacob's stomach to clench. Was he part of the community? Would they come together in unity and determination to raise this child?

Joannicus straightened his scapular as if he were preparing to perform an exorcism. "How do I achieve this bedtime thing?"

Joannicus bent down to pick up the trail of clothing across the floor. Jacob's heart grew heavy at the memory of his children bouncing and snuggling on the bed as he settled them down for the night. They had a communal sleep arrangement. Not helpful.

"Tuck him in and read him a story. I am sure he will sleep. He has had a busy day."

"So, I heard."

Jacob tried to look innocent as Paul bounced on the bed, singing, "Bless me, Father, for I have sinned. I have jumped on the bed again. I have learned my lesson, though, so off to a new bed I go."

"I did not teach him that. Rose did." Jacob grabbed the child in mid-leap. "Naughty little boy."

Paul giggled, squirmed, and grabbed his braid, pulling his face close. The youngster smelled of life. Jacob held back his tears.

Joannicus huffed and crossed his arms.

"Read him something? Like what? We don't own children's books."

Father Jacob pulled himself away, placing a hand on the child's curls and giving him a weak smile. "The Rule. That will render him unconscious for sure," he said.

Joannicus pulled a chair next to Paul's bed and reached into his cassock pocket. A worn copy of the Rule lay in his hands. Jacob stumbled for the doorway, using the wall for support as tears raced down his cheeks. He sank to the floor, taking comfort in the words of the Rule of Saint Benedict. "Listen, my son, to your master's precepts, and incline the ear of your heart..."

CHAPTER 5
THE DECISION

Psalm 14: 1
Lord, who shall be admitted to your tent?
And dwell on your holy mountain?

After Sunday Mass, Father Joannicus tried to exit the church, avoiding college females or lonely widows flirting with monks. Spring Sundays were troublesome, for the sun seemed to bring them out as it coaxed the branches to blossom.

"I will protect you," Jacob said as he came up behind Joannicus, wedged between the large philodendron and wall.

He didn't need protection, just an escape route. Father Joannicus didn't understand why students flocked to him. Jacob pointed out his passionate Bible narrations. "You make the stories come alive," he'd said.

Joannicus didn't believe that was the reason. He shuddered. The Bible was a family history. Like the psalms they recited daily, the stories were living, changing words. Words were what life was all about.

"How come you aren't at your parish?" Joannicus asked, worried that nobody was attending to the Catholics at Saint Clare's Parish.

"Rebecca is there. Who is that with the kid?"

Joannicus watched the slender woman wearing a pastel lavender suit with matching shoes march toward Brother Ambrose and Paul. Her pretty face scowled as she untied the boy from the massive monk's scapular. The woman bent to be at eye level with Paul. Joannicus had seen her before on the morning that Paul had arrived and guessed she was from social services.

"How was your visit? Were you a good little boy?" She asked, tucking a lock of brown hair behind her ear. Her sincerity reeked of falsehood.

Joannicus found the question insidious. She wanted them to fail.

"There's a cow. I gots to ride it. It was a big boney cow. And there are chickens and ducks and geeses, but no horses anymore. They have food called oats smeal, and I like it very much, and I got to eat it every day. And I got to ring the bells that call everyone to prayer time, louds, and whispers. And they have a rule of deathly silence. What chapter was that in?"

Brother Ambrose laughed and picked Paul up, tossing him in the air like a rag doll. "It's Chapter 42–no speaking after Vespers. It's called the great silence, not deathly, you silly boy."

Father Joannicus held his breath as the woman removed the giggling and squirming Paul from Ambrose's enormous hands. Joannicus read her face. All she saw was a large, untidy man who endangered a child. She drew Paul to her, gripping his shoulders.

"She's an official something," Joannicus said as the space grew quiet.

Brother Mellitus rolled past them with the speed reserved for a motorized wheelchair, forcing people to jump and move out of the way. He stopped next to Ambrose. Brother Mellitus pulled a lavender aerosol can from the depths of his robes and squirted Ambrose with a flowery air freshener.

"You stink."

The sickening sweet layer was mixed with the tobacco and incense.

"I wanna squirt," Paul said, escaping the imprisoning arms of the woman and climbing into the wheelchair.

"Mellitus," Ambrose said, coughing. "Give me that."

"Hey, it's protection against farters."

Seeing Joannicus, Paul shouted and dove out of the wheelchair.

If it hadn't been for Jacob's swiftness, Paul would've planted face-first on the aggregate floor. Instead, the boy landed in Jacob's arms. Paul wiggled free and bounced first on one foot and then the other, unaware of social protocol. Sweat formed at Joannicus's hairline.

"What on earth is happening here?" the woman asked. Her voice took on a mother-superior tone.

You left him here. What did you expect? Paul held the can, trying to push the button pointed at his face.

The woman's eyes traveled up Joannicus's habit, from his sock-and-sandaled feet to his face. Her face was filled with assumptions, while his flushed red.

Indignation bubbled within him. He was not this child's father despite the similar curly hair. Joannicus grabbed onto the can, but Paul didn't let go. A minor struggle occurred, with Joannicus winning the battle.

"I'm Barb Carr, Paul's caseworker."

"I'm a virgin," Joannicus said, his words hanging in the air like flies on a balmy day.

Joannicus stuffed the can into his cassock pocket. The atrium became suddenly silent, and the holy water fount bubbled merrily.

"I am Father Jacob, and this is..."

"Reverend Joannicus Brookes," Joannicus said, staring at Barb's stylish shoes but holding out his hand. "The Guest Master."

Paul peeked from behind Ambrose, who stood with his arms crossed, which pulled his habit up, revealing sagging red socks on hairy legs.

"I want to see my mama. Are we going to see her now?"

A false smile appeared on Barb's face. A hint of compassion rose in her eyes, and Joannicus winced. The answer was obvious. Sarah Warner had passed away. He remembered the grief that Jacob had experienced when his family had died. That sorrow was so heavy that one could almost touch it. Joannicus felt the urge to run as if military mortars were falling.

Paul crossed his arms. "I want to see her now."

Mellitus backed away, missing toes by millimeters. Joannicus drew in a breath. Any second, Paul would explode. He had seen this sequence of events when they said no.

The woman grabbed Paul's hand. "We can discuss this in the car. Come along." Paul wiggled free.

"I don't wanna go. I want to stay here. I want my mama." Paul sat defiantly on the floor.

Ms. Carr ignored the plaintive plea and headed out the church door to the courtyard as a swirl of snow greeted her.

A throbbing pain filled Joannicus's head. Brother Mellitus rolled away towards the monastery, chuckling to himself. Joannicus stared at him, puzzled. Nothing was amusing about the death of Paul's mother. The howling wind punctuated the silent moment as Father Jacob cleared his throat. The door remained closed. Brother Ambrose ran a rough hand through his bushy beard.

"Ah, dag-nabbit," Ambrose muttered as he grabbed Paul around the waist, heading out as echoes of Paul's protest mingled with the cries of the wind.

Joannicus sat in the community room, trying to read. The wails of the storm reverberated in the silence. Nobody tugged at his robes. There were no yawns or sighs for him to hush, no slamming doors or running feet on the highly polished hallway floors. Only a paper trail of childish drawings left behind by Paul haunted him. Joannicus heard the murmurings of other monks and their desires for fatherhood. He did not share that desire. Paul's visit had proved what he had suspected. Children were noisy, nosy, and a constant reminder of worldly vices.

The echoes of the protesting Paul disturbed him. The orphan youngster filled him with sadness, but he knew parenting was not for him. Guilt tinged his discernment. Should he have helped them take Paul away? He figured Paul would not accept his mother's death gracefully, even though he suspected Sarah Warner had prepared the child. For himself, death wasn't so bad.

He was prepared to go to his heavenly home.

Paul didn't have that knowledge. For some, a heavenly reward didn't bring joy.

Brother Mellitus and Brother Moses entered the room, bickering. Joannicus rose, grabbed his coat, and headed to the frozen outside. The snow had stopped, and the sun strained to warm the earth. He knew the reality of death. In a few years, Paul would not remember his mother. All he could recall of his favorite aunt was the aroma of lilies.

The debate raged in his mind, and he shook his head to dispel the words of his confreres. Moses believed God had given them a message in the scripture at noonday prayers, Second Corinthians 6:18: "Then I will accept you. And I will be a Father to you, and you shall be sons and daughters to me, says the Lord Almighty."

Brother Mellitus had accused the Abbot of picking the reading for the day. Could the old one be right? Had the Abbot picked that reading? It shook his beliefs and filled him with suspicion, and Joannicus didn't like doubt.

His toes ached as he walked outside from the monastery to the church. The cruelty of Mellitus to Moses stung. Moses was kind to everyone. The man's simplicity showed that God didn't just call scholars into His service. However, Joannicus didn't share his desire to have a playmate.

The crunch of snow underfoot felt comforting, as did the gust of warm air when he entered the church. He had an hour before dinner to be alone. He stood at the window, letting the heated air from the vents caress him. His mind settled like the snow covering the ground. If this was God's will, then they needed to talk. He would go to the sanctuary and pray in solitude. That was how he had become a monk—he had spent hours praying in the little Catholic Church on Jean Pierre Street, twelve blocks from the Baptist church his minister father led. Joannicus had grown up Baptist. All religions had rules, many of which said *do not* rather than *do*. He could see that raising a child fell into that category, for he had spent most of his time correcting Paul's actions.

As the day faded, Joannicus watched community members making their way to the refectory. The youngster would grow up alone. Who would guide him? Where were the straightforward answers? But like the sun, those answers retreated from him.

He struggled to decide. In the past, his choices were clear and direct, with no second-guessing the will of God.

The monks gathered for a meeting in the chapter room, a small space resembling a lecture hall with rows of chairs and pilfered pews. These old seats reminded Joe that nothing was useless or outdated. In the monastic tradition, items found a new use, and nothing was tossed out. Several ringer washers had become wool-dyeing vats.

Father Jacob slipped into the seat next to Joannicus with a cup of coffee and a doughnut. "This should be over rather quickly. I hope Abbot Gordon is ready."

Jacob is voting no. He had seen the struggle in Jacob's eyes as he watched Paul. The deaths of his children still caused Jacob pain. *He needs a healing prayer.*

"How do you know that? I haven't decided."

The doughnut hovered between mug and mouth. "Joe, if you choose yes, it will boost the number to three–you, Moses, and the Abbot."

Monks filed in and found places, whispering. Joannicus strained to hear their discussion. He could not read their faces.

Brother Moses sighed as he sat down next to Jacob.

"I miss him," Moses said. His round cheeks looked moist.

"So, was it you who prayed for money?" Jacob asked, putting an arm around the man's shoulders.

"Well, I did sort of," Moses confessed, fiddling with the tissue in his hand. "Rose needs a new tractor."

Jacob laughed. "Might I suggest that next time you ask God to send the money, have Him send it in unmarked tens and twenties?"

Brother Moses punched Jacob's arm. "It's not about that. I like children. They're fun."

"It is about the cash," Jacob said. "Or we would not be here."

Father Joannicus understood money, even though he didn't

want to. *We need the money.* Paul was a financial gain. The abbey couldn't make it on the teaching salaries alone. Brother Mellitus had created a list of everything money could buy, and temptation forced Joannicus to read it. Money would afford him more time in contemplation and conversation with God.

Joannicus thought about the sticky fingerprints that Paul had left behind. The child was messy. He glanced at the pile of dishes still in the sink, waiting for someone else to wash them.

We can't raise a child. We are monks, not social workers. His heart raced, and his breath was labored. *Where are the child's relatives?* Joannicus found playing God with someone's life made him queasy. *Calm down. Would it be so hard? If we all helped, it would not be overwhelming. Stop. The boy is noisy, demanding, and undisciplined.*

Reaching into his pocket, he fingered his rosary.

What if this is God's call? It couldn't be. God didn't toy. The idea dripped with absurdity. The room was filled with conversation and a hint of excitement.

It's ridiculous—as ridiculous as a boy raised Southern Baptist, converting to Catholicism, and becoming a monk. The clarity of the statement caused him to shiver. Miracles happen.

On the whiteboard, Abbot Gordon wrote the first word of the Rule, 'Listen.' The words comforted Joannicus until he asked himself, *am I listening?*

Abbot Gordon addressed the community. Midway through the man's lecture, Father Jacob rose and poured himself a cup of coffee.

"Brothers, we've prayed with open hearts and minds after joining our spirit with Paul. We have a decision to make. Will Paul stay with us, or will we turn him away? I want to remind you that this is a long-term commitment fraught with joy and daily struggles. It will take most of us working and praying together to achieve success. Brothers, let us put our vote to paper, and may God bless us as we make our determination."

Jacob walked past the whiteboard that held the word:

LISTEN

He picked up the pen and wrote:

MONASTERY FOR SALE: $1.5 MILLION

Without turning around, Abbot Gordon said, "Father Jacob, kindly erase whatever you wrote."

"Fine, but it divinely inspired me," Jacob said, writing a different message on the board. The motto of Saint Alberic's Monastery, coined by the saint himself:

'DO BECAUSE IT IS RIGHT, NOT BECAUSE YOU CAN.'

CHAPTER 6
WELCOME

Psalm 22: 6
Surely goodness and kindness shall follow me
all the days of my life.
In the Lord's own house shall I dwell,
forever and ever.

Father Joannicus stood at the monastery's entrance as Brother Ambrose escorted Barb Carr, Paul, and two lawyers across the courtyard. He watched Paul skipping, oblivious to the events that would change his life. The boy did not act grief-stricken. Barb grabbed the boy's hand, slowing him down. Her soft charcoal suit and stern face made her appear matronly, but the deep plum blouse was a hint of sun on an otherwise stormy morning.

Father Joannicus held the door open as Ambrose led the group through the small hallway opposite the angel-flanked gates that protected the cloistered monastery from the public.

"Hi, Gabriel and Michael," Paul said as he waved to the stoic iron angels.

When did they get names? They were generic. He peered closer at them. Had he missed something about them? Paul freed himself from Barb and quickly found a leg within the layers of habit and clung to Joannicus.

"Momma is dead. I don't know what that means." Paul's voice cracked. "The house where I stayed smelled funny. They had tons of kids. The woman yelled at me about starving people in India. I just want to go home." Tears rolled down Paul's rounded cheeks. Joannicus looked at Barb and then Ambrose as his leg dampened.

"Paul," Ms. Carr said in a business-like tone. She stuck out her hand.

Joannicus wondered at her sudden aloofness. Did Paul's cries unnerve her, or was she trying to keep a professional appearance? This grief was normal. Paul's mother had died. Her coldness disturbed Joannicus.

"Ah, you poor boy," Ambrose said, reaching for Paul and whisking him onto his large shoulder. The massive hand thumped Paul's back.

Worried that the man would break a rib, Joannicus reached out and stopped the repetitive motion. Brother Ambrose scowled at him. Paul's sobs became sniffles.

"Please follow me–Abbot Gordon is waiting," Joannicus said. He sensed the tension rising as his cheeks burned. He turned and headed to the Abbot's office.

"Father," Paul said from Ambrose's arm. "People say Momma's in heaven. I don't know where that is. Can you show me the way?"

The expectant brown eyes, hopeful for an answer, tugged at Joe's need to save another soul.

Why is he asking these questions? Was it the Holy Spirit begging Joannicus to act? He was unfamiliar with children, only college students, and they were challenging enough. The child would never understand the theological explanation of heaven. A line of scripture came to him, Matthew 18:10: "See that you do not despise one of these little ones, for I say to you that their angels in heaven continually see the face of My Father, who is in heaven."

Joannicus glanced at Paul, whose wet cheeks glistened. He trembled, wondering if this was the face of God.

Brother Ambrose beamed, waiting for the answer. When nobody answered the child, he scowled. "Certainly, we can show you the way."

The two young lawyers' heads shot up. Their faces filled with anticipation as they turned to look at Father Joannicus. Barb came to a complete stop. Her eyes were wide with disbelief.

"You're taking the boy, aren't you?" she said. Her voice was shriller than Joannicus remembered.

"I believe Abbot Gordon would like to speak to you," Joannicus said. Her perfume, like an invisible cobra, surrounded him.

"Of course we are," Ambrose said. "Why wouldn't we? It's the Christian thing to do."

"This isn't the usual place for children," Barb said. The two young lawyers stood frozen as Joannicus held the office door open.

"Nonsense, all are welcome," Ambrose boomed.

Paul squirmed out of Ambrose's arms

"I don't think you understand the gravity of the situation," Barb said. Her face held a hint of contempt for the enormous, unkempt man before her.

"He's an orphan, and we're taking him," Ambrose said, his eyes narrowed in challenge.

Ms. Carr stood straight and stiff. "You're doing it for the money. Don't deny that. I think there's a better solution."

"Foster care? With a woman who yells about starving children in Africa? Or perhaps place him with someone who would use up all his wealth?" Ambrose snorted.

"India. Where is that?" Paul skipped into the office. The room held several chairs arranged in an inviting circle and a large desk by the window.

"Seriously, the money weighed on our minds," Joannicus said. "Isn't that why Ms. Warner dangled that in front of us?"

The shocked face of Barb Carr caused Joannicus to regret his comment, but there was truth in the statement. Everyone benefited financially from this venture. Ambrose and the lawyers followed Paul.

"I'm sure Ms. Warner felt this would be a beneficial setting for her son, or else she wouldn't have asked," Ambrose said, placing a protective hand on Paul's head.

"A home filled with compassion, understanding, safety, and guidance. She wanted an environment of balance. I believe that's what Ms. Warner said," the blond-headed lawyer said.

"There will be two accounts. We hope we can continue to diversify your account for you," the second lawyer added.

"This is all wrong. A desperate plea from a dying woman. They are men, for God's sake." She disagreed with this arrangement. Her eyes moved from Paul to Joannicus, making a comparison again.

"I'm not the father." Joannicus moved to stand behind the green sofa. "I'm here to save souls."

"So, you say," Barb said, entering the office.

Joannicus shook his head. It was not his son. If it were, he would not abandon him.

"Do not judge what you don't understand," Joannicus said. "I agree with you. This is no place for a child. I want to know why he isn't with his father or relatives. Isn't that the logical choice?"

Ambrose smacked Joannicus on the arm, causing him to wince.

"That's not nice to hit people," Paul said.

"What are you saying?" Barb asked. "Are there deviants here hiding behind closed doors?"

"We're celibate. You have a dirty mind, Missy," Ambrose said as he stood close to her, overshadowing her and smelling like an old bear.

"They are monks," both lawyers said. "Men of God."

Barb whirled around, facing them, daring to turn her back on Ambrose. "Men of God sin, too. There's nothing normal here."

"Well, they have a microbrewery where they make Absolution Ale. It is 'forgiveness in a bottle,'" Lawyer One said. "For every sin, there is ale, a dark brew for mortal sins, amber ale for venial ones. For everyday mistakes, there is the original brew. It seems like someone here has a sense of humor. Ms. Carr, this isn't a prison."

"Just great, a group of humorous alcoholics raising a child," Barb said.

Ambrose began a low growl, and the lawyers took a step back. The door at the other end opened.

"Good day," Abbot Gordon said as he entered the room. "Please, come in, sit. Paul obeyed, climbing into a velvet chair, his feet dangling inches above the floor. Barb and the lawyers filled the empty chairs. Brother Ambrose and Father Joannicus stood on opposite sides of the desk.

Abbot Gordon smiled at Paul. Paul grinned back.

"How are you today?"

"Good," Paul said. "Momma is dead."

"Yes, I heard. I'm sorry. Would you like to live with us?"

Joannicus held his breath. What if Paul said no?

"Momma said I was gonna live here. Cans I have oatsmeal?" Paul asked.

Joe's head snapped up. Sarah Warner knew. A faint trickle of shame pricked him like a needle. *Could this be God's will?*

"Yes," Gordon said.

"Okay, I'll stay."

Abbot Gordon nodded and turned his attention to the adults in the room. "After prayerful consideration, we are honoring Ms. Warner's request."

The attorneys simultaneously snapped open their briefcases and scrambled for the documents. Father Joannicus felt light-headed.

What if we mess this up?

"Are you sure?" Barb asked as the lawyers gave her a wide-eyed stare of disbelief.

"Certainly," Abbot Gordon said, taking a seat as the lawyers arranged papers before him.

Joannicus watched the birds at the frozen feeder. Just like them, he felt thwarted from his heart's desire. He could change his stability to another Benedictine house. He liked the Gethsemane monastery. He could become retreat master for the monastic communities. They had requested him. He counted the number of monasteries and was up to 49 when he realized he could expand to the women's houses.

"Where's my room?" Paul asked, tugging on Joe's sleeve. "Father, are we going to be roommates?"

Beads of sweat formed on Joe's forehead as Barb's eyes opened wide. Her mouth moved, but the words seemed to stick inside.

Ambrose scooped Paul off the chair and set him down on the floor. "No, no, Little One. That was because you were a guest. You're one of us, and you get your very own cell."

"Cell? Take me there." Barb demanded.

"Can't, no women allowed," Ambrose said, stepping toward her, daring her to move around him.

Paul pouted. "I don't like to sleep alone."

Barb grabbed Paul's hand.

"You'll adjust," Ambrose chirped, taking Paul's other hand. "Let's find your cell– er, room."

Visions of Solomon flashed in Joe's head, the story of dividing a baby between two warring parties.

"Do I have to wear black? I like pink. Can I wear pink?" Paul said, looking from one adult to the other.

"This is a good thing," Ambrose said, leaning inward, inches from Barb's face.

She didn't appear the least bit fazed. "Says whom?"

The Abbot and the lawyers looked up.

"We need your help," Abbot Gordon said. "Let me explain a few things. A cell is just a bedroom with no locks or bars. It's not a prison cell."

"Raising a child isn't... this can't happen... I mean, there are no rules to guide you. You're not prepared," Barb said, dropping Paul's hand.

"Fear not. All things are possible with God's help." Gordon's voice was soothing as he moved from his desk to put a comforting arm around Barb's shoulder. "And with your guidance, I'm sure we can work this out."

We have a Rule, thought Joannicus, and he bit his lip to prevent that piece of wisdom from escaping his mouth. The Rule of Saint Benedict had guided lives for centuries, old and young alike. The Abbot has a plan. Father Joannicus wanted to hear the details.

Brother Ambrose had already escorted Paul out of the room.

Father Joannicus winced at Barb's look of piercing sadness and bewilderment. He turned and exited the room, heading toward the doors marked private. Once past the angel-flanked gates, Joannicus breathed more easily, knowing she could not follow them into this part of the monastery.

"That went well," Brother Ambrose said as Paul ran down the dim hallway. "No spilled blood."

"Seriously?" Joannicus said. This woman would not just leave. He had seen that expression on many a determined student. "She'll make Paul her special project and will visit, making all our lives miserable."

Brother Ambrose shook his head. "She has a job and more cases than she can handle."

Paul poked his head out of the cell that belonged to Joannicus.

Father Joannicus opened the door opposite his cell and waved Paul into the room. "She has weekends."

"We're busy on weekends."

Was Ambrose suggesting that he deny hospitality to this woman? They entered Paul's cell. The space was filled with a bed, a desk, a chair, a closet, and a sink. Ambrose pulled the heavy drapes, and sunshine rushed in, making the surroundings even more austere. Paul climbed up on the bed, drawing the bed curtains closed. He poked his head out.

"A tent for me."

Ms. Carr would say 'tomb,' thought Joannicus.

"Father, you worry too much. This is good. He'll adjust. He'll be sad for a while, and, like Jacob, he'll grow accustomed to us."

Joannicus didn't believe that. Jacob grieved for two years.

Ambrose opened a box, took out a soft blue velour baby blanket, and tossed it onto Paul's bed. He then placed the photo of Sarah and Paul on the shelf next to the crucifix. Paul squealed, pulling out a raggedy white tiger, and hugged the droopy animal.

When did the boxes arrive? Joannicus wondered if voting had all been a pretense.

"I miss Momma," Paul said, looking at the picture. Ambrose took the blanket and swaddled Paul like an infant. He sat in a rocking chair that yesterday had been in the community room.

"Some of us went to the apartment where Paul lived. We met the landlady, a pleasant woman. She told us all about what happened. Ms. Warner lapsed into a coma after Christmas. The visiting nurse didn't come until after the holidays." Ambrose lowered his voice. "Paul thought his mother was just sleeping. The nurse found him dehydrated. We should teach him who to call when he needs help."

Paul sniffled, and Ambrose rocked in the chair.

God, that's who we call when we need help. We're doomed. We know nothing about children.

"You voted no, didn't you?" Ambrose asked.

"No, I didn't vote." There, he confessed his weakness, his inability to choose.

A huge smile graced the wooly face. "Not to worry, I voted twice."

CHAPTER 7
MAP TO HEAVEN

Psalm 77: 70-71
He chose David, his servant.
And took him away from the sheepfolds.
From the care of the ewes, he called him.

Father Jacob stood away from the community. The day was bitterly cold as he watched the ceremony and the sobbing child. His heart ached with each ragged breath Paul took as they interned Sarah Warner in the secular section of the monastery's cemetery. He looked several rows ahead, past mothers and sisters of monks, to the row where his wife and children lay. He understood. His family didn't belong there. He hadn't been a member then. The community practiced kindness to a stranger. This tendril bound one to the monastery. The living always came back to visit their dead.

Brother Ambrose carried the limp child up the hill. "There, there, Little One. Things will get better tomorrow."

Would it be better tomorrow? How long would it take? Becoming a monk took four years and a lifetime of adjustments. He looked from Father Joannicus, who appeared born into his habit, to Brother Vincent, all starry-eyed and hopeful. There were still times when Jacob questioned if he was a monk.

The Abbot required that the monks at parishes come home weekly. Today was that day. Two days at the monastery, reacquainting himself with the rhythms of the monastic day. The early rising, the reciting of the psalms with his confreres, community meals, and the silence. He found comfort in the routine of monastic living.

The bells rang for evening prayers. Father Jacob made his way to the church, reflecting on the changes he had seen brought about by a small child. He took his assigned seat in choir, directly across from Brother Ambrose, watching as Paul crawled into the lap of Brother Moses. Father Joannicus frowned, and the creases on his forehead deepened. The boy was quiet. This was good, as Joannicus had complained that Paul was a significant disruption during prayers. They are taking the easy way out. Nobody wanted to take charge. Paul was bright, and his requests soon became demands as he cowed the monks into compliance.

After evening prayers, Jacob made his way down the darkened hallway on the first floor to Joe's cell. He knocked and entered. Like all cells, this room was small. The shelves groaned with books, and the wooden file cabinet lay open with stacked files. His unit was austere in comparison. He moved the folded clothes from the chair to the unmade bed. Jacob turned and suppressed a laugh, seeing cotton balls hanging from Joe's ears. Before he could ask why, a loud wail shook the halls of the otherwise silent monastery.

"What the?"

"Paul," Joannicus said, pushing the cotton tighter into his ears.

"Are you going to help?" Jacob asked, standing up.

"Why? This has been happening every evening."

The wailing grew louder.

"When does it end?"

"I don't know," Joannicus said with a shrug. "I leave, and I go to my office down the hill. When I come back, all is quiet."

Jacob frowned. Now, that was a change. "Are you sleeping down there?"

"Sometimes that child is not a quiet neighbor. If he's not crying, he's singing nonsense songs at the top of his lungs. I've talked to Abbot Gordon. He handed me a book on grief. I need a new cell."

"You are welcome to mine," Jacob said, thinking about the lumpy sofa in Joe's office. "It is not every day you become an orphan. Singing is good."

Joannicus slammed his book closed. Another shriek echoed like a military shell on the land. Paul had seemed content at prayers. The sound was disturbing, and Jacob felt compelled to move toward it.

"Come on, maybe we can help."

Father Joannicus shook his head as Jacob grabbed his elbow.

They entered the community room. Paul sat in the middle of the floor, with an audience of monks forming a semi-circle around him. Brother Moses sat with him, twisting his scapular into a knotted mass of black material.

"Your turn," Brother Ambrose said, nodding towards Jacob.

"Bedtime, little boy," Jacob said, trying to sound authoritarian, figuring this was a ruse, for he saw that Paul's face was absent of tears.

"I want Momma."

Cold, hard reality time, thought Jacob. "She is dead and buried; it is time for bed."

Brother Moses gasped, and Jacob felt a prickle of guilt for his harsh words.

"Wake her up," Paul demanded, rising from the floor clutching his raggedy white tiger, the white spaces almost gray.

"I do not have that power," Jacob said, crossing his arms under his scapular.

"What kind of holy man are you? Merlin said blue eyes can perform the magic. Is your wand broken? You don't need one for the waking up," Paul said as he stood on the sofa to be nose to nose with Jacob. "I woke him up. He was dead, and now he's okay." Paul pointed to Brother Ambrose.

"No, Little One. I was asleep. You woke me up from sleep," Ambrose said, adjusting the belt of his habit, causing his cassock to ride up. "Dead people don't breathe."

Paul flopped onto the sofa with a thud.

"Brother Moses said Mama's asleep in Christ. She's in that box, in the ground. How will she get out?"

All eyes turned to Moses–magic, special powers. Already, the child was confusing faith with fantasy.

"Paul, your Mama is not asleep. That's just a metaphor, a kind way to say she's dead," Ambrose said, picking at a loose thread on his habit, pulling and watching it unravel. Now, his right sleeve was longer.

Paul stood up, hopped off the sofa, and marched over to Brother Moses. He kicked him in the shins. "Mama's dead, not asleep."

Brother Moses cried out in pain. Jacob winced at the boldness and marveled at the community's tolerance of the brazen action.

"I told you not to lie to the boy," Ambrose said as he helped Moses to the sofa.

Paul turned, advancing toward Jacob, who stepped back, bumping into Joannicus.

"That Jesus guy woke up Laser Breath. Can't he wake Mama up? I need her. I want her now. Can we ask Jesus, please?"

"He is dead," Jacob whispered.

Joannicus elbowed him. It was the truth, and he would not take a foot to the shin for a bible story.

"He doesn't live here," Ambrose said as Moses' mouth hung open. "It's too late for this, way past our bedtime. Tomorrow, we will talk."

Jacob glanced at the grandfather clock in the corner. The boy was getting up at six every morning. It was after nine. Most monks went to sleep after evening prayers. Father Joannicus began turning the lights out in the room, a subtle hint to end this nonsense. Monks left in the glow of night lights.

Paul's face scrunched up, and his voice quivered. "I just want Momma."

The few remaining monks stared at the floor in dismay.

"Pick someone else," Ambrose said, his words clipped with frustration.

Paul stood straight. "I want Father Jonah."

Brother Ambrose yawned. "We don't have a Jonah."

Paul pointed. "I want him, Father Jonah."

Jacob coughed. Joannicus shook his head.

"Excellent, go to bed now. Tomorrow, we'll talk more," Ambrose said. He left the room, shedding parts of his habit as he exited.

Paul popped his thumb into his mouth and took the stunned monk's hand. Moses tried to straighten his mangled scapular, and the remaining monks headed to bed. Joannicus grabbed Jacob's arm and steered him down the hall. The possessed child had

66

disappeared. In his place, a complacent one followed the two monks.

Joannicus turned down the sheets on Paul's bed. A fresh scent caressed the room.

"It's not fair. I want to go home. I miss Momma. He's always saying tomorrow," Paul said, climbing into the bed. "Why do you have cotton in your ears? Do you have an earache?"

Joannicus pulled the white stuffing out, refusing to answer the questions peppered at him. He tucked the blanket around Paul and deliberately made the sign of the cross on the child's forehead. Paul fell silent, inserting his thumb and turning away from them.

"Oh, you got the magic touch," Jacob whispered as they left the room.

Joannicus stopped in the hallway. "I'm not the one."

"The one for what?"

Jacob followed Joannicus to his room.

"Seriously, you haven't heard. Caretaker, guardian, keeper, nanny, Abbot Gordon has a short list."

That would never happen. Everyone knew Joannicus didn't want the task.

"Well, it would be convenient. His room is next to yours."

"This is not funny. He doesn't sleep through the night. Nobody hears him crying, which I can't believe. He seeks me out. There are 40 others here. Someone else needs to step up and do the job."

Jacob opened his mouth, but Joannicus continued, "Don't even go there. This isn't the will of God. I understand the will of God. He would never make me choose someone over Him. He wants me to save souls."

Paul had a soul, but Jacob would not point that out.

The cell door opened, and Paul walked in. "Do you have a

map? If you have a map, I won't bother you cuz I can get there myself."

"A map to where?" Jacob asked.

"A map to heaven," Paul said, looking at Joannicus with raised eyebrows.

Joannicus turned away. "Sorry, I haven't been there, so I can't draw you a map."

"Then how does anyone get there?" Paul crossed his arms, taking the ready-to-argue stance.

"It's possible to achieve heaven by going to bed on time."

Jacob tried not to smile at the academic answer. Paul's face scrunched up, and he put his hands on his hips. "You don't know what you are talking about. Christ has died, Christ is raisined, and Christ will come again. But you don't know when—nobody can tell me. I don't believe you, fathers that aren't fathers, bread that is body. How come I can't have a zword. I wouldn't sleep with it. You wait until I learn how to read. Then I'll read that book of answers."

Jacob pushed Paul out of the room, seeing the narrowing eyes and the dull sound of grinding teeth coming from Joannicus.

"It is *risen*, not *raisined*, as in *rose from the dead*. Do you mean the Bible, and it is a book of stories? And nobody has a sword."

Paul sighed. "That big book you have in the church. Merlin told me the truth is in that book. Weren't you listening? You read about the *zword*."

Safely outside of Joe's cell, Jacob recalled the reading at prayers, "Do you mean the knife in Chapter 22 of the Rule, the one about how monks should sleep?"

"Yes, I need a zword."

"No," Jacob said, moving Paul across the small alcove between the two cells.

"Merlin said I'm old enough. He said you lost yours cuz you were always playing with it. I won't do that."

Jacob laughed. Dogma, fantasy, reality, and faith were being thrown into a mixture of a potentially explosive philosophy. He held open the covers to Paul's bed. "Who is Merlin?"

Paul yawned. "The man in the wheelchair. It's really a horse."

"It looks like a wheelchair, but perhaps it is a horse's ass-set," Jacob said, changing the word that almost tumbled out of his mouth. That would get back to Brother Mellitus. Where was the old monk? He wasn't in the community room watching the drama. Jacob wondered if Brother Mellitus had orchestrated the evening antics.

"That's because you're looking at it with your eyes. Use your soul." Paul dove headfirst into the blankets and peeked out at the foot of the bed. "I don't like to sleep alone."

Jacob raised his eyebrows and moved the pillow to where the head was. He noticed someone had placed a colorful tapestry on the wall, filled with angels' faces. Jacob sat in the rocking chair, watching as Paul studied him. As a child, he'd had trouble learning to sleep alone. This memory softened his original thought of staying aloof.

"We cannot sleep with you, but you can sit in my lap if you wish."

Paul needed no further encouragement.

"You know, I would pick someone other than Father Joannicus."

"No. He will do."

"Why him?"

"I like his smile," Paul said as he snuggled close and sucked his thumb. Jacob rocked and closed his eyes against the trickle of moisture that threatened to escape. He missed his children. The pain in his heart pounded. After a while, Paul's breath became soft even as his body weight grew heavy. Jacob moved the limp, sleeping child to the bed. He turned to leave and ran into Ambrose, who handed him several tissues.

Jacob mopped his wet cheeks. *How long had he been standing there?*

"Where's Mr. Compassionate?" Ambrose asked as they walked down the dark hall.

"Brooding."

"Well, he best Christian up. The boy has made his choice." Ambrose stopped, and his face softened. "You're a good man."

"I think the term you are looking for is foolish."

CHAPTER 8
EASTER

Psalm 52: 3
*God looks down from heaven on the sons of men
to see if any are wise, if any seek God.*

Father Jacob stood in the alcove between Paul and Joe's cells. Paul stood with his hands on his hips and his legs spread wide, trying to prevent Jacob from coming in.

"So, where's Father Joannicus?" Jacob said, finding the game tiresome.

"I don't know."

Jacob lifted Paul out of the way as he stepped into Paul's room.

"No."

Paul's voice was far too loud for the monastery hall.

"Morning, Father Joannicus," Jacob said. He noticed several pictures of saints, angels, and icons with bland faces and drippy eyes decorated the walls. Someone was trying to make it feel like home.

"Shh, he's sleeping."

"No, I'm awake. Paul, you need to keep your voice softer when you're in the halls," Joannicus said. He rolled his head from side to side, releasing the kinks.

"You woke him up," Paul said, stomping his foot.

"Are you coming to graze?" Jacob asked, ignoring Paul.

Joannicus frowned and rubbed his face. Jacob had heard the details of how Paul's snoring disrupted the meditative silences of the Easter vigil. When the bells and organ rang out, Joannicus left with a wailing child. Jacob knew this wasn't how Joannicus intended to celebrate the most sumptuous feast in the Christian calendar.

"Give it 365 days, and Easter will come again. If it makes you happy, I will co-celebrate with you this evening."

Joannicus stood, scooping up his liturgical robes. "384 days."

"What?"

"384 days. Seriously, Easter came early this year and is late next year."

"I am disturbed that you know that," Jacob said.

"So, where's that Jesus guy, anyway?" Paul asked, pushing his way between the two monks.

"This is a celebration of His resurrection, not His Second Coming," Joannicus said, the sarcasm missed on the child. He crossed the small alcove into his cell and tossed his robes on his unmade bed.

"So, he's not visiting today? But it's Easter," Paul said with a big smile, digging through a stack of clothing.

"I heard he upstaged the Lord," Jacob said.

"He ruined... never mind." Joannicus yawned and marched down the hall toward the community room.

The room had been transformed into a smorgasbord of baked treats, candied fruits, and sugary desserts. This day offered the opportunity to eat until dusk. At noon, the wine, meat, and cheese would appear. The feasting would continue until evening, when lamb and roasted vegetables would add to the full bellies of the monks.

Paul ran outside and scanned the yard, diving under bushes and turning over stones. Then he searched the community room, opening drawers, peeking under cushions, and behind books.

"What'd you lose, Little One?" Ambrose asked, helping himself to a second cinnamon roll.

"Nothing," Paul said, scratching his head.

Father Jacob spent the day enjoying his confreres, for today they were jovial and relaxed. Jacob liked this part about monastic living when they came together to celebrate. It reminded him of tribal gatherings, with their smiling faces and delicious dishes.

At dusk, they sang Easter prayers in the church and walked to the refectory for a special dinner with conversation, a welcome change from the silent meals. Jacob sat with Ambrose, Joannicus, and Paul, whose voice rose and fell with excitement about the day's events. After forty days of starkness, Jacob had to admit that the Easter celebration glowed.

After supper, Jacob took a short walk around the grounds. The sun setting brought a quick chill to the air, reminding all that spring was still in its fledgling stage. He returned inside to a glowing fire. Jacob sat on the sofa and reached for a piece of homemade baklava. Brother Ambrose poured sweet wine into his glass. The man tossed his head toward the sour-faced Joannicus.

"Lent is over," Ambrose said.

Jacob smiled when Paul ran into the room dressed in his spaceman pajamas. His suggestion of a bedtime routine seemed to work for everyone.

"Father Jonah, is today Easter?"

"Yes, all day," Joannicus answered, his voice ragged with irritation.

Paul leaned on Ambrose, who dipped a slab of gooey Easter bread into cocoa, offering it to Paul.

"Are there two Easters?"

"No, only one," Ambrose said. "I don't think we could survive the forty-day preparation twice yearly."

Paul pulled the massive, bearded face so that their noses met. "Are you sure?"

"Yes, Little One, I'm sure." Ambrose placed cookies before Paul, who licked his gooey fingers before grabbing an oval cookie.

"Oh," Paul said, biting a white puffball. "But today is Easter, right?"

"Seriously, everyone has answered that question a million times now," Joannicus said through clenched teeth. "Why do you keep asking that?"

"Because it doesn't feel like Easter," Paul said, wandering away, renewing his search through the community room. Joannicus looked questioningly at Ambrose, who shook his head and shrugged his shoulders.

Jacob asked Paul what he was looking for.

"I'm looking for Easter eggs. Did you find them all?" Paul crawled from under the table, placing his hands on his hips. "You supposed to share. Saint Benedict says so."

"There are no Easter eggs," Joannicus said. "Seriously, eggs aren't a part of Easter."

Paul laughed. "Yes, they are."

"We had eggs for dinner," Ambrose said, licking his fingers.

Paul scrunched his nose. "You're supposed to find them first."

Joannicus rose, walked to the kitchenette, and put his glass away. "Easter isn't about eggs. It is about Jesus. I told you the story about him. Don't you remember?"

"Yes, I know that. But doesn't the Easter bunny hide eggs here, like he did at my house? Mama got a white bunny and me a brown one. We'd eat the ears and tails."

"Paul, there is no Easter bunny," Joannicus said.

Jacob walked to where Joannicus stood and elbowed him before shaking his head, fearful of the drama he knew would follow at the revelation of Jesus replacing the Easter Bunny.

Paul's eyebrows knitted together. "You mean he just doesn't visit here?"

"No, he doesn't exist. It is just a story we tell children," Joannicus explained in a gentler tone.

Ambrose hid his face in his hands.

"I'm a children," Paul said, his jaw jutted out.

"Yes, I know that, but seriously, we don't do eggs, bunnies, or ducks."

"Are you sure?"

"Yes."

"Oh." Paul's lower lip stuck out as he put down his half-eaten cookie.

Brother Ambrose groaned and tossed a cookie in Jacob's direction. It bounced off his chest and landed on the counter, breaking into pieces.

"What do you want me to say? Joe's a liar? We just forgot to give the Easter Bunny your new address," Jacob said, feeling sorry for all of them.

Paul sniffled loudly and ran to the door.

"Where are you going?" Joannicus asked.

"I'm going to bed," Paul squeaked, disappearing into the hall.

"Brush your teeth, please."

Brother Mellitus hobbled into the community room, leaning on his cane. "What did you do to him?"

"I told him the truth," Joannicus said, brushing the crumbled cookie from the counter.

"The truth? When has that ever helped anyone grow in faith? Just because you didn't celebrate as a child doesn't give you the right to deprive Paul."

"We are not pagans," Joannicus said. "Would you rather I tell him a lie? That Easter is for finding eggs and eating chocolate bunnies."

"It always was for me," Brother Ambrose confessed. "Love those yellow marshmallow chicks."

Why can't both beliefs co-exist? Was all faith composed of controlling doctrines?

The Warrior inside of Jacob threw back his head and laughed.

Mellitus wobbled. Father Joannicus reached out to steady him, but the man batted his hand away. "Nor are we puritans. Your Southern Baptist roots are showing, Father."

"I told him the truth, our faith, and he must learn it," Joannicus said.

"Oh, please. The truth is that Paul's mother is in the cemetery, buried in dirt with maggots eating her rotting body. Do you suggest we tell him that truth next?" Mellitus said, collapsing into a chair.

"What's the big deal? The boy will learn the facts on his own when he is ready. Little lies do no harm," Ambrose said, wiping his mouth on his sleeve. "Besides, what is the difference between a story, fable, lie, and parable?"

"You guys can't be serious. The truth is the difference. We are baptizing him Catholic next week. It's time to stop riding on the back of paganism," Joannicus said, his voice quaking. "Easter is about Jesus, his sacrifice, and God's eternal love and forgiveness."

"Yes, Professor, a lesson you obviously haven't learned. Even Chief has an egg hunt at his parish," Mellitus said, placing his cane tip over Jacob's heart, leaving a bullseye.

"Tons of kids become good Catholics who once believed in Santa, bunnies, and miracles. Lighten up, Joe. He's just a kid, not a novice," Ambrose said, rising from his seat and lumbering to the sink with dirty dishes.

"Symbols help children understand salvation, the seeking after something, and finding it. Eggs and rabbits are symbolic of life," Jacob said, knowing that converting from one religion to another didn't erase the foundation of earlier beliefs. He was still Apsáalooke, and Joannicus had ties to his Baptist upbringing. In his culture, everything about a rabbit screamed life, from its rapid heartbeat to its wide range of vision and radar-like hearing. And they were cute.

"Lovely metaphor, but I won't tell him lies," Joannicus crossing his arms and huffing.

Everyone tells lies, eventually. Brother Mellitus banged his cane on the table. "Fine, send him to me. I'm not so worried about my immortal soul that I can't delight in the joy of a kitschy metaphor. I don't understand why the boy even likes you. Jesus is just a name in a story we tell him. The story means nothing unless it becomes real. You've robbed him of salvation. You should be ashamed of yourselves."

The three monks silently hung their heads as they headed to their cells.

Jacob sat quietly, watching the moon rise. *Why are we arguing? Nobody's belief fits into the textbook of Catholicism. Faith didn't work like that. Joannicus knows this. Why is he so upset over bunnies? He's taking faith doctrine to an unhealthy level. None of us see being Catholic as clearly as the Pope and Joannicus.*

Jacob rose before the bells for morning prayers rang and went to the church. Paul raced past him. Jacob smiled, grateful that children's memories proved short. Brother Ambrose was right. A little lie would've made bedtime pleasant. As he entered the church, he watched Paul squeal and bounce in excitement.

He sat in his assigned seat.

"Father Jonah, look what I found."

A rainbow of plastic eggs spilled out from the makeshift shirt basket, rolling under chairs and across the carpet.

"Eggs."

"*Shh*, I guess I was mistaken about Easter."

Paul crawled under the chairs to retrieve the runaway eggs, his eyes dancing with joy as he returned to Joannicus. "You think so? I want to hunt more."

"After prayers," Joannicus said.

Jacob grinned as he noticed an egg nestled in the Easter floral arrangement below the lectern. Another egg sat perched on the candlestick.

In between the reciting of the Psalms, Paul would gasp as he spied colored ovals around the church. At the end of prayers, Ambrose appeared with an egg basket from the farm. Paul shouted and darted, gathering eggs.

"Excellent recovery," Jacob said, standing with Joannicus, watching the exuberant boy.

"This doesn't mean what you think. Easter is about the resurrection," Joannicus said.

"One act of kindness is all I see," Jacob said, knowing how hard it was for Joannicus to compromise.

Basket laden with eggs, Paul skipped down the hall that connected the monastery to the church in front of the two monks.

"I like holidays," Paul said. "Merlin said our next big one is Holy Spirit Day. A spirit is a ghost. I like ghosts."

CHAPTER 9
JESUS AND JAM

Psalm 31: 8
I will instruct you and teach you the way you shall go.
I will give you counsel with my eye upon you.

Father Joannicus walked to Abbot Gordon's office, hoping the man had chosen someone else to care for Paul. As the Guest Master, he felt he had gone beyond his obligation to be hospitable.

"The Lord be with you, Father," Abbot Gordon said.

"And also with you, Father Abbot."

"I wanted to go over the ceremony for Paul's baptismal day. Have you met Gracie and Patrick Hoffman? They are an older childless couple from Saint George's Parish."

Joannicus nodded as dust floated in the sun through the blinds. Father Pius spoke of their involvement and generosity at

Saint George's parish. Father Pius was the pastor of Saint George, and Jacob was the pastor of Saint Clare.

"They are to be Paul's Godparents. Not that Paul's spiritual development will ever be neglected. I believe they'll add normalcy to his life. And a boy needs a woman's touch."

Joannicus watched the steam rise from the wooden fence in the courtyard behind the office and wondered why the Abbot was discussing women with him.

"There are some conditions with this title. Gracie wants the child to visit her. Gracie is a warm and kind woman. I'm hoping that you would encourage this relationship. We'll need to ease into this since Paul doesn't handle change well. Ms. Carr suggested we go slowly and stick to a routine."

Joannicus viewed two birds flittering and twittering at the feeder, vying for the right spot outside on the patio.

"Me?" Joannicus said, quaking inside.

"Paul seems to respond to you. He emulates your actions?"

A dread filled Joannicus, making him dizzy. Paul mimicked everyone, from words to actions. This morning, he witnessed the child bending and touching his toes, not realizing the gesture of a bow at the altar was one of homage, not exercise. Yesterday, Paul butted a pile of sofa cushions like a baby goat. Joannicus leaned on the corner of the large gleaming desk.

Why is he telling me this? There are 40 men here.

Joe's hands gripped the edge of the desk.

"What are you saying?" Joannicus asked.

"Your new assignment will be caretaker of Paul."

"Seriously? Paul?"

"I would call it guidance master, but I'm sure Ms. Carr would object. It is like taking care of our guests and novices. Paul is young. He'll need supervision and instruction."

The door to the office banged open. Joannicus expected to see

Paul, but he saw Brother Mellitus being pushed in his wheelchair by Father Jacob.

"See what prayer and faith can accomplish. We are now rich. Abbot Gordon, what shall we do? A vacation in Disneyland, fix the brewery so it's automated, a new car for the monastery carpool, a Jacuzzi hot tub," Jacob chirped.

"No, Father Jacob, nothing has changed. We are not spending money until we fulfill our obligation," Abbot Gordon said.

Everything had shifted. Joannicus felt immobilized. *This can't be happening.* He was clueless when it came to children. His only sibling was ten years his senior.

The wind blew petals from the flowering tree across the patio.

"This is so unfair. After all our discernment, we get nothing. I was not asking for me. At least consider a motorized wheelchair for Brother Mellitus," Jacob said as Abbot Gordon shook his head.

Joannicus turned toward the door. He had no words he could utter that didn't sound like direct disobedience. Panic filled him.

What would he do with the child? He couldn't assign him work and study like a novice.

He watched Mellitus and Jacob poking one another like siblings in the back seat of a car.

"Good day, Father Jacob," Gordon said, amusement playing in his voice.

Brother Mellitus whacked Jacob with his cane.

"Ouch, that hurts, old man," Jacob said, wheeling Mellitus out of the office.

"A fat lot of good you did me. I'll do the begging next time. Thank you very much."

Joe's mind grew foggy as he wandered the dim hall. What if he lost his temper and struck the child? He prayed fervently, asking that this not be his burden. Abbot Gordon seemed content with the decision, and Joannicus was an obedient monk.

He didn't like children. They were unreasonable. Echoes of questions volleyed in his mind. Where are the angels? Why can't I go to school with you? Why do you drink blood? Where is the body you eat?

His theological explanation fell on innocent ears beyond comprehension. In Paul's eyes, he was sure that he appeared to be a liar.

Baptismal Sunday arrived, and as with any celebration, plans don't always work out. With a deepening frown, Joannicus trudged outside to the patio. His head throbbed. He watched as Paul ran the length of the space and, like a goat, head-butted Ambrose's leg. Ambrose pushed him away as if shooing a fly. Jacob sat at one of the picnic tables. The smell of tobacco filled the air.

"You were late to the baptism," Joannicus said, waving his hand to break up the smoke cloud. That was a lie. He knew Jacob had not attended the ceremony.

"Well, I thought if lightning struck, someone should be outside," Jacob said, scapular dangling in front of Paul like a matador's cape.

Ambrose threw his head back and laughed. Paul dashed through the black cloth.

Jacob exhaled, blowing a smoke ring. "I was there for the exorcism part. His head did not spin around. There was no reference to Abbot Gordon's mother's ability to procreate."

Paul charged again, and Ambrose caught him and hung him over his massive shoulder as the child climbed down him like a tree.

"He doesn't know those words," Ambrose said, bouncing Paul like a yo-yo as the child clung to his forearm.

"Seriously, I think you're mistaken," Joannicus said, having heard Paul playing in his cell. "He knows how to take the Lord's name in vain."

Ambrose stopped, slid Paul to the ground, and, glaring down at him, said, "You weren't supposed to repeat that."

Father Jacob laughed and put out the cigarette he shared with Brother Ambrose.

Depression, like a cloud of smoke, seemed to surround Joannicus, darkening his thoughts and heart. Joannicus remembered his baptism. Even though it was against his parent's wishes, the spirit of God had filled him with strength and peace. Today, he appeared disheartened. "It's not funny. None of this is entertaining. This was to be a solemn occasion."

"Dignity goes out the window when you have children around," Jacob said, brushing the dirt from his scapular.

Father Joannicus wished he could erase the images. He was certain that his arm would have bruises on it, for Paul had clung to him like a baby orangutan. Nobody, not even Brother Ambrose, could pry him off. Joannicus had suffered like a gorilla on display rather than the master of ceremonies at a holy sacrament. It all went wrong, from the water to the oil.

"They always cry when they are infants. That is how you know it took. Who wants to give up sinning?" Jacob said.

Joannicus recalled how Paul kept blowing out the candle every time Gracie lit it. He only stopped when Joannicus, in frustration, scolded him. Then the tears and Gracie's burning gaze, as if he had slapped the child instead of saying, please stop that.

Paul twisted himself up in Ambrose's already wrinkled scapular.

"So, if you blow out the candle of everlasting life, does that mean you are destined for hell?" Jacob asked, amusement dancing in his blue eyes.

"Hell is now," Joannicus said, shocked to hear the words coming from his mouth.

Brother Ambrose and Father Jacob exchanged glances.

"There will be other sacraments. He will get those right. The next two are rather simple," Jacob said.

Joannicus crossed his arms under his scapular. Nobody had helped, and he wasn't sure they would assist in the future.

"I got saddled with this, so you're doing the next one."

Jacob shook his head, and his braid whipped from side to side. Ambrose detangled Paul.

"Seriously, this is a community effort, remember? Abbot Gordon will be delighted to hear you volunteered so early," Joannicus said. He was not giving up so easily.

"Joe, do not be an ass," Jacob said, his face pinched with pain.

Paul took a swing at Jacob but only hit the massive cloth folds.

"Stop that," Ambrose said, grabbing Paul by the shirt collar but glaring at Joannicus.

Frustration filled Joannicus, and the words of anger tumbled out. "Nobody was laughing at you. They are calling me Joe Mama. Baptism is not a circus show. Abbot Gordon thinks I'm the one for the job. I'm not."

"Do I get a black robe next time?" Paul asked.

"No. Robes are only for monks."

"I want to be a monk," Paul said.

"You will help," Joannicus said, trying to lighten the moment. "We all have to do our part."

"Joe, I am not doing it. I will leave first," Jacob said, his face darkened.

"Jacob," scolded Ambrose, pushing Paul aside.

Jacob turned and marched towards the backyard gate in long strides.

"Joe?" Ambrose pleaded.

"Rose," Joannicus said, nostrils flaring.

"Go," Paul shouted after Jacob.

Ambrose glared at Paul. "Little One, you're cruising for a bruising. Don't be like Gracie," Ambrose said to Joannicus.

"I don't like her," Paul said. "Do I gotta stay with her next weekend?"

"Yes," Joannicus said, his voice sounding shrill. "And you'll like it, or you'll go visit until you do."

Paul stomped his foot. "I just don't like you anymore." Crossing his arms, he bolted into the community room.

"That won't last too long." Ambrose reached into his breast pocket, pulling out his pouch of tobacco. "Joe, ease up. The baptism was delightful. I'm sorry if it embarrassed you. The candle blowing was endearing. And I wonder what he wished for."

The sound of a motorcycle revving alerted Joannicus of Jacob's departure for Saint Clare's.

Shame rose. He would have to say an extra decade of Rosary for penance tonight.

Ambrose squared his shoulders. "Don't worry, Jacob will be back. He's probably going home to prepare for Paul's First Communion."

"I doubt that. I only hope he isn't preparing his letter of dispensation."

"You know Jacob, he's a spark, you're a slow burn. You balance each other out," Ambrose said as he patted Joannicus on the shoulder. "Come, let's open that package Gracie left for Paul."

"We can't do that," Joannicus said. Disbelief tinged his voice.

A wicked smile grew on Ambrose's lips. "Yes, we can. You're like his personal Abbot and novice master, all rolled up into one. You can do anything."

A jolt went through his soul. The words of the Rule concerning the Abbot came to Joe's mind. "... let the Abbot always bear in mind what a burden he has undertaken and whom he will have to give an account of his stewardship..." (RB 64).

Father Joannicus hung the Christmas lights in Paul's room. They created a soft glow in the darkness, an endless reminder of the birth of the Savior. He wondered if he could tell him a story about Jesus and light, Matthew 5:14-16. What if he fears the dark? The tale of Chanukah.

"Who are my godparents again?" Paul asked, diving into the blankets on his bed.

"Gracie and Patrick Hoffman," Joannicus said, attempting to straighten the mess of clothing, shoes, and toys on the floor.

"Right. I like them. It's Christmas in my room all the time."

Didn't Paul complain earlier that he didn't like them? Joannicus was sure he could never keep up with the sudden changes in loyalty. Was this how people related to God—by worshiping one second and sinning the next? No wonder God was disappointed.

Paul smiled. "What did you change me into?"

"You're Roman Catholic," Joannicus said, sitting on the bed's edge. He noticed a box of toys that looked familiar. A Native American baby doll and several red and yellow trucks peeked out. He knew the items belonged to Rosie and Elias, two of Jacob's deceased children. Joannicus hung his head. Even Jacob pushed past his pain and gave something to the new life Paul was beginning.

"So, is that Jesus guy a Roman?"

"No, he's Jewish."

Paul slumped onto his pillow. "I wanted to be what he is. What are you?"

"Roman Catholic," Joannicus said. His joy at his baptism had been tainted because he knew how disappointed his Southern Baptist parents were at his choice.

"Do I get that flatbread now? It was not good of you to give it to everyone but me."

"That's Communion. Nice or not, it happens when you're eight." He prayed that someone else would administer that sacrament.

"Oh God, that's forever."

Joannicus leaned forward. The kid was beginning to sound like Brother Ambrose.

"Excuse me?"

Paul pulled the covers over his head. Joannicus smiled. Sometimes, the child's antics made him endearing.

"Seriously, oh God, sounds like you are praying now," Joannicus said as he made the sign of the cross over Paul. "Let's say the Lord's prayer."

After prayers, Joannicus tightly tucked the covers around Paul, who threw his arms around the contemplative monk.

"I love you, Father Jonah. I'm ready for the coming of the moon. I liked them best with jam, grape jam."

Joannicus trembled, flustered by the sudden embrace and confession.

"You mean Communion. You might be ready, but I am not," Joannicus said, grateful that he had sent his letters to other communities offering his service as retreat master.

He could see Paul raiding the tabernacle in the Blessed Sacrament chapel and eating the hosts like crackers. Jesus-n-jam. Joannicus made a mental note to remind the sacristan to keep the tabernacle doors locked.

CHAPTER 10
THE GRAVEYARD

Psalm 85:13
Your love for me has been great.
You have saved me from the depth of the grave.

The early morning held a slight chill. Jacob kneeled near the grave of his wife and children. The Japanese maple's red leaves on umbrella branches seemed out of place, just like he and his family. Maple among cedars. They reserved this sparsely-populated, secular graveyard for spinster sisters and widowed mothers of monks.

Jacob stood as he heard a rustling behind him.

"Why are you crying?" Paul asked, peering at him.

Jacob wiped his face with his hand. He scanned for another adult. His eyes met shadows of headstones forming graceful arches in the pre-dawn light.

"I was not crying."

"Yes, you were," Paul said.

"What are you doing here?"

"I came to meet Jesus."

The simple answer made Jacob laugh, but he stopped when he saw the serious look on Paul's face. He stood and noticed that Paul was in his pajamas and bathrobe. His confreres were unaware of the boy's escape.

"He is not coming today. It is his day off."

"He is not coming."

Several thoughts ran through Jacob's head, but the loudest one from the Warrior and Elder shouted, *Leave now!* Paul walked over to his mother's grave and sat in the moist grass. The sound of the motor of the old farm pickup pierced the morning. Jacob jumped the low wall and zigzagged through the rows of headstones to the massive gate of the graveyard. He glanced back, barely making out the shape of the boy. As he contemplated whether Brother Ambrose would see him, let alone stop, the headlights came into view. Jacob slipped through the wrought-iron gates adorned with crosses. The truck slowed and stopped without him having to wave it down.

Ambrose stuck his furry head out of the window. "We don't pick up hitchhikers."

"How did you know it was me?" Jacob asked.

"I always know where you are. You're my cross."

Jacob rolled his eyes. It was too early in the morning for cryptic revelations. "The boy is in the graveyard."

Brother Moses peered around Ambrose's massive body. "Not again?"

Brother Ambrose grunted and pursed his lips as he turned the truck towards the gate's entrance. The lights cast a crosshatch shadow across the yard and bounced a glare off the Abbot's wall at the front of the cemetery. The barrier was low and made of polished marble. It held the bodies of the Abbots of Saint Alberic's. A massive, life-size bronze crucifix stood behind the graves, looking down at the peaceful dead.

The truck door groaned as it opened. Brother Ambrose slid out. His boots made a squeaking sound as he marched up the walkway toward the wall. Moses scampered after him.

"He's just a little boy."

"It's time for limits. He can't be running off in the dark."

Paul sprang up over the low wall that separated the two cemeteries.

"Jesus, I'm over here," Paul shouted.

Jacob chuckled at the thought of Jesus entering a cemetery.

"You're not him," Paul said, shoulders slumping in disappointment.

"Time to head to prayers, little boy," Ambrose said as he stepped toward Paul.

"No."

"I wasn't asking," Ambrose said.

"I'm staying."

"Not."

Brother Ambrose scooped the child up. Paul fussed and tried to escape. The large man carried the boy over his head. Paul kicked and flailed like an upside-down beetle. He placed Paul in the cab. Paul scooted across the seat and exited out the opposite door. Ambrose moved with swiftness and seized Paul from the rear of the truck.

Jacob grimaced, and his heart thudded in his chest.

"Mother of Mary," Ambrose exclaimed in pain as Paul delivered a massive kick to the man's shin.

Brother Moses cried with Paul when Ambrose swatted the child. Jacob was astonished by Paul's determination. Despite the spanking, Paul continued to fight. Ambrose dropped the child to the ground with a thud. Although shaken, Paul shook off the encounter and ran through the graveyard to his mother's grave.

"Oh, my goodness," Brother Moses said. "He bit you."

Jacob watched the droplets of blood forming around the circle of indentations.

"Damn child, I better not get rabies." Ambrose wrapped his arm with a blue bandana. "This isn't my problem. Moses, let's go."

"But Paul," Moses said, sniffling.

"Finders keepers," Ambrose said as he climbed into the truck, slamming the door.

Jacob walked past the dead with a slow, sinking spirit. He had no answers and prayed that Abbot Gordon would send reinforcements soon. The bells rang with loud clarity, a clarity Jacob did not share.

"You are in trouble," Jacob said. Paul ignored him. Jacob had expected this moment to arrive. To tell Paul that resurrection wasn't happening would be useless. He remembered when his father, Endow, died. He missed the man, even though he was alone in that sentiment. Even after the death of his family, he found no comfort in words, religious or otherwise. Paul's grief was so raw it burned.

Jacob watched a field mouse dart from headstone to headstone, pausing at each for shelter. With each run, the timid animal took a leap of faith. The creature was adaptable and fiercely determined to brave the open space to make it home to the brush pile. Message received, little mouse. Stay focused on the little things to achieve the bigger picture.

"Paul, I promise you, life gets better." Most likely, he'll forget because he was so young.

Paul stood silent and stoic.

"Child of God, this will not bring her back." Jacob sat on the low wall. "Come with me to the monastery."

He wondered how many times this event had occurred in the last week.

Eventually, hunger or cold will send him home. The Elder in him shook a finger. He wouldn't be here today if the monks hadn't spoon-fed him when his family died. *Try again.*

"Paul, it is time to go."

"No, I'm waiting until Jesus comes." Paul folded himself like a gargoyle.

"He's not coming. He said he would send a letter, you know, like the letters we read in church." It was a lie, but a clever one. Jacob's stomach rumbled. "We are missing breakfast."

"Fasting is good for you. Father Jonah says it clears your brain."

The influence of Joannicus had already taken root in the child. The sun peaked orange over the clouded horizon.

"You know you are hungry."

With a wave of his arm, Paul shouted, "Get away from me, Satan!"

Jacob wondered who was working for the devil.

"You are mean, and maybe I should just let you freeze," Jacob hissed. "And his name is Father Joannicus, not Jonah."

Someone cleared his throat. Jacob froze.

"I would not do it," Jacob said as he scanned the graveyard for reinforcements.

"I'm staying," Paul said. "You can't make me leave."

"Child, we discussed this yesterday. He's not showing up today or soon," Joannicus said. He handed Paul a warm roll and helped him put on clothing over his pajamas.

"All of this waiting can happen elsewhere," Joannicus said, helping Paul into his coat.

"He's coming. I asked him," Paul said, straightening the flowers in the urn beside his mother's grave. "You told me he answers prayers."

The sun warmed Jacob's black habit as he accepted a thermos of coffee and a roll from Joannicus.

"Seriously, I have a class to teach. I can't be sitting awaiting an event that..." Joannicus paused and turned away.

Jacob smiled a rueful smile. There wasn't an acceptable ending to the sentence that didn't dispute everything they believed. The warmth of the coffee caressed Jacob's lips. They could just leave him. He would eventually return to the monastery.

Jacob watched as Joannicus walked between the rows of headstones of the monks, stopping at each grave as if seeking wisdom from beyond. The white clouds in the sky changed to gray. Rosary beads clicked, and he wished he could pray and ignore the stubborn child. But he couldn't. The graveyard never comforted him; an eternal reward was not a concept he rejoiced in.

Joannicus stopped in front of Sarah Warner's simple white marble square headstone and looked down at Paul, who sat there like an idol worshiper.

"He always listens, but that does not mean he will give you what you ask."

"That is just mean," Paul said.

"It takes ten pennies to make a dime. If you pray for ten pennies and God sends you a dime, was your prayer answered?"

Paul shrugged his shoulders. Jacob realized that a catechism parable would not convince Paul.

They stood and waited. Theology classes would not happen today. The sun played hide and seek with earth, warming and chilling, a gentle coaxing for seeds to sprout. It was the best way to get the child home.

The bells for noon prayers clanged, and Joannicus turned and looked up the hill. Jacob feared Joannicus would leave to pray, so he began the noon office.

"You can't pray here," Paul protested as a rumble of thunder backed him up.

Father Joannicus followed with the proper response. "Seriously, you can pray everywhere."

"Just like you can wait for Jesus anywhere," Jacob added as the sun ducked behind a blackened cloud.

Jacob and Joannicus sang a hymn, and Paul listened. They recited a psalm. For a reading, Jacob said, "A reading from the gospel according to Jacob."

"That is not true. I learnded there are four gospels: Matthew, Mark, Luke, and John. Right?" Paul asked, eyeing Joannicus for confirmation.

"A woman in heaven saw her son sad. She wanted to be with him. She had work to do, like getting the rooms ready for visitors. When he grew up, he and the grandkids would come to visit her. She called down to him, I love you, and everything will be all right. She asked the Lord for help. He told her to tell him to eat oatmeal. So, she did, and he felt better."

Paul gave Joannicus a look reserved for seasoned skeptics as the sky darkened and the air turned frigid. Jacob's scapular flew up and whipped at invisible demons. His cassock flapped around his legs. The air smelled metallic.

"Jesus is coming!" Paul ran, waving his arms. "It's time. Merlin said the story was true, the one with the kings."

"Kings?" Jacob asked.

"Last night's reading from 1st Kings," Joannicus said.

"It is just a storm," Jacob said, angry at a doctrine that gave people false hope.

A crack of lightning beyond the hilltop brightened the sky. *This is not funny, Lord. Cut it out. This is not helping.*

Paul gasped, and Joannicus jumped as another bolt of lightning shot across the darkness, illuminating the graveyard. Jacob stood his ground. Perhaps the Lord wasn't such a great shot, missing him while in plain sight.

"You're wrong," Paul said with a stomp of his foot. "It's Jesus. He's coming. I told you he'd listen to me."

The day grew blacker. The promise of a warm spring day gave way to winter's last protest. Moisture hung in the air.

Paul whirled around and fell to his knees in the dirt as the clouds sent stabbing shards of ice down on them. The pelts turned to fat raindrops that sounded like heavenly applause on the brick walkway. Both monks pulled their hoods up and tucked their hands under their scapulars.

Like a beagle after a rabbit, Paul dug in the wet earth, ripping the tender seedlings that covered the four-month-old grave.

"Oh God, end this madness," Jacob mumbled.

"Lord, hear our prayer," Joannicus said in a voice drowned by the chaos.

Like guardian angels watching, they stood. Jacob was grateful they buried the dead deep. The storm dumped the last of winter on them. Mud caked Paul's jacket and jeans, face and hands.

The rain-drenched woolen habit hung heavy on Jacob's shoulders. The coffee curdled in his stomach, and he fought the overwhelming desire to scoop up the distressed child and squeeze comfort into him.

"Momma, wake up. Jesus is here." With a muddy hand, Paul pushed his wet hair from his face and continued to dig. "It's time for the esserection," the boy shouted over his shoulder. "Help me, I have to get Mama out. Why did you bury her? She can't get out."

Paul's words echoed a pain Jacob had suffered with the entombing of his love. When he had buried his family, it seemed like his ability to care was under all that dirt. Paul's despair forced tears to run down his face as his throat tightened with sorrow.

Paul collapsed in the mud and pounded his fists on the soaked earth.

"He didn't come," Paul said, his voice dry and rough. Tears drew clean lines down his dirty face. "He didn't come, he didn't come."

Jacob stared into the blank-faced monk as raindrops spiraled down the man's stretched curls.

Why didn't Joannicus react? Was he overwhelmed by Paul's emotions? Paul lay caked in mud. Joannicus did not move. Jacob couldn't stand idle any longer, so he squatted and reached for Paul.

"He lied to me. He said God listens," Paul said, swatting the palm away.

"What exactly did you ask of God?" Father Jacob asked.

"I asked him to wake up Momma so I can go home."

Jacob bent over and pulled the limp Paul out of the mud hole.

"I think he answered. You are home."

From Jacob's powerful arms, Paul turned and glared at Joannicus.

"I hate your God."

Father Joannicus took a step back as if stabbed, his face pained.

Jacob tilted his head upward and let the raindrops slap his face. Paul wailed long, loud howls of pain. Joannicus turned from them and walked out of the graveyard.

Jacob howled, too, and in the day's fake twilight, he heard the coyote's answer.

Yes, Brother Coyote, it is time to let go of certainties. The coyote brought hidden emotions to the surface, and that was uncomfortable, but the healing had begun. *Aho*, thank you, Brother Buattee.

How could Joannicus walk away? The words of Ambrose rang in his mind, "he better Christian up." He wanted to shout, *come back here, you wimp*, but he held Paul tighter. He carried the sobbing child to the hilltop as the cries turned to gasps and fitful hiccups.

Jacob stopped as they neared the monastery. Steam rose from the pavement like fog as the sun reclaimed the day. He took the end of his scapular and wiped Paul's face. The odor of wet wool and rich earth gave Jacob an odd sense of sadness and hope. Renewal. We begin again.

Paul heaved a resolved breath. "I want oatsmeal for lunch."

CHAPTER II
THE ONE

Psalm 55:13
I am bound by the vows I have made you.

Joannicus read the note from Abbot Gordon requesting his presence. This had happened three times this week.

Damn. Not again. What had Paul done now?

Teaching was easy compared to answering Paul's questions.

"Why are you a father and Ambrose a brother?" Paul asked.

"I'm a priest, so I'm called father. The brothers are not priests," Joannicus explained.

"But you are all monks. My brain is gonna explode," Paul said, shaking his head from side to side, causing his curls to bob.

The child needed a haircut.

"We are all monks," Joannicus said, leaving out the vows of a Benedictine.

"I live here, but you won't let me be a monk," Paul said.

Joannicus was sure his brain would explode. This wasn't a job for him. He could already sense his life out of balance. He would explain this to the Abbot, hoping he would understand.

His heart slammed in his chest as he knocked on Abbot Gordon's office door before entering. The sun glared behind the Abbot, making him appear angelic.

The Transfiguration. Did the apostles see a trick of light? Joannicus scolded himself. *Stop.* There's no room for doubt. Truth, not speculation.

Abbot Gordon looked up. "The Lord be with you, Father Joannicus."

"And with you, Father Abbot." Joannicus moved past the reception area to one of the two golden velvet chairs in front of the desk. Joannicus sat down, folding his scapular in his lap to prevent it from dragging on the floor. The Abbot closed the file he was reading, slipped it under a stack of papers, and took his glasses off, setting them on the desk. The oval lenses made two circular rings tinged with rainbows on the dark wood.

"There is trouble at the farm. I intend to speak with Brother Ambrose. I think Paul needs a little less structure in his day. What do you think?"

Joannicus had heard that Brother Ambrose was having the child move rocks from one useless spot to another. Paul hadn't complained about the task. Paul had already worn out his welcome in the tailor shop and kitchen to the point that Brother Barnabas had locked the kitchen doors.

"What would he do with free time? We can't leave him unsupervised," Joannicus said. "We could put him in a class with the novices." He shuddered.

"Father, he's a little boy. Children need free time to do things."

What did children do? Play sports? That thought depressed Joannicus. When some monks watched football, he was always absent. As a youth, he had avoided all participation in sports. He also wondered who would take Paul to practice? He did not relish sitting outside watching children kick or throw balls.

"What is wrong with the farm? He has chores there."

Abbot Gordon leaning back in his chair. "He is challenging Ambrose, so maybe you can speak to Paul. Explain the chain of command."

Joannicus bit his lower lip and shook his head.

Paul thinks he's in charge, and we're here to obey him. Our desires and daily routine mean nothing to him. He needs more structure, not less.

"He has taken to you, and you seem to influence him. Gracie tells me he listens to your teachings, often repeating them to her."

Joannicus swallowed, then folded and refolded his scapular. "Father Abbot, she's mistaken. You're mistaken. Paul doesn't listen to me."

"Don't sell yourself short. I have seen improvement. He is going to bed peacefully. He shows up for prayers regularly."

"That isn't my doing."

"I know this is a group effort, but everyone sees Paul responding to you. He wants to please you."

"I don't want him to," Joannicus blurted out. Abbot Gordon frowned.

"Father, you're a natural teacher. We've had this conversation before."

Guilt washed over Joannicus as he hung his head. *I want to pray, not teach.* However, others had pushed him, and now he was Dean of the Theology Department. Today, he enjoyed inspiring young adults to seek God and achieve their potential using all God had given them.

His heart dropped, thinking about how Paul had disrupted his thoughts and invaded his day. Paul overshadowed the balance of work and prayer, the foundation of his Benedictine life.

"Father Abbot, this is not the job for me. Seriously, I don't like children. We don't get along," Joannicus said.

"Paul likes you."

"Why? I have done nothing to foster that." Teachings rumbled in his mind. Perhaps something bigger was at work here. *Children are God's precious gift. Whoever receives one such child i*n my name receives me.

The room grew hot. Obedience had never been an obstacle. He could not raise this child, with or without heaven's help. The questions and challenges had disrupted his work and destroyed his prayers.

The Abbot expected him to do this job. He had been remiss in his duties, lingering instead of acting when dealing with Paul. Shame nudged him. He had sought escape by trying to find teaching assignments at other Benedictine houses. More to the point, he hadn't asked permission. He was a monk who vowed stability at Saint Alberic's Monastery, not at Saint John's.

He needed to correct this.

"Abbot Gordon, I..." Father Joannicus stopped.

Abbot Gordon picked up his glasses. The air in the room became heavy, and Joannicus felt the collar of his habit constrict. The Abbot folded his hands and leveled his gaze. His gray eyes were calm. Joannicus sat on the edge of the chair.

"Are you aware that Abbots often speak to each other? Abbot Brennen from Saint John's Abbey has talked to me, and I noted your protest. I can see you're uncomfortable with this assignment, but I don't believe I'm asking too much of you. Between three and

Mass, you'll have free time. I recommend you spend time with Chapter 68 of the Rule."

Abbot Gordon didn't have to say the words. Joannicus knew Chapter 68 in the Rule of Saint Benedict, "And if after these representations, the Superior persists in his decision and command, let the subject know that this is for his good, and let him obey out of love, trusting in the help of God."

Abbot Gordon smiled and nodded. Joannicus knew the dismissal had come. Like a knife cutting through an onion, the sting burned through to his heart. Joannicus headed to his cell, walking past the door to the community room. Before he could get down the hall, Paul was standing before him.

"Father Jonah," came the plaintive cry. Joannicus stared down at the child. A fearful emotion stirred inside him. One he had not felt in years. Anger. It rose strongly as he struggled to cover it with compassion.

"We don't talk in the monastery halls," Joannicus said curtly.

"But Father Jonah, you're talking."

Joe's vision blurred. His face became hot as he suppressed the words he wanted to scream. He didn't make the rules. He just followed them.

Paul peered up at him.

"Are you sick? Do you have a throbby head?"

"No. Go see Abbot Gordon. He wants to talk to you."

Joannicus stepped around Paul, continuing his march to his cell. As soon as he entered his cell, he closed the door and leaned against it. Would Paul follow him? Silence surrounded him as he exhaled. The stacks of research on the chair mocked him. *When will you finish this?*

The unmade bed teased him, and the piles of clean and unclean clothes called out that his life, like this space, showed signs of neglect. His refuge had become the belly of a whale. Jonah became the mocking echo of Paul's nickname for him. Exiting, he glanced down the hall towards the community room. Soon, Paul would be in pursuit. Where to go to be alone? He wanted to be alone with his Savior, not alone with Paul.

He moved down the hallway leading to the church, passing the individual chapels, where monks would sometimes say a private Mass. A closet-size space fitted for one to be alone with the Savior. The stations of the cross mocked his steps.

In the atrium, he blessed himself from the bubbling fountain. Mass would start soon. He had little time. Could he make a novena to Saint Jude the Apostle, the patron of hopeless cases? He paused and looked at the large fountain as his hand hovered over the gurgling water. Had he blessed himself? He rubbed his fingers together, feeling the wetness. Dread filled his mind. Had his life become a series of mindless gestures?

Joannicus passed the sacristy, where a tray with his silver chalice covered with a pall and draped with a veil stood. The sacristan had finished his preparation and gone on to other tasks.

He was alone as he entered the church. A sudden chill caused him to tremble even as the afternoon heat tumbled through the open windows. He continued to the small Blessed Sacrament chapel and kneeled before the tabernacle. The light through the stained glass bathed him in color.

"God, why is this so hard? Obedience is simple. Do it." Joannicus sighed as his spirit and head argued. He closed his eyes, and the warm breath of the air caressed his brow. His heart pleaded for him to turn to his desire. I'm here to pray, teach, and save souls. I am not here to raise a child. But the Abbot just ordered me to focus on Paul, on his needs. How can I not obey?"

The bells rang, dismissing the first round of the mental battle, declaring nobody a winner. Joannicus rose, and with weighted feet, went to the dressing room. He removed his habit, leaving him in secular clothing, jeans, and a tee shirt. He slipped the green chasuble over his head and struggled to pull it straight. Like a cross beam, it lay on his shoulders, heavily burdensome. Joannicus prayed, "While serving you, Lord, may I be unselfish and charitable."

With a quick glance in the mirror, he took his place in the hallway. As principal celebrant, he would be the last to enter. The order of entry was the servers, the cross bearer, the brothers, and the robed priests.

Paul ran up to him. "I'm walking with you."

"No, I'm principal celebrant. You'll take your seat in the church with the rest of the people."

"But I don't want to. I want to come in with you. I'll follow you."

"No."

"It's in the Rule," Paul said.

"Seriously. No, it is not," Joannicus said. This new habit of Paul's, making up additions to the Rule of Saint Benedict, was no longer cute. The music for the opening hymn began, and Paul's procrastination had won him the possibility of walking in with the monks. Just as Joannicus was about to break ranks, Ambrose marched back to where Paul stood and scooped the child up, tucking him under his arm like a football.

"Hey, I want to march in the parade," Paul said.

"No is no," Ambrose said. "You have a choice. Come in with me, or I'll take you to your cell."

What made Ambrose help? Was this divine intervention? Today, it didn't matter. Joannicus was grateful to the man. Paul's presence disrupted every aspect of their lives.

He had no influence over that child.

Throughout the celebration, Joannicus stumbled like a newly

ordained priest over words he had committed to heart a decade ago.

His focus danced like the leaves in the breeze. He feared Paul had replaced God.

Joannicus stood at the podium to deliver his homily. He paused, watching Paul sitting on the floor between two monks, facing his empty chair, playing with a pocket-size leather-bound missal, several rosaries, and holy cards with prayers and depictions of saints.

"Where did the Lord Jesus wander off to this time?" Paul said. "If he leaves without telling us again, I'll not follow him anymore." Paul moved a holy card with a picture of Saint George and the dragon closer to the piled-up rosary beads on the chair before him. "Don't worry, we got the Rule. It's more powerful than burning bushes, stronger than watery wine, and can build monasteries on hilltops. Holy Saint Benedict gave it to us, and all that Jesus guy left was this pile of rosaries. Ta-da!" Paul pulled the crucifix up out of the beads. "He's risen! Run, go tell the Abbot."

Ambrose and Jacob snickered into their folded hands as Brother Moses nudged Paul's foot. The child looked up, craning his head to where Joannicus stood.

"Seriously, are you through?" Joannicus inquired when he had the boy's attention.

Nodding, Paul put the cards in his pocket and handed Brother Moses a pile of tangled rosaries. He climbed into his chair, grabbed the end of a scapular, and draped it like a tent.

Joannicus looked at the community assembled before him. Usually, he saw a group of hungry men waiting to be edified, but today, he saw the seven dwarfs plus several deadly sins added to the mixture. He began his homily with, "The word *obedience* comes from the Latin root *audire*, meaning to hear or to listen..."

At the end of his sermon, he surveyed the community, heads

bent, eyes closed. Were they asleep? Paul had slipped away, too, moving from empty chair to empty chair.

Father Joannicus stood at the altar, preparing to acknowledge the sacrifice of the Mass. He placed the stiff white linen, called a 'corporal,' on the table. Its small, red embroidered cross glared at him like a mark on his soul. The memorized words rattled off his tongue as he prayed. He stopped, amazed that they failed to linger in his thoughts as they had in the past. Joannicus blinked and poured the wine into his silver chalice, staring at the distorted reflection before him. This was his moment, time savored, communion with his Savior, saying the words that Jesus said, and recalling the sacrifice of giving one's life for another. Today, the joy eluded him like a playful lover. The red wine sparkled inside the chalice, beckoning him to partake. Raising the cup, he said, "When supper was ended, he took the cup. Again, he gave You thanks and praise, gave the cup to his disciples, and said..."

In his mind, he asked where He was. He had given thanks and praise. Why did God hide?

He set the cup on the altar, genuflected, his hands resting on the table's edge, wondering if he should remain in this position and beg for mercy.

He glanced around and noticed that Paul was sitting with another child. Irritation rose in him, glaring like a sunrise, taunting everything he thought he was.

He knew he was a priest, not a caregiver.

Joannicus rose and continued with the Mass, joining the community in the Lord's Prayer.

"Deliver us, Lord, from every evil...." Joannicus searched for Paul, who was already shaking hands with people.

As people greeted him with a sign of peace, Paul ran across the church and dove into Joe's robes, hugging him through the layers of material. Joannicus waited. Paul stood next to him with his nose almost resting on the altar. Joannicus pointed to the chairs. Paul shook his head. Joannicus closed his eyes, chanting to himself. *Why me? Why me? Why me?*

Silence filled the room as Joannicus looked at his confreres, who stared at him with stunned, concerned faces, making him wonder if he had spoken his thoughts aloud.

Sweat ran down his back as he flipped the book's pages on the altar. What came next?

Jacob's voice broke the silence. "Lamb of God, you take away the sins of the world. Have mercy on us."

Joannicus proceeded to the fourth part of the Eucharistic celebration, communion. His hands trembled as he distributed the hosts. He avoided the recipients' eyes, fearful that they would see his falseness.

His heart was heavy as Joannicus led the monks out of the church. Paul's joyful shout of "thanks be to God" echoed in his ears. He hung his vestments up and headed down the hall to the monastery for recreation. Jacob grabbed his arm and pulled him into the reconciliation room. The place where confessions were made. This replaced the old box and screen confessionals of the past. Two chairs, a shelf with a stole, a bible, flasks of oil, and Holy Water filled the small space.

"Ditch the habit. We are escaping."

CHAPTER 12
THAT MONK

Psalm 15:1-2
Preserve me, God, I take refuge in you.
I say to the Lord; you are my God.
My happiness lies in you alone.

Father Joannicus stood in the reconciliation room. The dim light from the wall sconce made it hard to read Jacob's face. The sound of a zipper told him Jacob was climbing out of his habit. Joannicus unzipped his cassock and, uncharacteristically, folded it into a pile on the opposite chair. Together, they stepped out, closing the door behind them.

There was a voice from the hallway. "Recreation is the other way."

"Need a shove in that direction?" Jacob asked with a sugar-coated smile.

"Out of habit and dressed funny. Behave yourselves, Fathers." Mellitus called as he continued toward the inner monastery doors.

Joannicus looked at his clothing, wondering what was wrong with his attire—a plaid shirt and black slacks. He owned several plaid shirts in a variety of colors. What did it matter what he wore under his habit?

"Hurry, before Mellitus claims there is a fire, and they all come," Jacob said. He darted down the winding paths, passing a bench under a shade tree, to the old iron gate exit.

Immediately, Joannicus knew that Jacob had not gotten permission. Seven cars of various models and years stood waiting in the parking garage. They were allowed trips, but only after speaking to the Abbot.

"I have keys. I am answering to a higher authority. Do not ask so many questions. Practice faith."

"Seriously, our absence will be noticed," Joannicus said, slipping into the passenger side of the blue Ford Falcon.

"Or seen as a reason for joyful celebration," Jacob said, starting the car.

They drove silently to the next town–if one could call it a town. It had the essentials: a grocery, a gas station, a clinic, and several taverns. They pulled into the gravel parking lot of Dirty Dan's Bar and Grill.

Father Joannicus shook his head and followed Jacob through the fake western doors into the room where smoke lingered overhead, and music mingled with laughter.

"A pitcher of Absolution Ale," Jacob called to the bartender as they headed to a vacant table.

"What's the sin?" called the patrons.

"A wicked desire for," Jacob paused. "For a buffalo burger with BBQ sauce."

People laughed and groaned. Joannicus wiped crumbs from

the dirty table into a napkin as if cleaning an altar. The pitcher arrived, and the server winked at Joannicus. Jacob poured the amber brew into the mugs. He wasted no time and launched into the woes of his life.

"Everything. A lot of work is on my desk. I've no lesson plans and a child who doesn't leave me alone. The community trusts God is speaking to them. The problem is they are hearing a message, and it is not the one God is sending me. Ms. Carr wants to descend and conduct an inquisition about things that may or may not happen. Other than that, all is just wonderful."

Jacob leaned forward on his elbows.

Which problem should you tackle first?

"Seriously, Ms. Carr. One minute, she demands knowledge, and the next, she wishes to crawl inside my soul."

Jacob grinned. "Ms. Carr could be helpful; use her and keep the topic on Paul. Speaking of Paul, I think that these belong to you." Jacob reached into his pocket and pulled out several crumpled pieces of paper.

Joannicus recognized the logo of Saint John's University and Gethsemane Abbey. Anger and betrayal rose inside him. Who had gone through his trash?

"I believe Merlin sent him to raid trashcans. Mellitus collects information that does not belong to him. I fear he will publish a monastery newsletter soon. Just kidding, but with what he knows, he could try to blackmail others. I learned my brother Vincent gets an allowance from my stepfather, Terrence. Of course, he turns it over to the Abbot, the virtuous bastard. You would think he could at least share with me. Did you know dear Papa is making a substantial donation in honor of his profession? Is there no end to the man's generosity?"

Joannicus winced. The sarcasm-laden love made him feel Jacob's pain. Terrence Mackenzie was a generous man, but his acts often hurt Jacob. He swore his stepfather loved him. Joannicus had a tough time seeing that. He felt no affection toward Paul, and guilt sloshed like the drink before him. Scripture flooded his mind as alcohol slurred his reasoning. God so loved the world.

Jacob gulped the remains of his beer. "So, why are you planning on leaving?"

Leave it to Jacob to find the agate on the beach. The music twanged over the speakers. Joe's head tangled with his heart, stinging words like the bitter ale tumbled from his mouth, "I converted for God. Where I serve him is academic. How I serve him is all that matters."

"It matters to me."

The server came and took their order. She leaned forward and smiled at Joe, laughing and lingering too long. Heat filled Joe's cheeks as he watched the foam dripping down his mug and waited for her to leave.

A second pitcher arrived. Jacob's blue eyes pierced Joe.

"Seriously, Abbot Gordon said no, don't worry about it."

Jacob lined his silverware straight on the table.

"I'm staying," Joannicus said, pouring beer into his mug, watching the head threaten to crest the top. "I don't want to."

The food arrived, and they ate. Jacob squirted ketchup over his fries. Joannicus placed a small mound of the sauce on the side of his plate. In between bites, Jacob suggested Joe take command and schedule Paul's day like a novice master would. He recommended the farm since Ambrose enjoyed the boy.

Joannicus dipped and nibbled a fry. Could he make Paul meditate and study? Or teach him to read. He envisioned Paul silently reading, lost in a book of the saints.

"Why does Paul like me?" Joannicus asked, thinking he didn't encourage the boy.

"I asked him. He said because you're soft and smell nice," Jacob said with a grin.

"Seriously, that's creepy."

Jacob laughed.

"Kids do not have genuine reasons. He does not like me because I spend time with you. He likes Ambrose because... Well, it's a mystery why he likes Rose."

"Rose is a smart man. He could teach biology if he wanted to. He has a Ph.D. I wish Abbot Gordon had selected him," Joannicus said, wiping the sauce from the burger off his chin.

Joannicus had never thought about the reasons for liking or disliking a person. People were reflections of God's handiwork. Was Paul? He remembered when he first met Jacob, a young man who married and had babies. Jacob's bold questioning of the Creator and church shocked him and forced him to search for the answers and truths. He didn't understand what Jacob saw in him. What made a friendship? Was it essential to clarify? *I don't want a friendship with Paul.*

"If God wants me to do this caretaker thing, what does Paul want?"

A beguiling smile appeared on Jacob's face. "It is all about love. God so loved the world, he made us to share his love with."

"I don't know how to love a child," Joannicus said, unsure if he possessed that emotion.

After paying the tab and hitting the bathroom, they headed to the parking lot. Jacob swayed, stumbling over the gravel as he walked past the Falcon.

"Give me the keys," Joannicus said, trying not to slur his words and attempting to take the keys.

They struggled momentarily until a heavy hand landed on Joe's shoulder.

"Whatcha doing there, mister?" a voice asked.

Joannicus turned, peering into the black eyes of the man inches in front of him.

The man spoke to Jacob in Crow.

"It is all okay, Two Beaver," Jacob said, moving closer to Joannicus. "Just a little parking lot dancing."

"What? Are you denying my help? You gone white or just looking for trouble?"

The man eyed Joannicus and exhaled, his breath rancid with alcohol and cigarettes. Joe's stomach seized, and he raised his hand to keep the man's breath out of his face.

Things happened in slow motion. Joannicus dropped to his knees, assuming he would hurl. Two Beaver swung his fist.

The thud was distinct. The large man lost his balance after striking Jacob, who had stumbled backward from the blow and landed on the ground.

Bright lights blinded them for a second as a car door slammed. Jacob forced himself upright using the bumper. Joannicus recognized the shiny black boots of a state trooper and the arrowhead gleaming from the man's hat.

"Gentlemen," the man with a gun said as he leaned closer. "Karl? Karl Mackenzie Knows the Song?"

"Hey, is that you, Douglas? How is your uncle?" Jacob asked, rubbing his chin.

Douglas took a step back and eyed the situation. Jacob licked the blood off his lips.

"Oh, wait. Sorry, Karl," a distraught Two Beaver mumbled as Douglas helped him up.

"You're forgiven," Jacob said. Two Beaver sobbed like a grieving parent.

Two Beaver stumbled to the patrol car without being asked.

Joannicus stood, using the car for support. The gravel clung as if permanently embedded in his knees, and the wave of nausea was replaced by a sense of spinning.

Douglas held out an open palm.

"Do I need to call Rebecca?"

Rebecca was Jacob's sister. She had rescued him many times. Joannicus heard the keys jingle into the officer's hand.

As they stood pondering what to do next, a server came outside with four cups of coffee and a bag of ice. She handed them each a cup and Jacob the ice. Two Beaver, unable to get into the patrol car, returned calmer, to the group.

"We drive on the right side," Douglas said, handing Joannicus the keys. "Speed limit is?"

"75," Joannicus said.

"Come along, Two Beaver. Let's sober you up, then get you home." The officer opened the patrol car door, and Two Beaver climbed in.

Joannicus sweated as the patrol car tailed him until he turned off the major highway to the road that ascended the hill to the monastery.

They made their way in the darkness to the footpath. Jacob loosened a brick and pulled out a flashlight, gave it a whack, and the light blinked on. Joannicus stood in disbelief when the door they had exited opened. A small rock placed in the jam had prevented the latch from working. Had Mellitus–for once–been kind?

Jacob hummed as they headed down the hallway to the reconciliation room.

"*Shh*," Joannicus said.

Jacob weaved his way down the hall. Joe's stomach swayed with him.

"Jacob, what if He leaves?" Joannicus said as they headed to the reconciliation room.

"He is not going anywhere for at least 18 years," Jacob said. "Or do you mean God?"

"Yes, God," Joannicus whispered as he opened the door to retrieve their habits.

"He is not going anywhere. Trust me, I have tried to escape His voice. Ah, that is kind of cute," Jacob said, finding Paul asleep on the floor.

"Where were you?" Paul asked, rubbing his eyes.

"At confession, why aren't you in bed?" Joannicus asked.

Paul yawned. "You didn't tuck me under. Merlin said you were painting. What did you paint?"

Joannicus scooped up his habit and the child.

"You're smoky," Paul mumbled as he rested his head on Joe's shoulder.

"See you at Morning prayer," Joannicus said as he walked down the hall with his burden.

"It is what I live for," Jacob whispered as he headed up the stairs with his habit draped over his shoulder.

CHAPTER 13
CELIBATE FOR A DAY

Psalm 145: 5
He is happy who is helped by Jacob's God.

The bells for Mass woke Joannicus. He had fallen asleep again in his cell at his desk. Every time he sat to do Lectio Divina, he napped. He couldn't remember the last time he finished one private prayer. The afternoon sun shone through the colored windows, painting cheerful patterns on the floor as he headed down the hallway to the church for Mass. As he approached the vestment room, he heard voices.

"Ah, just ignore Chief," Mellitus said. "He'll mess you up."

"He's mean. I don't like him," Paul said.

"Brother Mellitus, that is not how we refer to Father Jacob, nor is it kind," Joannicus said as he entered the room, wondering why he had to remind a senior monk about behavior. "Paul,

Father Jacob has been nice to you. He left toys for you. Why is he mean?"

"He doesn't play fair," Paul said, poking his head out of one of the vestment closets that lined the long, narrow room. Each closet held unique items; one had the white albs used for Mass, and another, the colorful chasubles and stoles for the different liturgical seasons.

"We were playing hide and seek, and he never looked for me. And he lied. He said he looked for me, but I know he didn't cuz I found him sitting in the community room. So, I told him to go hide, and now I can't find him."

"Seriously, just because you can't find him doesn't make him mean," Joannicus said as he checked the vestment colors for the day. He knew Jacob was the principal celebrant for Mass, meaning he'd be off sweating somewhere. Of course, the monastery didn't have an actual sweat lodge, but Jacob would find a makeshift one. It seemed an odd way to prepare, but it was Jacob's way.

"I agree with Paul," Mellitus said. "Chief, I mean Father Jacob, doesn't play fair."

"Brother, seriously. Behave, you're a senior monk."

The old monk leaned forward. "You behave, Mister I'm-gonna-run-away. You sound like a novice who didn't appreciate shoveling shit. Run home to Daddy. At least Chief won't be doing that."

Father Joannicus pursed his lips as he hung up his black habit. His plaid shirt already showed signs of sweat. He tucked it into his black slacks and donned the white alb for Mass. He selected a colorful rectangular cloth with a bold green and black design. Brother Mellitus had found an accomplice in the boy and used him to create mischief. Recently, Joannicus had spent hours untangling the wild tales Mellitus had put into Paul's head. He had often spoken to Brother Mellitus about his influence but to no avail.

"Brother Mellitus, or should I call you Merlin," Joannicus said. He turned to look at himself in the mirrors, pulling the stole so it hung over his shoulders, the ends lining up midway down his leg. "I'm still here, and I need you to stop including Paul in your mischief."

"Is that an accusation?"

"I'm not making accusations. I'm warning you to behave and keep Paul out of trouble."

"What are you talking about?" Paul asked, trying to swim out of the vestment closet, which held the black pleated robes for Sunday Vespers.

"He's just mumbling," Mellitus said, extracting a worn copy of the Rule of Saint Benedict from his pocket and shaking it at Joannicus.

"Some things are private," Joannicus said, straightening his robe.

"We're a community. Nothing is private."

A fake smile graced the old man's face. Joe felt his face grow hot, recalling the humiliating moments at the hand of this monk. Mellitus had spent a lot of time targeting him, claiming it built character.

"Seriously, sending Paul into the private cells of our confreres is unacceptable."

"He was emptying trash."

"That's not true." Joannicus felt a slight empowerment as the old man sneered. "And might I suggest you put the correct name back on Jacob's mail slot in the community room before he discovers you switched it?"

"Jacob will think it's funny," Mellitus said with an air of superiority.

Paul stumbled out of the closet. "How did you know?"

"I know more than you think," Joannicus said, knowing that

switching the boxes made Jacob receive his half-brother's mail and messages. "It's not wise to alienate your only adult ally."

Community members entered the room to dress for Mass.

"What do aliens eat?" Paul asked.

Joannicus tucked Paul's shirt in and re-tied his necktie.

"Never mind, time for Mass."

Joannicus stood in the hall behind the other priests, wondering how Jacob had convinced him he could teach Paul. He had been a novice master, and his entire class had remained monks. Novices had enough sense to withdraw and contemplate. Paul just continued to ask more questions, and most of them were disturbing.

If it's Christ's body, why does it taste like cardboard? If we're supposed to be silent, why are people still talking? If I'm to be kind to everyone, why isn't everyone kind to me?

Paul ran back through the atrium, pushing his way past the line of monks to Joannicus.

"There are Indians with drums. Do I get to drum?"

"This is not drumming time."

"But they're drumming."

"Father Jacob is the principal celebrant, so there are drums. Go inside and sit."

"No. I'm mad at him. I don't want to stay. I want to watch TV."

Brother Mellitus smiled. "Smart kid, I'll supervise."

Joannicus frowned. "Join the celebration or go to your cell. I'll come and get you for dinner. You choose."

"What about recreation?" Paul asked. Recreation was a time between Mass and dinner when the monks gathered together socially.

"No recreation without participation at Mass."

Paul pouted. "Not fair."

"Oh, a mean monk contest," Mellitus said. "I like it already."

They entered the church to the rhythm of the drums. Paul forced his way between the priests in the first row and plopped next to Joannicus.

Jacob stood before the altar instead of sitting in the center chair reserved for the principal celebrant. He faced the monastic community, the five regular weekday liturgy attendees, and a handful of Apsáalooke guests. He wore a colorful blanket, made for him by the monastic tailors, instead of the usual vestments. His hair, unbraided, hung long and black, framing his angular face. He greeted everyone, speaking first in Apsáalooke and then in English.

Joannicus felt a tug on his sleeve.

"That isn't right," Paul said.

"Listen," Joannicus said, surprised that Paul had learned the protocols for Mass.

Paul sat on the floor at Joe's feet, wrapped his arms around folded legs, and perched his chin on his knees. Joannicus wondered if he should correct the posture. Paul learned fast, but he took his cues from everyone. If a monk used his sleeve as a napkin or picked his nose, Paul was sure to mimic the behavior.

When it came time for the homily, Jacob sat on the floor. Joannicus noticed he was barefoot. Paul scooted forward. Joannicus fought the urge to insist that he sit in the chair. After a few moments, Paul crawled back to Joannicus.

"Who is this Great Spirit guy?" Paul whispered.

"God by a different name," Joannicus said as he heard the grunt of disapproval from some of his community members.

"Yeah, right," Paul said in curious disbelief.

Jacob lit a small fire at the altar. The flames jumped as the sage crackled.

Paul gasped, "Oh my."

Joannicus sniffed the smoke. It reeked a little like marijuana.

When Jacob danced around the altar, Paul kicked off his shoes and moved to follow Jacob, but Joannicus pulled him back.

Two monks walked out of the church.

"It's not over. Where are they going?" Paul asked, watching them leave.

Joannicus wondered if he should tell Paul the truth.

"To the bathroom," Joannicus said, thinking their behavior of leaving was an overreaction. Even without the proper words, they knew the prayers. The essentials still existed. He wondered if the Pope had spoken in Polish, would they have dared to walk out?

After the dancing, the sacred part of the Mass began, and Jacob raised his chalice.

"That's an ugly cup," Paul said in a hushed tone.

"It's homemade."

The chalice Jacob used was large and lopsided, made of clay, and nothing like the ornate vessels that usually graced the altar. Jacob's wife Faith had made it as a fruit bowl, but in the firing process, it had collapsed.

"This is all wrong," Paul muttered, wagging his head like some monks behind him. Joannicus wondered how Paul had become so cynical in such a short time. Had he taught Paul to be critical? He understood the ceremony was unorthodox, but living in Montana, surrounded by Native culture, allowed Joannicus to accept the mixture. It was still Mass.

The community filed two by two to receive communion. Paul kept changing lines until Joannicus grabbed his sleeve and pulled him into one line. Too young to take communion, Paul usually received a blessing, but as Jacob raised his hand to bless Paul, the child stuck his tongue out at him. Jacob laughed. Joannicus fought the urge to smack Paul. It startled him so much that he stepped out of line for communion.

"Why didn't you get any?" Paul whispered.

"Shh, practice meditation," Joannicus whispered back, shame washing over him, causing him to sweat.

"Here? Now?"

Joannicus glared at Paul, who slumped back in his chair in exaggerated defeat.

Dear God in heaven, what is happening? Where did that feeling come from? Confreres in the past had angered him, but not to physical violence. In the silence, he heard someone crack their knuckles, and he glanced to his right at Paul. The boy sat still and silent. Joannicus sighed, thankful he had taught the child the art of silence.

He just wanted to guide lives and help others in faith, never questioning how one became faithful. He always had faith. He had absolute security that his actions matched the will of God.

In the meditative time between communion and dismissal, Jacob sang a song. Paul slipped to the floor and sat wide-eyed. Jacob's powerful voice caressed the walls. Joannicus recalled the first time he heard Jacob sing, two years after the death of Faith and the children.

It was not a hymn but a pop culture song entitled "Sunshine." After the song, Paul clapped. Joannicus attempted to make him stop.

"Seriously, we don't do that."

"But it was good, and I liked it. I like sunshine and loving one another, just like Jesus would."

"It was for God, not you," Joannicus hissed.

"God told me to clap," Paul said with confidence.

After Mass, Paul said, "That was not Mass."

"Father Jacob celebrates in his own way," Joannicus said. "Just because it is different doesn't make it wrong."

Paul gave Joannicus a hard-disbelieving stare. Joannicus made a mental note to move "right judgment" to the top of his "work with Paul" list.

A willowy woman with midnight hair that hung down her back in a thick braid approached Joannicus.

"Joannicus," Rebecca said.

"Rebecca," Joannicus said with guarded warmth. She did not love the Catholic faith, even though she understood it and had three vowed siblings. The only thing they had in common was their love for Jacob. Each approached that differently. They had a silent agreement with respect.

Paul scooted closer to Joannicus, trying to disappear in the skirt of his habit.

"Definite trouble," Rebecca said as she eyed Paul, who stood in his stocking feet. "I agree with Rose."

"Brother Ambrose exaggerates," Jacob said, entering the atrium, looking like every monk. He draped his arm over Rebecca's shoulder. Side by side, the biological resemblance shone greater than the one between Jacob and his half-brother Vincent.

"Can I call Brother Ambrose, Rose?" Paul asked.

"Seriously, you will call him Brother Ambrose," Joannicus said.

"He don't smell like a rose," Paul said as he peeked at Jacob. "An' you're a meanie, even if you are the principal celibate for the day, but I liked your song."

"Every monk is a celibate. You mean celebrant," Joannicus said, raising his eyes upward.

"I prefer celibate for a day," Jacob said. "I like the song too."

"You would." Rebecca laughed, leaning into him with a familiarity.

"Is he supposed to be doing that?" Paul said, stepping forward.

"It's his sister," Joannicus said, not liking the tone in Paul's voice. "It's a hug." He didn't see the point of explaining the complicated dynamics of Rebecca and Jacob. Their relationship had the closeness of a mother and child, not brother and sister. She had raised him from birth, protected him, and failed to protect him. Like blackberry bushes, their bond was tangled and thorny.

"Merlin said monks don't do that. They keep their body parts separate," Paul said. "I saw Brother Cyril kissing a girl, and Father Albert drinks a lot of Jesus. He's always in the sacristy."

"Perhaps he is a vampire," Jacob said.

"Seriously, Father Jacob," Joannicus scolded. He wished he had the power to silence the child, fearing a long night of having to separate fact, fiction, and fantasy.

"I'll pray for you, brother. I'll pray for all of you," Rebecca said, kissing Jacob on the cheek. "Now which one's Cyril?"

"Becca," Jacob said, becoming serious. "Prayer will not help." He kissed her on the cheek and pointed her towards the door.

"Brother Cyril was kissing the girl on the…" Joannicus covered Paul's mouth.

"Nobody likes a tattletale."

"I don't have a tail," Paul said, his voice echoing in the empty atrium.

"I know, but you are someone with a big mouth that reports everything he sees," Jacob said as he turned toward Joannicus. "Are you upset with me? I noticed you did not partake."

"It's not you. I didn't have a clear conscience."

Jacob gave Joannicus a penetrating glance. Joannicus hoped he wouldn't press him on the issue. Paul ran down the hall, closing all the side chapel doors as he went.

"Paul, why are you doing that?" Joannicus asked, opening the hall chapel doors. The rooms, which held a bench and an altar with a kneeler, usually remained open, beckoning one to come and spend time in communion with God.

"Merlin said the Great Spirit hides in closets," Paul said. Is the Holy Ghost the Great Spirit?

"Yeah, sort of," Jacob said, stopping the child from closing the last door. "He rules with Father Sun and Mother Earth."

Joannicus groaned. The information would not prove helpful. Paul had enough confusion with three persons in one and the difference between Saint Benedict, the Abbot, and God.

Jacob grabbed the sleeve of the mischievous boy and bent down to look at him eye to eye.

"Look, I will teach you as long as you promise to stop tattling on others."

"Fine, fine, I won't tell tales about you," Paul said as they entered the cloistered hall inside the monastery, heading to the community room.

The rich wood paneling bounced light from the polished floor. Paul ran down the hall in his stocking feet and attempted to slide into the community room. Joannicus held his breath as the boy skidded, missing a statue of Mary by inches. Jacob grinned, took off his shoes, and ran after Paul, sliding down the hall, scapular waving behind him.

CHAPTER 14
GOAT SACRIFICE

Psalm 50:14-15
Give me again the joy of your help,
with a spirit of fervor sustain me,
that I may teach transgressors your ways
and sinners may return to you.

F ather Joannicus sat in the dark church wrapped in a mantra prayer of Psalm 50 when the distinct odor of perfume offended his nose. Random lights flickered on and then off. The monk on his right clicked his tongue in a scolding.

Barb Carr had arrived and thought it was her job to illuminate the church. Joannicus stood, the morning peace shattered. He walked to the atrium.

"It's dark in there," Barb said.

Joannicus reached over and turned on the wall sconces. A soft light shot heavenward while keeping the sanctuary in a shadowy darkness.

Today, he didn't want to be the guest master or hospitable. She was here to create trouble. He nodded and handed Barb a set of prayer books as several monks filed by. The bells rang, the lights clicked on, and Father Joannicus led her to the row behind the choir. Joannicus faced the altar and bowed, feeling her eyes on him. Loud and fast footsteps entered the church. Paul skidded to a stop and, with a flourish, bowed to nothing in particular. The movement resembled a warm-up for gym class. His cheeks were still rosy from sleep. Paul's face contorted with confusion when he saw Ms. Carr.

"What's happening?" Paul asked as he approached Joannicus.

Joannicus shook his head and pointed to the empty chair. He was hopeful the invitation to sit beside him would keep Paul's reaction minimal. As prayers began, three students from Joe's upper-division ethics class entered the church. This group had attended before. They joined with psalters and sat beside Paul.

At the praying of the "Glory Be," the standing community bowed in unison. Paul continued his calisthenics performance, touching the floor with his fingertips with each bow. Joannicus pretended not to notice as he felt Barb's eyes on him, but student Sherry smiled.

Today's psalms spoke of the threat of enemies, and the words rang true. Ms. Carr was a menace, looking for something wrong with them. Barb's sudden appearance was upsetting to Paul. During the reading, Paul wiggled and squirmed. Joannicus placed a hand on Paul, and the movement quelled. The last time she visited, his mother had died, and she left him with them. Paul picked at the hole forming on the knee of his jeans.

Sherry's magenta nails distracted Joannicus, glaring back from the stark white pages of her prayer book. He watched them dance over the words as she pointed out each one to Paul while the monks recited the psalms.

The last 'amen' rumbled through the church, and the community headed to breakfast.

"I don't want to go. I'll be good and go to my cell at bedtime and not your bed." Paul pulled on Joe's sleeve and promised he wouldn't swear.

The Abbot turned and shot a glance at Joannicus.

Paul thought Ms. Carr was here to take him back. Did one monk threaten Paul with Ms. Carr to make him behave? And did it work?

Father Joannicus headed to the exit. Barb stood in his way. The three students glanced at him, and he recognized the concern on their faces. Paul wrapped his hands around Joe's wrist in a death grip. Joannicus, with Paul in tow, stepped around her.

"You're welcome to have breakfast with us."

"Then you can leave," Paul said.

Joannicus pried the boy's fingers off him.

"Paul, that's not kind. Ms. Carr is our guest, and we treat our guests with hospitality. In the Rule, it says we show visitors every kindness. We are to receive them as if they were Christ."

"I don't want her to take me away," Paul said, grasping Joe's scapular.

"She can't do that," Sherry said as she turned to Joannicus. "Father, can we talk to you? We heard rumors."

"What's a rumor?" Paul asked.

"Things that aren't true," Joannicus said. He needed to leave.

"Lies? Oh, you get punished for telling lies," Paul announced with a fist-to-palm motion. "Pow, straight to the moon."

Thank you, Ambrose, thought Joannicus, realizing he could not hide. He motioned for the group to follow him to the refectory.

"I've some questions," Barb said, eyes narrowing. "This Rule of yours talks of beating children."

David laughed, and Barb's head snapped in his direction. "There is nothing funny about this. A child's welfare is at stake."

Joannicus crossed his arms. "Why are you here?"

"I'm concerned about Paul," Barb said. Her voice cracked with annoyance.

"It has been over six months since you've been here. Everything is fine." Joannicus held the door open for the group and Ms. Carr. Paul ran down the hall to the refectory.

"I don't need to explain my visit to you. What are you hiding?" Barb said, her heels tapping on the floor as she marched down the hall. He wasn't hiding anything from her.

"Why are you so suspicious and condemning?" Joannicus asked as he opened the guest dining room. He tried to be positive, realizing that the constant sight of people at their worst moments could taint one's opinion of humanity.

"I'm not. I have seen things you can't imagine. You live locked away behind a monastic wall. There is evil in the world. My job is prevention rather than praying for good to come. So, I'm asking why you are sleeping with a child."

They set the guest dining room for three. The odor of coffee, pastries, eggs, and sausage wafted as he stepped into the space. This was too intimate. He didn't want to talk to her. Next time, she would eat in silence, like everyone else in the refectory.

The students lingered, and Joannicus was grateful.

"You are mistaken."

"Paul clearly said your bed."

Joe's jaw tightened as Paul entered the guest dining room with a sticky bun. Joannicus squeezed the rosary beads in his pocket, letting the edges bite into his palm. He inhaled deeply.

"Paul has trouble falling asleep. I let him fall asleep in my bed and then move him to his own cell."

"Why can't he sleep? What's happening here at night? A cell, is it locked?"

"Our doors do not have locks. Seriously, what do you think goes on at a monastery?"

"Drunken wild sex orgies," David mumbled, helping himself to a pastry.

"Silly, there are no ogres. We have magic and a lot of talk about Jesus, who isn't coming tomorrow," Paul said. "Did you know magic is like God? You gotta believe for it to be real."

Joannicus cringed and poured coffee into the waiting mugs.

Barb coughed. "Who told you that?"

"I don't remember. But everyone talks to God here. He lives here. I think maybe on the fourth floor. I haven't gotten there yet, but I will." Paul answered before stuffing the bun into his mouth. Joannicus handed Paul a napkin.

"Are we getting more children?" Paul asked, taking a seat at the table.

"No, you're enough for one community," Joannicus said.

"We heard you were leaving," Sherry said, her magenta-nailed finger pointing at Joannicus.

"If I go anywhere, it will be on a sabbatical, a temporary vacation. Monks do it all the time."

"But why?" the students asked in unison.

The question annoyed him. They sounded like Paul. He was not the kind of father Paul needed. A sabbatical would remove him from Paul and the monastery.

"You're abandoning the child," Barb said, unfolding her napkin as the fork and knife clanked together.

"I'm not the person for this job," Joannicus said. Where was Abbot Gordon?

Barb set her lips firmly.

"Yes, you are," Sherry said, placing a hand on Paul's head. Silence followed. She was mistaken. His cheeks reddened.

"This is a monastery where we pray and work, devote our lives to the Divine. I'm a monk. I pray. That's my work. Parenting is a secular job."

"I don't see how that matters. Both involve prayer and labor," David said, grabbing a mug and pouring coffee. Paul covered his head with his napkin.

"Children need two parents. Here are only men." That wasn't entirely truthful, for celibate men always attracted a strong following of women. Already, they were fussing over Paul on Sunday and in the college's offices.

"But Father, there are women around you. Celibacy doesn't stop you from raising a child. You know single parents raise children," David said.

Whose side was David on?

"Celibate, right," Barb said, stirring creamer into her coffee. "I saw the stares as they left."

There it was. She didn't believe men could be celibate or raise a child. Joannicus pulled off the napkin hat and pointed to the glass of milk in front of Paul.

"Oh, lady, that isn't lust," Sherry said. "That's fear."

Was Sherry right? In his case, yes. Other monks had no issues with women. Once again, the secular world condemned what it didn't understand.

"My dear woman, you're confusing wants with needs. You need food, but you have a choice of what you eat. The same is true for celibacy. It's a choice. We are human. Temptations come and go."

"Is that what you call women?" Barb asked, looking to Sherry for support.

"No, I call them balancers. We all play a role in the salvation of humanity. What religion are you, Ms. Carr?" Joannicus asked, curious about what other prejudices she was harboring.

"That is none of your business. The Catholic Church does not corner the market on abusive clergy. I've been around the block. I have heard it all and seen more than I care to remember."

"So, you're here to confirm your worst fears? Let me make this easy for you. We can make this a multiple-choice question. You pick: Are we a cold, austere group of men? A dysfunctional, backward group of men? A group of sick and perverted men? Or, men incapable of parental love? You can say all the above." His voice had reached a fervent pitch.

Ms. Carr flamed. "I'm here to save one child."

"He doesn't need that kind of saving," Joannicus said as Paul stood and stomped his foot.

"You're men, and you know nothing about children."

"I'm eating where it is quiet," Paul said, stomping out of the room. Joannicus let him go.

"Ms. Carr, you're welcome to visit. If you want to find something wrong with us, you will. I realize your job has tainted your views of the world. Let's agree to rein in our judgments. If you do not condemn our Rule and lifestyle, I'll tolerate your prejudices."

The three students stood wide-eyed.

"I'm not prejudiced. You're not seeing what I am seeing."

"True, but I prefer my world over yours," Joannicus said. Peace, balance, order—he didn't want to live in the secular world.

"That's my point. You are blind to the realities. There is a world out there."

"No, I know the realities. You can't expect a warm welcome when you enter, expecting a demon and criticizing what you know little about. Approach it this way. Everyone here is trying to improve himself.

"And what if they fail?"

"Your system fails too," Sherry said, her eyes narrowed with anger. "Father will succeed, he believes, and you're not leaving, right?"

The doors to the refectory opened, and Ambrose stepped in with Paul in tow. Both fists held sticky buns.

"I need to go to class. Paul spends his mornings at the farm. I'm sure they will welcome you there," Joannicus said.

"Not today, Father. We're sacrificing goats," Ambrose said.

Ms. Carr opened her mouth, but no words escaped.

The Abbot appeared in the doorway, and Joannicus exited with the students trailing behind him.

CHAPTER 15
KITTENS, CATS, AND OTHER FELINES

Psalm 58:3
*O rescue me from those who do evil
and save me from bloodthirsty men.*

J acob helped the farm crew with chores, and Paul scampered behind the various kittens. He had counted two dozen. Jacob knew kitten removal would occur soon. Most of the cats avoided the child because they were feral, which didn't stop Paul from chasing the curious kittens that the mother cats couldn't control.

Paul ran in pursuit of a black one. Scholastica, the Australian Shepherd, barked at his heels, trying to herd both. The kittens scattered in every direction, and Paul skidded to a stop.

"Hey, why do you have cats in a sack?" he called as Ambrose walked by with a burlap bag of noise and movement.

Jacob ushered Paul back into the yard.

"What does he mean they are going home? I thought this was their home?"

An orange kitten ran by, and Paul followed it behind a bale of hay.

Jacob sighed in relief. He didn't want to explain the destination of the sack. As cruel as it was, he knew the ways of barn life. Paul chased kittens and snuggled lambs. Scholastica ran herself ragged by chasing after him.

As noon approached, they gathered at the truck to head up the hill.

"Can I take this kitten?" Paul asked, holding on to a smoky gray bundle of fur.

"No," Ambrose said. "Animals stay on the farm."

"You're mean. I don't want to be with you." Paul stomped to the truck, slamming the cab door.

In the refectory, Jacob sat at the table looking at the monks. None of them acknowledged the sound of the little peeps that punctuated the clanking of silverware, the clinking of glasses, and the crunching of food. He turned, half expecting to see a novice in wet sneakers. Then he noticed Barb Carr eating her soup with the monks. Her last visit was a month ago, and she had no complaints then. Why was she still visiting? Her taunt face told him she disapproved of silent meals. Jacob wondered why she wasn't in the guest dining room.

Ambrose stuffed the last bite of sandwich into his mouth and scowled at Jacob, scraping his chair on the floor as he rose. As he left the room, Paul scampered after him.

The protesting in the hall was loud. Wide-eyed, Barb tossed a crouton at Joannicus, who was sitting opposite her. She shook her head, but Joannicus sat, ignoring her. Most of the community exited from a different door to avoid the hallway noise.

"What is going on out there?" Barb asked, breaking the silence.

Jacob watched as Joannicus sipped his tea. Finally, he walked as if they iced the floor, and his shoes were made of lead. Curious, Jacob moved in the same direction.

"Did you bring them up here?" Ambrose asked, holding Paul's red hoodie, which held eggshells and newly hatched chicks.

"No," Paul said.

Ambrose let out a slight growl, and his eyes narrowed. He looped his hand into his leather belt, making him look like an extra-large gnome. "Really? I'm sorry I accused you of something you didn't do."

"Let's take them back," Paul said.

"It's too late. They will die. Baby chicks need to be warm after hatching. This is very disappointing," Ambrose said, walking away, taking the hatchlings with him.

Father Joannicus cleared his throat and crossed his arms. Paul's expression changed from an innocent doe to a pained, weak smile.

"Rest time," Paul said, running to the exit.

Barb looked confused. "What just happened?"

"Paul has taken farm animals from the barn," Joannicus said. "And lied."

"How do you know?"

Joannicus stared at her in disbelief. "Seriously, read those child-rearing books you left me. If you'll excuse me, I need to talk to Paul."

Father Jacob followed Joannicus, proud of him for facing the self-righteous Ms. Carr. He was curious about what other critters were living in Paul's room.

They entered Paul's cell. Jacob noticed the bookshelf now held books and Disney movies. Someone had put up a bulletin board, and Paul's drawings crowded the edges. The space now resembled a child's room with monastic overtones.

Paul was under the covers with his eyes tightly closed. The sleep performance might have worked if they hadn't seen him awake five minutes earlier. They waited in silence and heard a muffled mew, and a kitty appeared out of the half-hidden burlap sack. In a matter of seconds, kittens darted around the room. A tabby attacked the bottom of Jacob's robes while a black and white tuxedo tried to climb his scapular. The smoky gray chased the orange one under the blankets that hung off the bed. Jacob suppressed a smile.

"Where did these come from?" Joannicus asked, stepping away from the kittens as if they were tigers.

"The barn," Paul said, giving a fake yawn as if he had just woken from sleep.

"What are you doing with them?"

"Merlin said every boy needs a pet. I'm just deciding which one. All the good saints had pets. Saint Benedict had a crow. What if someone tries to poison me?"

Jacob raised an eyebrow. The child was using Saint Benedict against them.

"Paul, did you bring those chicks to the hilltop?" Joannicus asked, arms crossed and trembling slightly.

"No, farm animals belong on the farm."

It impressed Jacob, the bold lie this time without remorse. The kittens settled into a furry ball of color in the middle of Paul's bed.

"I believe Ms. Carr wanted to spend the day with you," Joannicus said, his voice hollow and controlled. "She'll be in the parlor. Please meet her there."

Paul hastily exited the room.

"He lied," Jacob said, scooping the blanket of kittens and placing them in an empty box. "You know you have to punish him. Less than an hour ago, Ambrose told him no to kittens as pets."

Joannicus picked up the clothing on the floor and folded it. "Seriously, what do you suggest? Spank him. Barb thinks it's barbaric. She favors rewards."

"For lying?"

Joannicus turned and gave Jacob a look of impatience.

"Barb said. Since when is she an expert? She doesn't even own a child. Besides, you must use what works for you. Each relationship is unique. I never had a problem lying to my mother, but I did not lie to my dad."

"That's because he beat you," Joannicus said.

Ouch, that hurt. Sometimes, the truth did hurt. The fact of the matter was Terrence, Jacob's stepfather, often lost control when dealing with Jacob.

Jacob handed Joannicus the box of kittens, but Joannicus shook his head. "I'll let Ambrose handle it."

Sadness filled Jacob as he and the box of kittens approached the barn. Jacob released the captives. This was Ambrose's problem. The ravens argued from the roof of the slaughterhouse. It was a conspiracy of ravens and monks. He slipped out of his habit and hung it on a peg. As he entered the yard, he saw the rows of chickens hanging from hooks, and the smell of fresh blood filled the air. Several feral cats ran up, stealing morsels from the pan of chicken heads.

Jacob winced as the axe lopped off another head with a solid thud.

"We have a kitten problem. Joe wants you to handle it," Jacob said, stepping to avoid blood puddles in the dirt.

"Kittens?" Ambrose asked, placing twine on the feet of the decapitated hen.

"Paul took kittens to his room."

"I'm disposing of the rest of them today. Paul has turned too many into pets, and they have lost their natural ability to sense danger. He'll have to give up his Saint Francis dream." Ambrose placed a struggling chicken on the wooden block.

"No," Paul screamed, causing Ambrose to lose his grip on the bird. As the ravens scattered, the fortunate bird flew to temporary safety, alerting the next district of the news. "Where are my kitties? Where are Shadrach, Meshach, Abednego, and Ralph?"

Ralph? Jacob suppressed a grin. Paul stood brave and bold in front of the axe-wielding monk. A friendly kitten rubbed against Paul's leg.

"You let him follow you?" Ambrose growled.

"No." Jacob squared his shoulders. "Where is Ms. Carr?" He stepped toward Paul, who held a kitten point side out.

"Get away from me, you murderer."

Paul bared his teeth. Jacob stepped back, wondering why Paul accused him of being the splatter of chicken blood.

Paul ran past him in the general direction of the hilltop.

"Well, go after him," Ambrose boomed.

"Me? No way. Did you see his face?"

"You're bigger than him. Sit on him."

"I think he needs to be alone."

"Fine, when the Abbot comes looking for him," Ambrose said, wiping his hands on his blood-stained apron. "You explain to him how this happened."

Jacob followed Ambrose's lead in gathering the chickens and equipment and tossing them into the truck bed.

Ambrose washed up in the barn and hung the reddened apron on a peg. "It's farm living, and it isn't any more horrifying than those saint stories he has been reading, Saint Lucy and her eyeballs. Where's his keeper?"

"With the Carr woman," Jacob said. He put his habit back on, worried whether his comment was valid.

"She's after something, and it's not Paul."

"Yes, I think she has found it."

Ambrose turned and waved a finger at Jacob. "Then you best be there to advise him. You're the one with experience."

Jacob wanted to laugh as he climbed into the truck. The last advice he had given concerning women had ended in disaster. Joannicus asked how to deal with Gracie, Paul's godmother. She disapproved of everything Joannicus did. Jacob tagged along that day and corrected Paul in front of her. Gracie now had a personal vendetta against him. The upside was she currently thought Joannicus was perfect.

The truck rumbled up the hill to the refectory. He helped Ambrose unload the chickens at the back door of the kitchen.

His experience with women amounted to his wife, Faith, and his sister, Rebecca. He cared for his other sisters, and the relationship with his mother was toxic. Often, he wondered if that tainted his dealings with women. As a boy, he'd wanted to be an orphan. He no longer wished for her love but sometimes hoped. He knew that would never happen. This brief reflection soured his mood.

Paul entered the church late. Jacob noticed he sat as far from the community as possible in an octagonal room. After Mass, Paul stood in the atrium glaring and trying to be intimidating.

"Cut it out," Jacob said.

"Get away, you killer," Paul hissed.

"I was not holding the axe," Jacob snarled back.

Paul glared at Ambrose. "You didn't stop him."

Father Joannicus and Ms. Carr entered the atrium.

"Father Jonah, they lied. They kill things–the chickens and my kittens. I saw them killing everything in the barn," Paul yelled, running over to them.

Joannicus raised his eyebrows at Jacob and Ambrose.

"What? Are you crazy? Why did you let him witness that?" Barb said, shaking her head.

"Wasn't intentional. It's a farm. We eat meat. The kid needed to learn," Ambrose said, crossing his arm.

"We eat the animals," Paul said. Horror filled his face. "We eat kittens."

"No, of course not. But the animals at the farm serve a function. They're not pets," Joannicus said, moving toward the door.

Paul crossed his arms, reminding Jacob of Ambrose.

"My kittens were serving a function. They were playing with me."

Ambrose followed Joannicus out of the church.

Jacob was sure he liked what he heard. Ambrose spared the lives of kittens. Paul was changing his confreres. The order of life was changing all because of a child.

Barb and Jacob followed the pair, and Paul raced after them through the garden.

Ambrose stopped and turned. Everyone froze in place. "Listen up, Little One, the farm animals are not companions. You can't have them as pets. That is final," Ambrose said, raising his voice.

Paul crossed his arms. "Shadrach, Meshach, Abednego, and Ralph?"

"I spared Ralph and friends," Ambrose said. "But they are working cats. They'll not be pet-ified," Ambrose said as Paul stood toe-to-toe with the large man.

"I want them all," Paul said.

"No, too many cats."

Joannicus looked at the ground, avoiding conversation.

"You killed my kittens. You murderers," Paul shrieked, his face turning purple.

Jacob's heart ached for Paul as they entered the hallway outside the refectory.

"Couldn't you find homes or fix them?" Barb sputtered, taking up Paul's cause.

"Look, lady, you take care of your vermin your way, with your laws and rules," Ambrose said, stopping again and glaring at her. "I do it my way."

"You killed them," Paul said, anger dripping from every word.

Ambrose's face turned red, and his voice took on a menacing growl.

"It's the reality of farm life. Farm animals are not pets. Farm animals work or are food. We cannot have hundreds of cats running around. Pets are a nuisance."

"I'm a nuisance. You say that every day. You gonna kill me?" Paul shouted as tears ran down his face.

As shocking as these words were, this logic didn't surprise Jacob. It seemed sane from the perspective of an almost six-year-old.

"That is utter nonsense," Ambrose retorted. "You're a boy, not a kitten."

"I don't care. I don't like you. I'm never going to speak to you again. Never."

Paul ran away from them. Jacob's appetite drained. Ms. Carr was stunned. They needed help.

"Fat chance that will last," Ambrose mumbled, running his rough hand over his face. Jacob could tell from how he jutted his bearded chin that he felt guilty for being so blatant.

Ambrose marched to the refectory. Barb followed Joannicus into the room. Jacob stood in the hall, alone, conflicted.

Jacob left the building, heading to the kitchenette in the

community room. There, he filled two bowls with cereal and grabbed the milk jug. He walked into Paul's room without knocking to find Paul perched on the desk by the window.

"I'm mad," Paul said, wiping his tears.

"Yeah, I can tell. Sorry. Sometimes life sucks."

Paul glared at him.

"I brought you food. Do not worry. It is vegetarian."

"What's a veg-a-tin?"

"Meatless," Jacob said, sitting in the rocking chair.

Paul's face softened. Jacob could see the struggle between hunger and conviction.

"It's not right."

"It is what it is."

"I counted the chickens. We have 101, and I'm counting them every day." Paul picked up the bowl and ate.

Jacob smiled. There were not that many hens. He wondered how many chickens Paul would count tomorrow. There was no point in arguing. Life was hard to take. Moms died, and some didn't love their children: women who desired monks and monks who didn't want to be parents.

"How come Ms. Barb is here? She asks too many questions. Father Jonah was busy with her. I don't like that. He is mine. I wish I were like Saint Scholastica–she prayed, and God made it rain so hard her brother Benedict couldn't leave her alone. Only I want God to send her away."

The pure honesty amused Jacob. "Maybe Father Joannicus is telling her stories."

"Father Jonah reads to me all the time. I don't get his stories."

Jacob nodded. Heady theological metaphors didn't work on little boys.

"Once upon a time, a little boy was mean to his brother. His meaner father made him say sorry. Time passed, and the boy became a vegetarian. He listened to his brother and mean father, but he lived happily ever after. The end. Amen."

Paul peered over the rim of the bowl, slurping his milk.

"I'll put it under advisement," Paul said.

Jacob laughed and drank his milk from his bowl.

CHAPTER 16
IT IS WRITTEN

Psalm 88:29
I will keep my love for him always with him.
My covenant shall last.

Father Joannicus sat in the darkened church before morning prayers began, thinking of Ms. Carr. He found himself looking forward to her visits. His world was foreign to her, and she was curious. That pleased him.

Joannicus had left home at eighteen. Today, he realized he had more to learn about children. She could teach him. He knew she did not understand religious life. He wished to explain to her the joy he experienced being God's chosen. This way of life gave him joy and completeness.

The sweetness of her perfume tickled his nose. Joannicus

opened his eyes to scan the church. He saw her tiptoeing so her heels would not tap on the cement floor. The lights clicked on, and he rose to sit with her, which was his duty, but today, it was a privilege. She was helping him understand Paul. The bells for morning praise rang, breaking the peace of the night.

Barb's visits were now so frequent that Paul, upon seeing her, went to Joe's assigned seat between Brothers Moses and Barnabas. As amusing as it was, Paul's place was not in choir.

He needed to explain seating and inform the boy that it was according to when one was professed. He hoped that would stop him from sitting with them. Not likely.

Joannicus sat next to Barb and noticed that she had the right books with her. He reached over to flip to the correct page as his hand bumped her soft, warm fingers. He smiled apologetically and felt his cheeks burning.

The pitch of her voice rose higher than his confreres when she sang. Her singing sounded like a canary among crows.

After prayers, the community headed to breakfast, and Joannicus escorted Barb to the atrium, where he spotted her suitcase. He had planned her arrival, so her room stood ready. He picked up her bag and led the way. Outside, the air was crisp with the hint of winter.

They walked to the guesthouse. Barb spoke, "I tried to get here before prayers, but as usual, my timing is off."

Joannicus held open the door. "It's not a problem. I'm surprised to see you here so early. We wouldn't be converting you, would we?"

Barb laughed. The sound warmed the hall. "I like prayers. They are comforting. I enjoy the non-denominational quality it has."

"That's wonderful." Joannicus said, unlocking the room labeled 'Saint Hildegard.' This saint was a visionary, and he hoped her life would encourage Barb. A basket of fresh fruit and snacks graced the small side table in the modest space. On the desk, Joannicus had placed a stack of books.

"I see you have stocked me with more reading material. I enjoyed the tale of Benedict and his sister. She asked him to linger, and he didn't want to, but she prayed, and God made him stay."

"Paul likes that story, too. He seems to relish the gruesome parts rather than the virtues the saints exemplified. I'm teaching him about humility and good works on the level of an almost six-year-old."

"Hold on, I need to hang up this blouse before it wrinkles." Barb took it from her suitcase. A lacy undergarment dangled from the bottom button. Joannicus stood in the doorway. Should he turn away? The satin pastel peach fabric caused him to stare. Such pretty colors, but so sheer, thin. What protection did it give with winter coming soon? She wasn't wearing that now, was she? He stopped, mortified at where his thoughts wandered.

"There, let's go to breakfast. I'm starved," Barb said as she closed the closet door.

Father Joannicus nodded, deciding not to point out the garment. In silence, they headed to the guest dining room. The cool morning air helped to quell the sudden warmth coursing through Joannicus. They entered and saw that a table awaited them, set for three. Crystal goblets filled with squeezed orange juice glistened—a basket of fresh biscuits and cups of homemade freezer jam begging to be eaten. Paul had treated himself to oatmeal.

"This is wonderful," Barb said, lifting the lid of one of the floral-printed bowls. The aroma of bacon and sausage filled the room. Paul reached over and grabbed a link.

"Hospitality is a trademark of Benedictines," Joannicus said, blessing himself and saying a quick prayer while glancing at Paul. Paul stood with his forked sausage and bowed his head.

Barb gave Paul a wink as she waited.

"How are you, Paul?" she asked as they sat.

"They made me eat in here," Paul said as he wiped his milk mustache on his sleeve. Joannicus handed him a napkin. "They won't let me go to school. They said I had to wait."

"It seems pointless just because his birthday is in October, not September. They won't take him," Joannicus added. "I'm sure he knows more than any other child entering. They wouldn't even consider evaluating him for placement. In a year, he will have surpassed everything they could teach. I read smart kids become bored and end up in trouble."

Barb helped herself to a biscuit and jam. "You can teach him before school starts, keep him challenged. I can supply workbooks on addition and subtraction when I visit next time."

"I can add. I count the eggs. Fifty eggs make four dozen cartons with two left over."

Joannicus stirred his tea. The spoon banged on the sides. It amazed him, the patience she showed Paul. He would have scolded the boy for bragging. Humility was not a virtue that Paul possessed. Women must have more tolerance than men. Lately, he watched them at Mass, how they tended to the children, and kept them focused and quiet. He tried using their techniques with Paul.

"You could learn to print," Barb suggested, her eyes joyful at Paul's babbling. She bit into her biscuit and let out a moan.

Father Joannicus looked at his biscuit. Could their blueberry jam be that much better than store-bought? Paul liked the cereal at his Godmother Gracie's house. Joannicus had seen the variety packs she purchased. At the monastery, they had two types of breakfast cereal–cornflakes and something with bran.

"I write," Paul said through a mouthful of oatmeal.

"Good. Did you know letters make words?"

Paul nodded. Embarrassment filled Joannicus as he pulled a small notepad from his habit pocket and wrote the words humble, Benedict, and Ephesians.

"Those are easy words. You need to pick something harder, like *conspicuous* or *effervescence*," Paul said.

Barb's laughter permeated the room. Joannicus found himself giddy.

The thump on the wall alerted Paul that Ambrose was in the mudroom. He quickly finished his oatmeal and dashed out the door, his napkin marking the halfway point of his hasty exit.

Joannicus rose, folded the cloth, and placed it on the table.

"Seriously, he's not that smart. It's just that he lives with us, and we are intellectuals. Some of it rubs off on him."

The morning dampness evaporated, and the day's warmth filled the air. He kept these hours free, rescheduling student advisory and a couple of meetings. They headed down the hill on a gravel trail toward the cemetery.

As he listened to her speaking about Saint John of the Cross, it occurred to him that Jacob had been right. She was better as an ally. He sensed she had no plans to become Catholic. Her acceptance of who they were and what they believed had progressed. Last spring, she was ready to crucify him for being a male. Now, their topics of conversation included more things than religion and her job.

They climbed the back steps to the side garden.

"Don't you get hot in that dress?" Barb asked. Beads of sweat glistened on her temples. The rose bushes were holding on to their leaves until the frost. The rose hips were large and swollen, which hinted at a hard winter ahead.

"This is not a dress. It's a habit. It has pockets. Dresses don't have pockets. This is a scapular," Joannicus said, waving the long rectangular cloth that hung from his shoulders to his ankles. "We use cotton for summer, wool in the winter. In December, I thank God for my dress."

"I understand routine, but doesn't it get old, day after day?"

"There are times the silence is crushing. But the daily practice frees me. I came to know God, to pray, to form a relationship. I'm aware I sound crazy."

"No. We all seek wholeness and companionship, oneness." She pushed her brown hair behind her ear. "I think I'm a little envious."

"You can have this. Seriously, you can," Joannicus said with passionate enthusiasm.

"No nunnery for me. The office I work in has women in it. I'm not interested in living with them."

He had to agree with her. A house with one woman has one too many. He had given retreats to women's communities. He knew anyone could apply the Benedictine life and learn balance and peace.

They paused at a small iron gate before entering a tiny meditation space at the church's east end. There was a stone bench and a bamboo water feature. Joannicus shook the pebbles from his sandal as he attempted to stay on the large stepping stones. All the blocks had a Japanese caricature, evoking a monastic ideal. Silence, humility, hospitality, prayer, obedience, Joannicus stopped upon stability.

Barb sat on the bench. "So, you never wanted more?"

"No, my father is a Baptist minister. Religion has always been with me. Seriously, it's like when a student tells me they have found the one to spend the rest of their lives with."

"You can fall out of love," Barb said, running her hands over her skirt.

The yellow flowers contrasted against the dark wooden door. Joannicus shook his head. She was wrong. His passion for God was all-consuming and ever-growing. He could not imagine the emptiness one might feel without God in one's life.

Her patronizing expression made him aware that she didn't understand.

"You think me naïve," Joannicus said.

"Yes, and I'm jealous of your simplicity." She ran her hand along the richly stained bench.

"You can have this," Joannicus said. "Seriously, it's all a matter of balance."

"I hope nothing ever moves into your world and changes that."

Joannicus grabbed the heavy, rustic handle, which felt cool to his touch. "I hope something comes into your heart and changes you. Paul's presence has been a change—one I struggle with daily."

Joannicus realized that this pretty woman was his age and still single. He pulled on the door, but it resisted his tug.

"How is it a woman so dedicated to children is childless?" He said before realizing the question might be offensive.

"Mr. Right is unavailable."

The bells clanged, calling the monks to noon prayers.

"Have you looked for him?" Joannicus asked. They entered the church, and Joannicus handed her a psalter. She had a sad resignation in her eyes as she whispered, "Oh, I have, but I fear he, like me, is dedicated to his job."

Joannicus nodded as he stopped at the Holy Water font and blessed himself.

They stood opposite each other with the large slate fount between them. Joannicus looked at Barb, and she smiled. Joannicus glanced away. Her gaze upon him was intense. He sensed he was missing something.

Monks filed in, and the moment passed. They sat in the row behind the choir as Paul came in sniffling, his lip protruding in a pout as he made his way toward them. Ambrose followed on his heels. Paul latched onto Joe's scapular. Ambrose lifted the lad to eye level and hissed, "He'll not rescue you, but Jesus might. Pray, boy, pray."

Ambrose plopped Paul into the proper seat and moved to his place in the choir. Paul moved two seats away from Joannicus and hung his head. Barb leaned over, whispering into Joe's ear. It tickled, and he heard little of what she said.

Prayers began.

Her floral perfume wafted sweet. He wondered what her qualifications for a mate might be. A sudden breeze flipped the pages of his psalter, causing him to lose his place. She had a pretty smile, and she had a big heart. Just as he found it, the light above them sputtered and then went out, leaving him in a shadowy space. Joannicus moved two seats over, and Barb followed him. The speaker system squawked and crackled in protest at the words being announced. For once, Paul was the lesser distraction.

After prayers, Paul stood pouting in the atrium, flanked by Ambrose and Jacob.

"We've taken care of it, Father," Ambrose announced. Joannicus grasped that something serious had transpired. "Paul's going to clean everything he wrote on. Some wood may need sanding and repainting. The *Epistle According to Paul* on the floor tiles will fade in time. He'll be busy for days cleaning."

"What did he do?" Barb asked as Paul hung his head and scooted behind Jacob.

"He has written on every flat surface he could reach. He knows to only write on paper," Ambrose said, yanking Paul from his hiding place and roughing his hair. "A prolific writer, this one, all the damned boards in the barn. When does he find time?"

"For shame, you know better," Joannicus said. He hoped Barb would see how they supported each other and not notice that Paul had escaped a watchful eye.

"Who taught him to write?" Jacob asked.

"I only instructed him to read," Joannicus said, crossing his arms. "I'm not the one giving him spelling tests."

"He's a smart boy. He needs to exercise his brain and his body." Ambrose turned to Paul and glared. "You can read?"

Paul pushed up against Jacob and nodded.

"So why in tarnation am I reading stories about talking bears?" Ambrose said, his face scrunching.

"It's lunchtime," Paul announced, taking Barb's hand and towing her toward the refectory.

Barb glanced back at Joannicus.

"Where have you been?" Jacob asked.

"With our guest," Joannicus said. "Seriously, don't give me that look. We were talking about Saint Benedict."

"What was she chatting about?" Jacob asked.

"Don't go there. I thought we wished she was an ally."

"Of the monastery, but remember what happened to Saint Benedict and his sister. God listens to what women pray for over the virtuous intentions of men."

Joannicus crossed his arms. Barb wasn't the praying type.

"Jacob, that's insane. She wanted to understand ours and Paul's life. That's all."

He had done nothing wrong. Anyone could have seen and found him. They had just talked.

The holy water font bubbled, dancing to its own tune as Joannicus blessed himself before heading out the door.

"By now, she should be an expert," Jacob mumbled.

An anger rose in Joannicus, and he stopped at the heavy wooden doors and turned. "Is there something you're not telling me?" Fearful that his superiors were observing his behavior. If one of them uttered the words "exclusive friendship," Joannicus would make another visit to the Abbot's office. They did not discourage closeness but warned everyone about exclusivity.

Jacob looked away. "I am worried. Ms. Carr is a single woman and, frankly, cute. Her frequent visits suggest she is looking for something."

"Well, I'm not it," Joannicus said, his voice harsher than he had intended as he reached for the door.

"I hope not. I do not want to lose you." Jacob smiled. "I will fight for you."

Joannicus marched toward the refectory. Jacob jogged to catch up.

"If she wants a man, she should search for the kid's father. He has one, and nobody has mentioned him."

"He could be dead or undesirable. I'm sure there's a reason. Barb hasn't brought up a missing parent. Why would we care since Paul is now with us?"

"You are right. Leave well enough alone."

As they entered the courtyard, Joannicus stopped. Everywhere he focused, he saw the chalk message. *I love Father Jonah.*

"Oh, my," Jacob said. "Seems like important news."

Joannicus closed his eyes and bowed his head.

Jacob choked back a laugh. "Good idea. I will pray for rain too."

CHAPTER 17
FLIGHT INSURANCE

Psalm 53: 11
I will proclaim that your name is good
in the presence of your friends.

At eighteen, Joannicus asked God to announce His will. The day after graduating high school, he left Louisiana and entered the postulant program at Saint Alberic's Monastery. God had been explicit then. Now, he felt unsure of that call–doubtful. The community seemed to hinder his success. They told Paul fairy tales and stories, which Paul took as church teachings.

A tug on the hood of his habit brought Joannicus out of his contemplation. Joe leaned his head back and opened his eyes to see Jacob standing over him.

"I found you. I am warning you that Paul is looking for you."

Father Joannicus winced and glanced around the sanctuary before speaking, "Seriously, what has he done now?"

"He was with Merlin. Those two should not be alone together."

"I refuse to babysit Merlin. Brother Mellitus is the Abbot's problem."

"Come on, let us hide elsewhere," Jacob said, toting a wicker basket. Joannicus wondered if, following Jacob, he was being led into the woods by the Big Bad Wolf.

Jacob and Joannicus sat on a bale of hay in the barn loft as night settled. Pink and orange streaked the sky as the sheep called to each other. The monastery on the hilltop glowed, putting the cemetery below in a deep shadow. Tranquility descended and reminded Joannicus of a time before Paul.

He now thought in terms of 'BP' and 'AP.' Before Paul, there were moments laden with the splendor of God. After Paul, he had the constant, meaningless chatter of a child's day.

Father Jacob poured hot tea and a shot of brandy from a thermos into a plastic cup and handed it to Joannicus. "Do you have vacation plans?"

"Vacation? A before-Paul event," Joannicus said as regret filled him with remorse. He had always relished the return to the monastery. It was his yearly honeymoon. Since Paul's arrival, he stayed home, worried that he would never come back if he left.

Disappointment etched Jacob's face. "You cannot wait until he turns 18 to go on vacation. Everyone needs a change of scenery."

Joannicus downed the brandy tea, which burned its way to his stomach. "Seriously, that advice is about as helpful as when I was a boy. When was your last break?"

Jacob braided the long strands of straw together. "I visit my sister for respite."

"You visit her every Friday. That doesn't count. Paul won't tolerate me leaving." Joannicus remembered the last time he left Paul with his confreres and the thousand questions Paul had peppered him with for an hour after his return.

"When did Paul become an Abbot? Joe, send him to Gracie's, or maybe Barbie should take him."

Joannicus pondered the possibilities. Gracie loved Paul, but a week might change that. Barb had book knowledge, but it fell short when dealing with an actual child.

He needed a vacation, but he couldn't leave Paul behind. Could he take Paul with him? Would Jacob help?

Even though Joannicus found Jacob a little quick-handed, Paul responded to him. He could go home to Louisiana. His parents would be helpful, and a return to his spiritual beginnings tugged at his soul.

After checking their luggage and confirming their seats, the two men headed to the gates.

Jacob stopped. "Ah, damn, where is Paul?"

Joannicus scanned the vast space. Children with adults, none of them were Paul. A vision of Paul riding the conveyor belt with the baggage came to him. Had he made a mistake agreeing to this trip?

"I assumed you had his hand."

"His hand?"

Jacob frowned and headed back to check-in. "I will find him."

Elation filled Joannicus as he reached for Jacob's arm, stopping him from moving away. "Wait, do we want to find him? We could go, and they'll call the monastery. He knows the number."

They would forgive them someday.

"Can you live with the guilt? Rose would kill us," Jacob said as they continued to the gate.

A voice blared over the intercom system, "Father Jonah, and we know that isn't the correct name of Saint All Brick Monastery. Or Father Jacob from somewhere near there. Please pick up the white courtesy phone."

They both frowned and walked to the phone.

"He's in the security office on the first floor."

"Good, and when we get there, I will wring his neck," Jacob said.

"Seriously, we should have moved faster," Joannicus said as he crept through the airport, dodging luggage and stray children. "I told you to check him as baggage. You are the one who insisted that he was a carry-on."

When they entered the security room, Paul shouted, "Father Jonah!"

All eyes turned to them. Joe's priest collar saved them from unnecessary questions.

"Do that again and we'll leave you behind," Jacob scolded, putting away his identification and grabbing Paul's shirt at the shoulder.

Joannicus patted Paul's head. "Never mind, Father Jacob, he's feeling guilty."

"Why is he guilty? Is he going to hell?" Paul asked as he skipped beside them.

Joannicus wasted no time getting himself through the checkpoint, leaving Jacob to manage Paul.

He was traveling to Louisiana with or without them.

"I'll go around that," Paul said, looking at the large doorframe.

"Just walk through it to Father Joannicus," Jacob instructed.

The alarm rang. Paul shouted as he dodged security and dove for Joannicus.

"Hold on, little guy," the man said.

It didn't surprise Joannicus when they emptied Paul's pockets to see a mountain of Saint Christopher's medals.

"I suggest you grab his ankles and shake him," the man in uniform said.

Joannicus agreed as he sat smugly, waiting and reflecting on the question, "How much trouble can one child be?"

Now you know.

"Did you swallow any of these?" Jacob asked, impatience tinged the quiz. Paul shook his head, setting off the alarm again.

"Dump all of them now!"

Joannicus glanced at his watch. Forty-five minutes. The security guard laughed as he cleared them.

Paul didn't appear cowed by Jacob's glare.

"I need one," Paul said, walking barefoot after him. "For flight insurance."

Jacob growled softly as they weaved through luggage and long-legged sleeping bodies, finding seats at the boarding gate.

"Seriously, where did you get those?" Joannicus said.

"Merlin started a collection. He said we could buy our way into heaven if the plane crashed," Paul said, plopping his shoes, jacket, and backpack in the brown plastic chair. "Some gave two because his saint license had expired."

Joannicus sat in the seat facing the window. He planned to escape to Saint Joseph's Abbey if the chaos continued. That was his secret arrangement–a visit with Mom and Dad and then four miles north of Covington to the peaceful grounds of Saint Joseph's. Jet fuel wafted through the gateway door as the pilot and attendants, with little suitcases, boarded.

"You get to keep one medal. Give the rest away," Jacob said as Paul enthusiastically raced to protect the souls who flew that day.

"That'll instill confidence in the airline," Joannicus said. His hope for a peaceful trip waned.

Jacob leaned against the window as Paul watched the luggage cart backing up to the plane.

"We should've left him with security," Joannicus said.

Jacob laughed. "Lighten up. It was funny. This will be good for Paul. Doting grandparents are fun."

Joannicus didn't have cozy grandma memories. One grandmother was a Baptist. With her, there was no dancing, singing, drinking, or games. He didn't know his other grandma.

Why did he let Jacob talk him into this? His folks didn't like kids. There were rules and expensive things. Joannicus pictured the doily-covered chairs, the white sofa, and the antique-lined shelves. This house wasn't Gracie's. Paul won't be able to explore every nook and cranny to his heart's content.

Joannicus realized that the next two weeks would be torture. God had tricked him. He missed Ambrose, something he had never expected to experience. Paul would get bored without the farm. He should turn around and go home. Joannicus shuddered and became thankful for the monastery, which distracted Paul.

They boarded the plane, placing Paul between them. Joannicus settled down for the flight with a book. Barb had told him that children often slept on planes. He glanced at Paul, who fiddled with the pocket and tray in front of him. Joannicus missed naps. Those breaks were rare now that Paul was six, but when they occurred, he thanked God. As an alternative, he taught Paul meditation. Some days, he got a solid ten minutes of silence. While they flew, Paul ate the honey-roasted peanuts and drank his juice. He was mostly silent and still. Halfway through the flight, the peace ended.

"Paul, please sit still," Joannicus said after the tenth bump.

"How long till we land on Earth?" Paul asked.

Joannicus glanced up from his book. Had he heard Paul correctly?

"Four more hours," Jacob said with a yawn. "You can take your seat belt off for a while."

Paul frowned. "No, I don't want to stick to the ceiling."

Joannicus groaned, guessing someone had filled the boy's head with nonsense. Were they trying to ruin his vacation?

Jacob chuckled. "Where did you hear this? Never mind. That cannot happen. We are not in a rocket ship. Gravity still works."

Paul carefully unbuckled his belt and stood in the seat. He played with the buttons, sending an icy stream of air into Joe's face. Joannicus peered over his glasses at Jacob, who smiled sheepishly.

"Do you need to use the restroom?" Jacob asked when Paul squirmed again.

"No," Paul said.

"Yes, you do," Jacob said. "Come on, I will take you."

"No, I can hold it."

"No, you cannot."

Paul gripped the metal armrest. "Yes, I can."

Jacob ignored Paul's protests and carried him to the back of the plane.

Joannicus heard Paul over the engines' roar and pretended he wasn't traveling with them. He avoided the glances of the flight attendant and wished he had ordered a drink.

Paul returned with an extra bag of pretzels and a grumpy Jacob. "I cannot believe how cruel our confreres are by telling him that the toilet would suck him out of the plane."

"Everyone knows that happens only if you flush," Joannicus said.

Jacob re-buckled Paul. "Okay, listen up. Everything the monks told you about this trip was a big fat lie, not real. Do you understand?"

Paul nodded and began asking a series of questions about the plane's design. Joannicus fluffed up his pillow, popped his head-phones in, and pulled the little blue blanket over his shoulder, chanting to himself. *Not my problem.*

CHAPTER 18
OBEDIENT SON

Psalm 83:11
One day within your courts
is better than a thousand elsewhere.

The green and brown taxi pulled up under the large shade tree. The white picket fence shimmered in the sunlight as they walked to the door. Butterflies danced on the tops of pink blossoms. The splashing water greeted them as the cushioned chairs on the dark wooden porch begged a tired traveler to sit and rest. The rose-colored door opened, and the sweetness of cinnamon floated in the damp morning air. Marian Brookes wiped her hands on her floral print apron before hugging, kissing, and fussing over Joannicus in a manner that made both Paul and Jacob laugh. Her dimples and olive skin mirrored Joe's.

"Mom, seriously," Joannicus said. "Cut it out."

"How often do I see you, once in five years?"

"Three years. It's been three years," Joannicus mumbled. "I call you every week."

"Every other week," Marian said, smiling at Jacob and Paul.

"This is Jacob," Joannicus said. "And that's Paul."

"Yes, I remember Jacob from your ordination. Welcome," Marian said. "Oh, my goodness."

She approached Paul, who stood frozen and wide-eyed. "He looks like... come in honey, let's go meet the Reverend," she said, taking Paul's hand and leaving the suitcase on the walk for Joannicus.

Reverend Malcolm Brookes met them in the hallway. They shook hands. His curly hair and round face pointed to the genetic link between father and son.

"Malcolm, this is Paul. Amazing, don't you think?" Marian said, gently caressing Paul's curls.

"Yes, I do. A striking resemblance to our Collin," Malcolm said, using Joe's childhood name. "Son, do you have something to share?"

Angst washed over Joannicus. *Not his parents, too.* Did everyone think he'd abandon his calling because of a wink and a smile? Joannicus didn't see the resemblance to him, maybe to his twin brother, Conner, who had died when he was eight from Reye Syndrome.

"We'll get out the photo albums and compare," Marian said, as she patted her son's arm.

"Mom, please don't embarrass me."

"What's so embarrassing about a mother showing off her baby?"

"I adore looking at baby pictures," Jacob said as Joannicus hurried away.

Joannicus stood in his old room. Jacob appeared and closed the door as Marian continued to remark about Paul. Nothing had changed much in this room. There were still two twin beds with matching blue and red coverlets. The bookshelves held the novels he had read as a boy. Gone were his posters of the universe, replaced with watercolors of flowers, a tribute to his mother's painting adventures.

"Who is that woman?" Joannicus said, putting his suitcase on the bed.

"Ah, your mother?" Jacob said.

"Seriously, my mother doesn't fuss like that."

"Perhaps she is getting senile," Jacob said. "Wow, your room is like a memorial to a saint. When I left, Judith nailed the door shut."

There was truth in the statement. Jacob's mother did not appear to be fond of Jacob. Yet she adored her youngest son, Jacob's half-brother, Vincent.

The door to the bedroom opened, and Paul entered, dripping white frosting from a pastry. Joannicus watched the goop fall in droplets onto the Asian rug.

"Where am I sleeping?" Paul asked, mouth full of dough.

"Guest room," Joannicus said.

Paul's brow scowled as Jacob ushered him out of the space.

Throughout the evening, Paul tried to climb into Joe's lap.

"I'm not Ambrose," Joannicus said as he pushed the boy away.

"Hold the child," Marian said, shaking her head as a white strand fell from the red hair clip.

"He doesn't do this at home."

"This isn't home. I now understand why you joined the monastery. You're not fond of children."

"He likes me," Paul said with confidence. "He's just skittish, like a newborn lamb."

Joannicus marveled at the conclusions Paul drew, and he wasn't sure he enjoyed being compared to the farm animals. Marion looked up from her tatting, and Joannicus realized he had lost the battle and picked Paul up.

Joannicus couldn't sleep. He listened to the even breaths of Jacob in the bed next to him. He heard the familiar sounds of the evening—his mother to bed, his father to his office. Classical music filled the hall, and he watched the door to his bedroom creep open. Paul tiptoed in. Discovering Jacob, the boy moved to where Joannicus sat. Not wanting a scene, he allowed Paul to crawl into the warm bed. He sat on the floor and waited until Paul fell asleep. He entered his sister Daria's forbidden lair, which was now for guests. She was six years older and rarely wanted anything to do with him unless it helped her. He examined the frilly lace and lavender accents, then turned and headed to the living room.

The next morning, after an uncomfortable night on the family room sofa, Joannicus sat on the back porch and sipped his tea. Jacob yawned and added sugar to his coffee. Paul raced around the floral-laden garden, trying to catch a butterfly. He appeared with a handful of Marian's peonies, and Joannicus gasped. He waited for the scolding, the temper, or at least a reprimand, but his mother ignored it all.

"I don't get it," Joannicus whispered to Jacob. "Paul has left fingerprints on the windows and slammed the screen doors, let the flies in, filled himself up with treats so he eats nothing at mealtimes, and my parents have not complained."

"They do not want to interfere. Talk to Paul, remind him of the rules of behavior."

Joannicus borrowed his parent's car and drove to Saint Joseph's Monastery. He spent the day in prayer and quiet conversation with the Abbot. In the late afternoon, he returned home. The rich aroma of raisin cookies greeted him as he approached the front door. Paul's excited voice echoed through the house from the kitchen. He passed his father's study, where Malcolm and Jacob discussed Sunday readings.

The candy dish stood half-empty, and Joannicus knew his mother had filled it that morning. Paul raced past him, lifted the lid, and scooped a fist full of sweets.

"Paul, that's your last dip. No more today, got it?"

Paul nodded and ran away. Joannicus sat in the floral sitting room smoothing a crocheted doily. Isolation engulfed him and left him questioning where he belonged. Where did God want him to be? He fingered the envelope in his pocket. Louisiana winters were mild compared to Montana. He would visit Saint Alberic's often if allowed. His teaching skills would help the seminary more than the college. He had a Ph.D. in divinity, even though the Divine escaped him.

The glass lid on the candy dish made a gentle clink.

"Paul?" Joannicus said. "Come here."

Paul stood sentry, flour handprints painted his shirt, cheeks bulging.

"What did I just say?" Joannicus asked, noticing how Paul held his hands behind his back. Paul swallowed. Joannicus grimaced.

"No candy," Paul said.

"You took more candy."

"No."

"Don't lie. That doesn't make things better. Tell me the truth," his voice was loud, and it carried through the house. Jacob, Malcolm, and Marian appeared in the hall.

"Let me see your hands," Joannicus said, knowing what he would see.

Paul backed away.

"Seriously," Joannicus said.

"Oh my, we should remove the candy dish," Marian said.

"No," Joannicus said, hurt that his mother believed removing temptation would teach a better lesson. "The problem isn't the dish, it's the child."

"He's a child. Lessons take time. We learn by making mistakes," Marian said. "Let's just put it away."

"He has to learn to resist the impulse," Joannicus said, as he took a step toward Paul.

"A candy dish does not endanger his soul," Marian said, brushing a lock of hair from her flushed face.

"I said no. He can learn the hard way. Paul, naughty step now," Joannicus said, pointing to three steps in front of the attic door. His father called this step the step of contemplation, but Joannicus had always thought of it as the naughty step. A place to reflect on his misdeeds.

"You're overreacting. He's a child, he needs to have choices. This one will not ruin his life."

"One path leads to another," Joannicus said. "Mother, you know this."

"Is that what happened? We allowed you too many opportunities?"

"What are you talking about?" Joannicus asked. Choices? The right way and the other way. His parents were always clear on what path to take.

"I'm speaking about why you aren't preaching with your father. Why are you Catholic instead of Baptist?"

"Marian," Malcolm said, moving closer to his trembling wife. "This is not the time."

The disclosure hit Joannicus hard. His mother had never expressed her disappointment at his conversion. Had she hoped her only son would marry and have children?

"You don't approve?"

"I didn't raise you Catholic. I worked at making sure you would not be that. Sometimes curses are not breakable."

Joe's head reeled. Curses. Was Jacob right? Had she lost her mind?

He discovered Catholics had a propensity for mystical and karmic fate, and he was aware of voodoo and black magic in the surrounding culture. Yet his mother was Baptist; she believed in the practical. His parents' rigid beliefs made him look to the Catholic Church, the opportunity to believe in the mysterious, that which defied explanation.

Paul turned away from them. A sticky peppermint, like a bulls-eye, clung to the jeans.

"Get back here," Joannicus said, feeling a rush of confusion like a gust of wind trying to blow him off his feet. They didn't approve. They didn't accept.

Paul waved his hands in the air. "See? No candy."

Joe's mind swirled, and he raised his hand as if to strike the child. Jacob moved swiftly, firmly gripping Joe's forearm as he grabbed Paul with his other hand.

Jacob stepped between them and lowered himself to face the boy. "No candy means no candy. You disobeyed."

The Reverend and Mrs. Brookes jumped when Jacob swatted the child.

"You lied. Unacceptable. Do not lie." Jacob swatted again and Paul protested loudly. Jacob sniffed the air. "The cookies are burning. A fair punishment for creating all this drama. Next time, choose the right path."

"Oh my," Marian said, as she raced to the kitchen to rescue the batch of cookies. Paul sniffled.

"Go help Mrs. Brookes clean up," Jacob said, dismissing the penitent boy.

"How was that better? Seriously, what did he learn from that?" Joannicus asked, grateful Jacob had stepped in.

"It's over," Malcolm breathed. "Right or wrong, Paul will recover."

"Unlike you and Mom," Joannicus said, hearing the words coming from his mouth. Emotions churned, and he felt himself spiraling out of control. He wanted to stomp to his room and slam the door.

"Your mother spoke needlessly," Malcolm said. "We're proud of you."

Joannicus could not muster the air to snort or scoff. Deflated, he turned and walked down the hall as Jacob followed.

"It is a melt-away mint, not a mortal sin," Jacob said.

"This is not funny. I thought they accepted my vocation."

His mind reeled. Was he overanalyzing this? They lied to him. Curses, when did they believe in voodoo? He didn't even know he had a Catholic heritage. Now he knew why he only had one set of grandparents. They allowed him to become Catholic.

"They love you. They didn't sell you for thirty pieces of silver," Jacob said.

The words stung, and Joe reeled, taking a step back, thinking he was not Jesus, and God didn't sell his son.

Joannicus felt his stomach contents climb up his esophagus. "It's all a joke with you: life, death, your monastic calling, your belief in God and redemption. My relationship with God is everything."

Joannicus saw the slight flinch on Jacob's face and squelched the guilt he felt for allowing his tongue to be a sword.

"True," Jacob said. The mask of compassion faded to tangible pain on Jacob's face as his blue eyes narrowed. "God is where you seek him. I am curious: where does Paul fit into your God's world?"

"I serve God," Joannicus shouted. "Stop being so self-righteous. Is Paul going to replace the children you lost? You come, interact, and then rush back to your safe hermitage. I'm shocked you're here now trying to be a father, stepping up when at home you can barely stand to be with him." Part of him regretted the words tumbling out, and part of him winced as his friend bled from the cuts he had made in Jacob's heart.

"Serving God does not exclude others," Jacob said, rising tall to tower over Joannicus.

"Are you serving God in that parish of yours? Are you converting souls?" Joannicus asked, his tongue stinging.

"I do not know. I am telling stories. That is all I can do. That and listen," Jacob whispered. "How was your visit to Saint Joe's?"

Joannicus took a step back. How did Jacob know? He had told nobody of his plan.

"What's going on?" Paul said, bottom lip quivering as he and Marian stood in the doorway. Jacob stepped into the hallway.

"A minor disagreement, nothing to concern yourself with," Marian said, putting an arm around the boy.

Jacob smiled at Marion. "I am sorry, but I cannot join you for dinner this evening."

They watched him walk out the door.

"Is he gone forever?" Paul asked.

"No, no," Marion said.

"Drats," Paul said.

"Paul Warner, sit," three voices said, pointing to the step.

"He didn't hear me," Paul whined as he sat.

"I did. You can get up when you've figured out what you'll say to Father Jacob when he gets back. Here is a hint. You begin with I'm sorry," Joannicus said as he plopped down next to Paul. He had the same task ahead of him.

Joannicus heard the singing long before Jacob stumbled up the walk. He had been sitting on the porch wondering how his mother could believe in curses. He knew she had Cajun roots. Cajuns were Catholic. Now he understood why he had never seen her side of the family. She broke tradition when she converted to Baptist. Joannicus reverting to Catholicism must have crushed her world. He also realized his rebellion made him more like her.

A beautiful tenor voice filled the streets. Jacob staggered to the porch and collapsed in the chair.

That was not a hymn.

Jacob grinned at Joannicus. "Good morning." The sweet liquor breath mingled with the honeysuckles. "You waited up for me. You did not need to."

"I prayed for you," Joannicus said, as the sun pinked the sky.

"Hm, that is a good thing. We should all do more of that."

"Jacob, I'm sorry."

Jacob ran his fingers through his unbraided hair. "Nah, you are not. You spoke the truth. I have no wish to be pierced with the love of God."

"Funny, I miss the piercing," Joannicus said, thinking Paul had overshadowed God.

"I admire you. I used to think you were naïve, but now I am in awe."

Joannicus felt sullen. His life as a monk was faltering in faith, and the prayerful atmosphere of St. Joseph was intoxicating. He could be alone with God again.

"Not sure I deserve your admiration." Joannicus looked over his cup of lukewarm tea. "If I go, what will happen to you?"

A sad smiled graced Jacob's lips. "Me, I go where the Abbot sends me. The obedient one is me. I only look like the wicked son. I will miss you."

CHAPTER 19
BROKEN

Psalm 16: 9-10
My foes encircle me with deadly intent.
Their hearts tight shut; their mouths speak proudly.
They advance against me, and now they surround me.
Their eyes are watching to strike me to the ground.

Back in Montana, Jacob and Joannicus dressed in the vestment room for Mass. The door opened with a creak, causing Jacob to jump. He needed to calm his nerves. His family would be present as his youngest brother, Vincent, was about to make his final profession. Jacob was pleased with his half-brother's decision, even with the strained family dynamics.

"There you are," Paul said, entering the room and approaching Jacob. "Merlin said you ran away and joined the Indians."

"Paul, I am an Indian," Jacob said.

"What kind?"

"Apsáalooke."

"Merlin said that's Crow, and they are tricksters."

"Seriously, haven't I explained to you that Brother Mellitus tells more tales than truth?" Joannicus said as he shooed Paul out the door. Moments later, they heard a scream, and Paul darted back into the space, diving into the closet of robes.

"There's a lady dressed as a monk, only in a funny colored robe–pale yellow. We should get those colors. Rainbow monks."

Jacob laughed as Joannicus shook his head.

"She is a Benedictine nun," Jacob explained. "And my sister, Sister Marie."

Marie's community wore habits minus the hood. After today, there would be three Benedictines in one family.

"Does everyone in your family take the black?" Paul asked, his voice muffled from where he hid inside the vestment closet.

The door banged open, and the tip of a cane kept it from bouncing closed.

"The natives are making me restless," Brother Mellitus said, pointing his cane at Jacob. "I think we should limit the number of guests at these celebrations."

From the closet, Paul's head appeared in a vestment sleeve. Joannicus attempted to free the boy from the tightly packed robes.

"You got the weirdest family–nuns, brothers, fathers, half-ies, and steps. Is it true that Brother Vincent is a twin?"

"Yes," Jacob said, helping to untangle Paul. Where did Paul get his information?

"I didn't see anyone who looked like him. Are you sure?"

"Quite sure, his twin is a girl."

"Eww," Paul said in a disgusted tone. "How we gonna know which father Mackenzie they are calling when Brother Vincent becomes a father?"

Jacob stepped back as if someone had gut-punched him. It was approved that he would be a priest. Nobody had mentioned that to him.

"Where did you hear that?"

Paul ran over to Mellitus and took his hand.

"It came to me in prayer," Paul said, tugging on Mellitus.

"Don't look at me," Brother Mellitus said. "God and the innocent know all."

Mellitus knew too much about everyone. A mirage of emotions danced without the rhythm of drums: jealousy, joy, and pride. He wondered if anyone from his family knew and how they would react. He remembered when he made vows that only Rebecca and Terrence had been there. He silently moved on to the priesthood but not without the scathing judgment of his mother, Judith. There were no proud or joyous family moments then.

"Paul, don't use prayer like that," Joannicus said, waving his arms to shoo the spying duo out of the room.

"But Father, you said wonderful things happen with prayer. Brother Ambrose says to pray all the time. He even prays in the bathroom. He says, 'Oh thank you, Jesus,' and flushes."

Jacob looked at Mellitus, who started to giggle, and then they both laughed long and hard until Ambrose lumbered in with a newly pressed cuculla, a robe with many pleats symbolizing that one had made final vows.

"Brother," Mellitus said as he exited. "Might I suggest more fiber in your diet?"

Confusion knitted Ambrose's brow as he shook his head. Jacob dried his cheeks, grabbed Joannicus, and headed to the church.

During the ceremony, Paul squeezed in between the chairs to be closer to the front. Jacob pulled him back.

"Sit," Jacob whispered. Paul plopped to the floor at his feet.

"Why's the Abbot wearing that pillar on his head?" Paul asked, pointing to the hat on Abbot Gordon's head.

"It's a miter, and it makes him appear official."

"Or corny," Paul said, leaning forward.

Jacob secretly agreed. Brother Ambrose, as Junior Master, looked exceptionally polished as he walked the junior monks around the church and led them to Abbot Gordon one by one. There was an intimacy about this ritual that Jacob liked.

"Come, my son, and hear me. I will teach you the fear of the Lord," Abbot Gordon sang.

"Oh no," Paul said when the three juniors knelt before Abbot Gordon and read their vows before signing them at the altar.

"Brother Ambrose said I wasn't to write on that table ever again."

Good, Jacob thought, remembering the weeklong clean-up job of the epistle according to Paul. Although there was still a board in the barn that held these words: *I love Father Jonah.*

Paul watched with rapture as each man chanted three times, "Uphold me, Lord, according to your promise, and I shall live. Let my hope in you not be in vain."

The words echoed in Jacob, and he worried that his monastic hope was misplaced. It was enough for now.

"Oh my God, oh my God," Paul said as he pressed closer to Jacob.

Each man prostrated himself on the floor covered with a black shroud. The child shivered, and so did Jacob, remembering the spine-tingling sensation he had the day he made his vows. He lay with his nose pressed to the incense-infused carpet, a cloth draped over him–a symbolic gesture of death. The words of Ezekiel murmured in his heart. 'Put off your old self, which belongs to your former manner of life and is corrupt through deceitful desires. Be renewed in the spirit of your mind, and put on the new self, created after the likeness of God in true righteousness and holiness.'

Paul expelled a long breath as they dressed the solemnly professed in a pleated cuculla.

"You got one of those," Paul exclaimed, recognizing something familiar in this strange ritual.

Jacob nodded and glanced at Joannicus, who didn't look as awed as he had seen him at other ceremonies of profession. Was he thinking about his vow of stability and whether it was to Saint Alberic or St. Joseph in Louisiana? He feared Joe's choice. He would miss him if he left.

The celebration was in full swing. Jacob had lost track of Paul in the mêlée of children that ran around the grounds between the monastery and the refectory. Various aromas of smoked goose and roast beef filled the air as he stood in line for food. He was hungry, for he had skipped breakfast, nervous at the appearance of his family. Joannicus stood in line behind him as Ambrose elbowed his way between them, his plate heavy with food.

"Not much fiber, Brother," Jacob said, smiling as a mischievous child.

"Fiber? What's with all this fiber? I want meat. You two stick with me. We will be the three monkateers."

Jacob snickered, wondering if the man had meant to say *musketeers*. Did he expect Mackenzie drama at this crowded public gathering? When the Mackenzie family was together, explosive moments happened. Yet he felt safe in Ambrose's shadow.

Paul scurried past them as they weaved their way to a table. Jacob wished he could sit with the other Apsáalooke.

Ambrose firmly elbowed Rebecca, Jacob's sister, out of his way.

He planted himself like a sentry among the Mackenzies on a bench that groaned as he placed his massive girth upon it.

Voices mingled, mixed with the laughter and cries of children as they ran around the tables. The sunset colored the sky with warm hues of peach and blue.

Teary-eyed, Paul ran up to Joannicus. "Someone punched me and called me something. And they won't let me play with my ball."

Paul turned to Brother Ambrose. "Make them give it back."

"No, Little One, share or find something else to play with," Ambrose said, licking his fingers.

"I shared my cookies, my blocks, and my marbles. They called me nasty names and took everything. I have nothing but a smack on the head and a punch in the arm. I don't like these kids."

"Try dropping the word *my*," Father Joannicus said, handing Paul a handkerchief. Paul elbowed his way into Ambrose's lap, bumping the beer in his hand. Ambrose blotted the spill with his habit sleeve.

The atmosphere shifted with Paul's presence and displeasure. Judith's face pinched with disapproval. He followed her gaze and watched Ambrose dangle loose meat above Paul's mouth as if he were a baby bird being fed worms.

Joannicus nudged Ambrose to stop the play. Brother Vincent stood in his new habit.

I want to say thanks to Father Joannicus. He inspired me to enter the priesthood."

Jacob felt a slight tap on his soul. Good for Joannicus.

"Wonderful," Terrence, Jacob's stepfather, said, embracing Vincent. "This is an honor. Our son, a priest."

Paul's head shot up from dipping the carrots in the chocolate pudding on Ambrose's plate. "You have a son who is a priest already."

A frozen smirk appeared on Jacob's face.

Judith looked directly at Paul. "Vincent is our blood."

"So?" Paul said, his face showing his innocence and confusion. "Father Jacob is blood, too. He's not adopted. He calls you Mom and Dad—adopted means chosen. I'm adopted, and I chose Father Jonah."

Ambrose covered Paul's mouth, muffling the words. "Come along, Paul. I think you are hungry."

"No, I'm not. I don't think that Father Jacob belongs to that tribe. They don't act like family. They are mean." Paul's voice trailed off as Ambrose removed him.

"Out of the mouths of children," Rebecca muttered, hiding a smile behind a piece of fry bread.

Joannicus held his breath. Jacob felt a thickness around him like a shroud. He traced his fingers on the pattern of the wooden table. *Ambrose, things are going to get nasty.*

"Well, don't you have something to say to your brother?" Judith asked, purposely not using his title. The bells rang, announcing the time and cutting off the conversation. Was it time for prayer or sleep?

What should he say? Congratulations?

"Thanks for the compliment, Brother Vincent, but a calling to the priesthood comes from a higher power," Joannicus said.

Jacob almost laughed at Joe's attempt to drain the air of tension by invoking God's name.

Paul re-entered the group with wet cheeks. What had Ambrose done? Paul stood in front of the Mackenzie children.

"I have to go to bed now. Can I please have my ball?" Paul said, words clipped.

The boy quickly glanced at the adults and gave Paul the ball with a mighty throw. It bounced off Paul's chest with a loud thud, causing him to fall backward. Jacob caught the ball one-handed, glaring at his nephew.

"What?" the boy said in a half-hearted challenge.

"Front and center," came a growl from the boy's father.

The tone made Jacob grimace as he helped Paul up, and they headed to the monastery—a perfect escape.

Jacob stood at the window in Paul's cell as he washed his face and brushed his teeth. Voices rose and fell. Judith railed about Jacob's rudeness and ruining the day for his brother, even as Vincent explained that Paul was always like that.

Jacob drew the curtains shut.

"Tuck me in," Paul said to Jacob.

"You okay?"

Paul nodded. "I don't hurt too much. I don't like those people. They left me broken," Paul said, sniffling, on the verge of tears.

"Yeah," Jacob said with a heavy sigh as he picked up the boy and carried him to the rocker. "I know."

CHAPTER 20
SCHOOL

Psalm 61:13
You repay each man according to his deeds.

Father Joannicus counted the red squares of light on the carpet in the church. The heating system clicked on, and the air hissed. Vested for Mass, he sat waiting.

Prayer didn't come.

The bells tolled, releasing him from the torturous hour. He rose and walked back to enter the church with his fellow monks. Few people attended the daily celebration. Some appeared lost; others were joyous for a moment of peace before facing the next challenges of their days. Joannicus felt like a hypocrite. He glanced around, wondering where Paul was.

Throughout the liturgy, Joe's mind wandered from Paul to parenthood to prayer. He looked up to see Father Bede turn to leave the altar to distribute the Hosts. In slow motion, the man fell forward, and the tiny discs of Jesus went flying. A gasp of horror rippled as monks tried to rescue Jesus, punctuated by Brother Mellitus in a hiccup of laughter. Prostrate on the carpet, Bede lay clutching the golden plate. Amidst the chaos, Joannicus watched Paul crawl out from under the brown altar cloth and exit the church.

Paul sat in a chair in the garment room, his feet swinging and hands gripping the armrest. The hall echoed with amazement at Paul's diabolical skill in tying knots.

Father Joannicus took off his liturgical robe and stood with his arms crossed.

"We don't tie our confrere's shoelaces into knots. What possessed you to do that?"

Paul stood and crossed his arms. "I was mad at him. He yelled at Merlin."

Father Joannicus slammed the closet door. "What will happen to me when I'm done yelling at you and Merlin?"

"Nothing," Paul shouted, putting his hands on his hips, imitating Ambrose's wide stance. "I still like you."

"Seriously, you need to use more discretion when choosing who you like and defend."

"What?" Paul's face scrunched.

"You need to rethink who you play with," Joannicus said, hanging up his liturgical robe.

"You like Father Jacob, and he's mean."

Jacob was Paul's default sibling. The one you blamed when you didn't want to be in trouble. The missing brother. That was Jacob's explanation when Joannicus wondered why Paul pointed an accusing finger at Jacob.

"He's not mean. He holds you accountable. I can say no to

Father Jacob. Can you say no to Merlin?"

"Of course he can," Brother Mellitus said, standing in the doorway.

"Look at my shoes." Father Bede roared from behind Mellitus. The laces dangled at uneven lengths with tightly fixed knots.

The vein on Bede's forehead pulsed.

Joannicus rubbed his temples, thinking they all needed a time-out. This was an emotional minefield. They needed a silent meal and time for tempers to dissolve. Joannicus grabbed Paul by the arm and headed into the hall as the community called after him, Bede, the louder, leading the chorus.

"Father Joannicus," Abbot Gordon broke through the cacophony. "We need to settle this before dinner."

No, we don't, Joannicus thought.

Abbot Gordon turned and led the way to his office. Paul sat sideways in a chair. He appeared to be unaffected by the bedlam. Joannicus plopped himself on the small sofa, away from the others. The unfairness of this moment simmered in his brain and gut—it wasn't his problem.

"Father Abbot," Bede said with a stomp of his foot. "This has gotten out of hand. Practical jokes are not funny."

"Wasn't a joke. I was mad," Paul yelled.

Joannicus closed his eyes as hunger growled in his belly. Hadn't Paul learned the lessons from the lives of the saints and martyrs? Fire leads to ashes.

"Paul," Abbot Gordon said as if dealing with a novice. "Revenge isn't a monastic virtue."

It was a nice monastic lecture. Joannicus wished he could escape. Guilt surfaced. Saint John's University had offered him a way out. He wondered if the Abbot would let him go.

Joannicus focused on the clock. Its pendulum ticked, and his stomach rumbled. He listened to "he said, he did" for the fifth time. They sounded ridiculous arguing with a child who was in the wrong. Each round became louder, and nothing changed. Joe placed his head in his hands and closed his eyes.

"Let's take a moment," Abbot Gordon said. His voice was tinged with frustration.

Brother Mellitus poked Joannicus with the end of his cane, leaving a dirt mark on his shoulder. "Wake up, sleepyhead."

Joannicus opened his eyes. This ancient monk aided and baited Paul. He was a negative influence, and Paul couldn't see that. The child only saw a magical monk. Dread crept into Joannicus. How many awful kids would Paul follow at school, and to what result? He envisioned visits to the principal's office at Chet Huntley Elementary.

Bede was right. This must end.

Joannicus stood and straightened his habit. "Brother Mellitus, this has to stop. You know Paul admires you. I implore you to use that for good."

Joannicus realized, from the smirk on the old monk's face, that Mellitus didn't respect his authority. Mellitus had tortured many a young monk with his caustic humor.

"Who died and left you in charge?" Mellitus asked. A wooly gray eyebrow rose.

After months of reading about power struggles with children, Joannicus saw Mellitus for what he was: a big child. Rule number one in parenting: never threaten what you can't deliver.

"If you don't cease, your time with Paul will end. But for now, I'm limiting your visits. One hour a day," Joannicus said, hoping he would not have to supervise too.

Mellitus stopped smiling.

Joannicus had won for the moment. He turned to Paul and put his hands on Paul's shoulders. "Stop the jokes. They're not funny.

If you're angry, use your words. If that doesn't work, forgive the person. That is the monastic way."

The clock on the wall filled the room with gentle tick-tocks.

He continued, "No recreation for you tonight, Paul. I want you to do something for Father Bede. Now that we settled this, I'm going to dinner."

Joannicus marched out of the office, leaving them in stunned silence.

"Maybe he is the Abbot," Mellitus said with a chuckle.

The day had arrived. A glimmer of hope shot through Joannicus as he drove to Chet Huntley Elementary School. Five days without Paul—there would be no more interrupted lectures by an inquisitive six-year-old.

"I don't want to go to school, Father." Paul crossed his arms and refused to get out of the car.

"All children go to school," Joannicus said, unbuckling Paul's seatbelt.

"I can stay home, and you can teach me. You're a teacher."

"Not for little kids. Seriously, you must go to school. You'll enjoy it. There are children of your own age. You will learn things. You're going, so you may as well come and check it out."

Paul groaned and exited the car. Joannicus tucked in Paul's shirt and tried vainly to tame the curls on the boy's head.

"I won't learn nothing," Paul said. "I'll miss prayers and my time on the farm. Brother Ambrose needs me."

Prayer without Paul–the thought made Joannicus euphoric. They walked into the building, which smelled faintly of perfume and disinfectant. Brightly colored animals carrying books and wearing backpacks covered the wall at Paul's eye level. They made their way to the office. Joannicus handed the completed paperwork to a woman with wispy brown hair. She looked it over and sent them to a classroom. They passed a scene of a boy on a haystack reading a book.

Class pictures of goofy smiling children and posters of information on programs and services hung outside Room 3.

"Why is everything above my head?" Paul said, looking up at the displays.

Joannicus pointed to the parade of animals leading to the kindergarten room.

"This is for babies. Everyone knows elephants are bigger than monkeys. None of them read."

"Behave, or I won't show you where the library is," Joannicus said.

"The library. What is that?"

"It's where you borrow books and bring them home to read. Not saint books."

Paul's eyes danced. Joannicus recognized he had won the first round.

A thin woman with short brown hair and tiny ankles that defied the body they supported appeared in the hall. "Hello. I'm Mrs. Piasano. I'll be teaching your son," she scanned over the paperwork, "Paul this year."

"I'm Reverend Joannicus Brooke, and he's not my son," Joannicus said, annoyed that his priestly collar didn't tell her that.

"She didn't read the papers," Paul whispered with disapproval.

"Oh," she said as she looked again at the forms. "You're Paul's guardian. He's an orphan. How interesting."

Paul peeked out behind Joannicus. "What's so interesting about that?"

Mrs. Piasano smiled. "Hello, Paul, I'll be your teacher this year."

Joannicus pulled Paul in front of him, surprised at Paul's sudden shyness.

"Nice to meet you," Paul said darkly.

Mrs. Piasano talked to Paul about what he would learn in kindergarten. Joannicus surveyed the colorful, busy room with its miniature desks that came up only to his knees. Mrs. Piasano explained the games on the shelves and the free time reward for completing assignments. Joannicus recalled his education classes; the keywords for elementary school teachers were to keep the children busy.

"Here is our circle, where we sit, observe, and note the weather. Each week, we pick a helper."

Joannicus noted that Paul was more advanced than this. A slight worry crept into his mind. *Would they be able to keep Paul busy?* That wasn't his problem. It would be theirs.

Paul crossed his arms. "I know that stuff. I can count to a hundred. I can read and write my name. I can add and subtract. I count the chicken eggs all the time. I know twelve makes a dozen. I can spell Louisiana, capital-l-o-u-i-s-i-a-n-a. Want to hear me read or count?"

"Stop with the attitude," Father Joannicus said with an apologetic smile. A quick hope ran through him. Paul would be there all day if they advanced him.

Paul flopped himself in a blue plastic chair. Joannicus looked for a seat, but there were only miniature plastic chairs. Feeling awkward, he sat, his knees rising to his shoulders. Mrs. Piasano perched in a larger version of the tiny chairs.

Paul looked at the stack of papers on the desk and read: "This says, 'Welcome to kindergarten. Your child will need crayons, glue, twelve pencils, a large box of tissue, and a book bag. We are...'"

"Excited," Mrs. Piasano said.

"We are excited that your child will be with us this year," Paul continued.

"Thank you, Paul," Mrs. Piasano said. The warmth in her voice evaporated. "Do you have any questions about kindergarten?"

Questions? How many hours will you keep him?

"What kind of writing do you call that?" Paul asked, pointing to the printed alphabet on the wall.

"That is printing. You'll learn how to print this year."

"Why? It's kind of ugly. I like to write my name like a grownup."

"Well, kindergartners print."

Joannicus gripped his knees with his hands. Could she turn them away?

Paul's face collapsed. "When do kids get to write?"

"You learn cursive in the third grade."

Paul turned to Joannicus. "Father, I want to go to third grade. I can write cursive now."

The interview was over. Joannicus gathered the papers and left. Once outside in the parking lot, Joannicus tried to calm himself. He had never felt so embarrassed. Could a school reject a kindergartener?

"What about the library?"

"Not today. We need to work on your humility," Joannicus said.

Joannicus got in the car, slamming the door behind him.

"You're not being fair. I don't want to go there. I won't learn anything. I need to be with Merlin and Ambrose," Paul said, climbing into the car.

"Seriously, you don't know everything, and you will go to school."

Paul pouted, and Joannicus jerked the car into reverse, wondering if they had boarding schools for kindergartners.

CHAPTER 21
GRACIE

Psalm 38:1
I will be watchful of my ways.

J oannicus put the last stamp on the envelope addressed to St. Vincent's Arch Abbey. He slipped the letter between the stack of papers as he heard Brother Mellitus enter the community room. He glanced up to see Mellitus pushing Paul in a wheelchair.

"Where have you been?" Joannicus asked Paul as Jacob appeared from outside, heading straight to the coffee urn.

"In the church," Paul said.

"You don't want to know. But since you asked, we were praying like all good Benedictines, *Lectio Divina*," Mellitus said.

"Can I have coffee?" Paul asked, climbing out of the chair and peering over the counter.

"Seriously, no," Joannicus said, "And no snacks, it's too close to supper."

Mellitus grabbed a handful of cookies and slipped one to Paul. Father Joannicus pretended not to notice. He was not in the mood to play Inquisition.

"When do I get a habit?" Paul asked, standing on the sofa.

"You're not a monk," Joannicus said.

"You have a habit," Jacob said, making his way to the table. He eyed the cookies. "It is annoying others, and you are good at it."

Paul bellyflopped onto the sofa and asked, muffled by the cushions. "But I want a dress like yours. Can I have communion at Mass? It's not fair I have to starve when you get a snack."

"Communion is not a snack. When you're in the second grade, after instruction, you can receive," Joannicus said, watching Mellitus empty the plate of cookies into his habit pocket.

"Do I go to school for that?" Paul asked, bouncing on the sofa.

"Seriously, yes, you must learn about the sacraments to participate in them."

"Don't fret, kid. There is nothing to it unless you're a Baptist," Mellitus said, handing Jacob the empty plate. "Don't give me a dirty look, Chief. I was just keeping you from temptation."

"What's a Baptist? Oh, wait, I know that was what John was, a Baptist."

Jacob scooped Paul off the back of the teetering chair as Paul tried to bridge the span between the sofa and the armchair.

Mellitus reclaimed his wheelchair, an enormous grin on his face.

"I'm not playing Too Many Questions."

"It's twenty questions," Paul corrected. "Can I have a sleepover?"

"Seriously?" Joannicus asked. Visions of children running down the monastery halls, jumping out, and shouting 'Boo!' at unsuspecting monks caused him to hold his breath. The clock on the wall ticked.

"Oh, please," Paul said. "Charlie won't be any trouble. I promise."

"I'll consider it," Joannicus said, wondering if Mellitus had anything to do with the unusual request. Paul had been in school for months now, and never had he mentioned sleepovers.

"Can you do it before Saint Teresa of Avila day?" Paul climbed into Mellitus' lap.

"Come on, let us leave Grumpy and Busy alone so they can perfect their habits," Mellitus said as they rolled away.

"Sounds like Paul has a friend," Jacob said. "Friends keep kids occupied."

"I don't want to open my weekends to little boys and mischief. Mellitus is enough fun for anyone. He's up to no good. Those two spend too much time together."

"I thought you had limited it to an hour a day."

"More or less," Joannicus said, wondering when he would need to supervise.

"You could send Paul and his plus one to Gracie's," Jacob suggested.

"Oh right, one more thing to add to her list of things we are doing wrong," Joannicus said, shoving his papers into his briefcase.

Jacob balanced on the back legs of the chair. "She has a list?"

"Seriously, she does, doesn't every woman? So do the other members of the 'Concerned Citizens for Paul' women's club." That sounded unkind. He didn't mean it to come out that way. The critiques designed to be helpful did not help him control Paul.

Jacob's chair clunked on the floor as he rose. "And here I thought I was Grumpy."

Instant guilt washed over Joannicus. "Don't be like that. Just help me fend off the well-meaning women."

"It cannot be that bad," Jacob said. "Paul talks about how fun it is at Gracie's, and it gives you a free weekend. Barb is the one who concerns me. She is too interested in us."

"She seems to have a dual purpose when she comes to visit. I can deal with her. You could help by coming with me this Sunday to the Hoffman's. I hate picking him up. They want to socialize, and that leads to the list."

"Have you considered structuring it so you drop him off and they bring him back Sunday evening?"

Joannicus knew Barb would disapprove, for she believed that the custodial parent should be the one to retrieve a visiting child.

Sunday afternoon arrived, and Joannicus approached Jacob in the community room.

Jacob looked up from the beer he was drinking, sighed, and gulped the rest before standing and following Joannicus to the parking lot.

They drove to Gracie and Patrick Hoffman's home. Joannicus parked the car in front of the immaculate two-story houses identical to those around it. A green lawn and a rainbow of geraniums in pots welcomed them as they headed to the door. Paul ran out, barefoot and covered in white flour, arms waving.

"We're baking," Paul shouted, stopping and frowning. "What are you doing here?"

"Monks come in pairs," Joannicus said, hoping Paul would believe him.

"Welcome," Gracie said, smiling as Paul raced back inside.

As they entered, the bakery's aromas enveloped them. The entryway opened in three directions. The upstairs was graced with a carved oak rail. The living room was heavy with wooden furniture. Down a passage lay the kitchen.

"This is Father Jacob Mackenzie Knows the Song," Joannicus said.

Gracie tilted her head to look the tall man in the eye.

"I've heard about you," Gracie said. "The Mackenzie family from Saint George's parish?"

"Yes, my parents are parishioners, and we attended school there," Jacob said.

"Fine school," Gracie said with approval. "I don't understand why Paul can't go there."

"Public school is fine," Joannicus said, wishing to avoid a lengthy conversation about the conditions in Sarah Warner's will. Explanations would cause her to volunteer to drive, and he was sure seeing her every day would test his vows. He was already wavering in stability and obedience. He didn't need to add *conversatio morum* to the mix.

The two monks sat in the living room on the floral-printed sofa. The smell of roasting meat drifted towards them. Jacob's stomach growled in the silence.

Paul appeared flour-free. "Can we stay for dinner?"

Joannicus shook his head.

"Why not?"

"We will miss prayers," Joannicus said, seeing Gracie's hot, disapproving look.

"It's your fault," Paul pointed at Jacob as he stomped up the stairs, slamming a door.

Gracie headed upstairs. Joannicus turned toward the dining room and observed a table set for four.

"It appears they were planning on you staying," Jacob whispered. "We could stay. It smells delicious."

"And reward his negative behavior?" Joannicus said, not wanting to socialize.

Patrick Hoffman stepped into the room and introduced

himself to Jacob.

"Ah, you're the mean one. Paul blames you when he's here. I guess you're his sibling. I used to blame my dog when things went wrong. He likes you a lot. You're like an older brother to him. He shares with me all the adventures, some I'm sure are exaggerated."

Joannicus glanced at Jacob, who smiled sheepishly—sibling rivalry. Joe had skipped that chapter in the book that Barb had loaned him. Did Paul see the community as siblings?

Patrick smiled. "Can I get you some coffee or tea? Those two mean well, but perhaps they need to be less impulsive."

Jacob chuckled as Patrick explained that Gracie and Paul had plans.

Guilt cornered Joannicus, and he caved in. He wanted to be home, at prayers, not practicing social graces he didn't have.

Puffy-eyed Paul came down the stairs to the living room. Joannicus informed him they would stay, and Paul perked up.

After setting an extra place, they sat. Joannicus draped his napkin across his lap and studied the floral print on the dish before him. Scrumptious aromas rose from the serving bowls. Paul piled his plate with mashed potatoes and declined the meat.

"We don't get to talk when we eat," Paul announced through a mouthful of food.

The conversation stuttered and started until Patrick talked about the ancient church. Joannicus found himself in teacher mode.

"I want another roll," Paul said, and Jacob pointed to the half-eaten one on the child's plate. Paul reached across the table, and Jacob slapped his hand. Although Paul did not fuss, Gracie breathed rapidly.

"How dare you, in my house, to my godson," Gracie said, turning bright red, unable to contain her disapproval. "You're the one who spanks, aren't you? Are you aware that is a barbaric method?"

"Gracie, it's not our business," Patrick whispered.

Joannicus cleared his throat, hoping they would catch on. Barb said never to disagree in front of the child. Even the Rule favored discretion when correcting faults. Yet Joannicus knew all the expert advice, books, and suggestions were worthless. Each event had its own timing and solution.

Paul ate the remaining piece of his roll.

"We use what works for us," Joannicus said, stabbing his green beans.

"He doesn't like it," Gracie said, glancing at Paul, who was silent.

"He doesn't want to go to bed or brush his teeth," Joannicus said. He wondered why she was being protective. What tales had Paul been telling her? Did she think they were mistreating him?

"That's not discipline. Everything that happens to Paul is our business. We professed before God and that community we would watch over him."

"Over his soul," Joannicus said, setting his fork down as Paul snatched a second roll. Why was he misbehaving? They all stared. Joannicus cleared his throat. Jacob's eyes narrowed, and his jaw tightened.

"Right now, his soul is connected to his body."

Paul played with his mashed potatoes and gravy, making brown rivers down the white sides with his finger. The raised voices unnerved Joannicus, but he saw nothing wrong with Jacob's actions. Jacob was always reasonable concerning Paul's behavior.

Joannicus couldn't stand it any longer. Some behaviors were unacceptable, even if it was Gracie's house and her rules.

"Paul, you're being wasteful and disrespectful. Leave the table until you are ready to behave," Joannicus said.

Paul's mouth hung open, as did Gracie's. The cuckoo clock squawked. Jacob pushed his beans around his plate.

Paul rose and folded his napkin with extraordinary care, lingering over every crease, glancing first at Joannicus and then at Gracie. Patrick patted Gracie's clenched hand. Joe chanted in his mind: *Go now before I lose it, go now before I lose it.*

As soon as the upstairs bedroom door closed, Gracie exploded. "For God's sake, he's just a child. Children make mistakes."

"Seriously, Paul is playing you and me for fools, and we all failed by not being a united front," Joannicus said. "He was out of line, and we realize that. Father Jacob was the only one who confronted him. We all owe Father Jacob an apology. If Paul misbehaves in my presence, I will correct him here or at the monastery. If I'm not here, I trust your choices."

Gracie rose stiffly and cleared plates. Joannicus could see Paul's shadow lingering on the stairs as Patrick escorted the monks to the living room.

"Come here," Joannicus said.

Paul apologized before Joannicus could scold him and then dashed into the kitchen.

Joannicus stared at the velvet painting of a matador, wondering if he had just ended his free weekends. He traced the flower on the arm of the sofa as Paul entered, carrying a small cake.

"Happy birthday," he sang out.

Joannicus tried to remember what day it was, April 21st—his birthday.

"Thank you," Joannicus said stiffly. Paul told the tale of making a cake. After the cake, Gracie sent Paul upstairs to pack.

"I understand that you have yet to celebrate Paul's birthday," Gracie said.

"We don't celebrate birthdays. Our old lives are in the past. We commemorate feast days, and Paul joins in those celebrations," Joannicus explained. "You're welcome to celebrate his birthday. I believe it's October 24th."

"Little children need recognition. It makes them feel special."

"Yes, I agree. Seriously, this is not a contest. We both want what's best for Paul."

Paul thumped his suitcase down the stairs. Joannicus rose. It was time to leave. "But since we are discussing what is best for Paul, I would prefer that he not watch monster movies while he's here."

"Monster movies?" Gracie's cheeks reddened as she looked at Paul.

"Yes, the kind with ghosts in them. They give him nightmares, and we both know how important it's for children to sleep well."

Paul hugged Gracie and darted to the car.

"Well, that was fun," Jacob said as they left the Hoffmans' home.

Joannicus climbed into the car and turned to glare at Paul. "Don't play me against Mr. and Mrs. Hoffman again. Or I will not be the one picking you up." Joannicus handed Paul a rosary. "Since you were so awful to Father Jacob and me, pray that I don't banish you to your cell for the rest of the evening."

Words of protest formed on the boy's lips but did not erupt. *Good*, thought Joannicus.

He has learned something.

CHAPTER 22
OLD MEN AND WOMEN

Psalm 80: 12
O that my people would heed me,
that Israel would walk in my ways!

I t would have been an ordinary Mass during ordinary times
if someone hadn't glued the other chalices to the serving
tray. Joannicus watched Paul and Mellitus try to restrain
themselves during the antics. Merlin sat in his chair and
grinned.

"Looks like we will have to sip our Jesus or lap Him up," he
said. "Oh, let's be Byzantine today, a little Eastern and Western
mix of rites. I have a gold spoon for dipping."

Mass took longer because there was one spoon and many
partakers. Paul and Mellitus giggled at the sight of monks opening
their mouths for the wine.

This has to stop, thought Joannicus. Invading the sanctity of the Mass was grievous. Yet the old monk sat delighted in himself.

After Mass, Joannicus crept down the hall, wondering why he was summoned to the Abbot's office.

"How do we remove the chalices?" Abbot Gordon asked as Joannicus entered the room.

"Wash them off. It's just water-based glue," Mellitus said.

Abbot Gordon reprimanded Mellitus and Paul while looking at Joannicus.

"We were learning about other Catholics," Paul said in a rehearsed tone.

"Doesn't hurt to branch out occasionally," Mellitus said, winking at Paul.

Abbot Gordon continued to stare at Joannicus as he spoke.

"Brother Mellitus, please try to restrain yourself. Paul, you have an hour in the corner in the community room."

Joannicus turned to leave, still wondering why he was there.

"Now, is that fair, Father Abbot? The brat catches trouble, but I don't. I'll accept this silly punishment, along with the little troublemaker."

"Brother Mellitus, really," Abbot Gordon sighed.

"No, no, I insist. It's only right. I was the accomplice to this heinous act. You must punish me. I expected something a little more creative from you, Father Joannicus."

"Shh, Merlin, don't," Paul said. "This is good, Father Abbot. I'm going now." The child headed out the door, passing Joannicus.

Brother Mellitus sat next to Paul, who faced the wall. Mellitus had placed a sign on his chest: "Being punished." The man looked foolish. He hoped the shenanigans would end. The old monk relished the attention, the stares, and the snickers. Joannicus reflected on their first meeting–how unpleasant Brother Mellitus was and that he remained so. Mellitus took pleasure in breaking novices by collecting their faults as a sweater collects lint. The man had a nickname for everyone. Mellitus perceived Joannicus as less than a monk because he had been a Baptist before converting to Catholicism—a spy among us, a traitor to his own kind. Joannicus ignored the ridicule, for he knew God called him. These days, the old man called Joe "his holiness." That was harder to endure.

He was far from perfect. Perfection was not what Joannicus saw when he looked at his soul.

Three days later, Paul raced past him at turbo speed. Joannicus headed to the community room, where they celebrated the Saint Benedict feast with sweets, drinks, and appetizers. Mellitus and Paul sat side-by-side, snickering and pointing. Joannicus moved closer to them.

"Oh, my goodness," Paul said, giggling. "Brother Moses now has a white habit."

"A true splasher."

Joannicus looked and gasped. The front of the monk's black habit showed white dots as if an ink pen had exploded. Brother Ambrose had a streak of white from one shoulder to the next across his scapular.

"Splasher or dunker. Dunker." Mellitus said to Paul.

"His middle dot is on his belly," Paul giggled.

It didn't take long for others to see their black habits were speckled with white.

Mellitus laughed at the mayhem. "His holiness is a dabber. Three small, perfect dots."

"It's okay, Father," Paul said. "I have a black marker to fix the white."

White was not the color Joannicus was seeing. Paul cheerfully went from monk to monk, repairing the damage when each monk had blessed himself at the holy water font. The water had been replaced with bleach.

"Seriously, Brother Mellitus, this is not teaching good steward-ship," Joannicus said through clenched teeth.

"Oh, Father, I was correcting habits–bad ones at that. The community should be aware of how reverent they are. It was a tool for learning, not for causing problems."

"You need to stop."

Joannicus sat baffled. They were not that angry.

Sleep escaped him that night, so he pondered what Mellitus was teaching Paul. They were more like siblings; he didn't relish disciplining an old monk. But he knew Paul enjoyed Mellitus. Paul had explained that Mellitus was Merlin the wizard and knew magic. Then, he compared transubstantiation and miracles to magic, concluding that it was all magic.

How to explain to a child the difference between miracle and magic. Joannicus didn't even try.

One afternoon, after Mellitus rolled into the community room alone, Joannicus steeled himself for the talk. He glanced at his watch. Joannicus had practiced the opening lines and the reasons. Mellitus would not get to him.

Brother Mellitus parked his wheelchair and walked to the kitchen area, where he fixed himself a cup of coffee. It was a day for fasting, yet Mellitus placed scones on his plate. He moved with perfect balance towards Joannicus. The helpless monk he portrayed to others was an act. Joannicus could feel his chest tighten.

"I'd offer you some, but I appreciate how you love mortifica-tion," the old monk said.

"Where's Paul? Doesn't he spend the afternoon with you?" Joannicus asked.

"He's busy."

That did not sound good. Joannicus opened his eyes wide, a stare that he used on Paul whenever he had something meaningful for the boy to remember.

"Father, that doesn't work on me. That x-ray vision stare does not cow me."

For a monk of 72 years, Joannicus expected more. "It's not meant as a game."

"Everything is a game to Paul," Mellitus said, biting into the wafer.

"If you continue setting up Paul, you will both lose."

Brother Mellitus shook his cookie, letting the crumbs fly. "Hell's bells, you're frightening me. If you haven't noticed, you're not the Abbot."

"I am where Paul is concerned. Stop using him as a pawn in this sick game of yours. Pranks make people not like you. Paul doesn't need that."

"Life is a game. People are awful. They betray you and hurt you. That life lesson one should learn early to survive, or else one becomes a wimp like you. The world is not simple."

Things were not going well.

"You're a monk. Can't you at least set a Christian example? Do kindness instead of pranks."

Mellitus shook his head.

Paul raced into the room. "Merlin, I did it. It's done." He froze and looked at Joannicus.

Did what? Dread filled Joannicus, but he held his tongue.

"Good boy. Now you can fetch me my cane, wheelchair, and a novice, preferably that pudgy one," Mellitus said. "I can walk, but my helplessness makes the young ones feel pious about helping an old monk."

Joannicus shook his head. The sentiment of compassion didn't come easily when dealing with Mellitus. Even if Joannicus tried, he had a tough time putting a positive spin on how Mellitus lived his monastic calling.

Joannicus spent the next day waiting to see if the mischief would appear. When nothing happened, he prayed a small thank you as he walked into the church with his conferrers for Sunday evening vespers.

Paul sat with Gracie and Patrick Hoffman—it was Paul's weekend with them. Gracie's intense gaze seared Father Joannicus. Why can't she be more like her husband, Patrick? He was a calm, sensible man. Prayers ended, and Joannicus wished he could exit out a side door. He was not in the mood for a second sermon.

"Father Joannicus," Gracie began as soon as he entered the atrium. She stood so close to him he could smell the scent of roses. "I thought we had an understanding about the rigors of monastic living. We discussed how children need to feel special."

Joannicus looked over Gracie's shoulder. Ambrose stood a short distance from her, making faces. Patrick studied the pattern on his shoes. What tales had Paul spun? They did not force him to pray. Didn't she know Paul chose to pray? He sighed, turning back into her tirade.

"And fasting for Lent, we both understand children are exempt from those practices."

Paul wasn't fasting, and Joannicus didn't even suggest it.

"I think you're mistaken. Our monastic Lenten practice is to select a fault and work on it. I believe Paul has been working on gratefulness."

The tight lips on Gracie's face told Joannicus that she remained unimpressed.

Paul grabbed Joe's arm. "Father Jonah, can we get chocolate cereal? I like it and raisin toast."

"No, I don't think so."

"Why don't we go to the store and buy new cereal?"

They had three choices of cereal, and Paul preferred oatmeal. Paul hopped on one foot and then the other. Joannicus wondered how much sugar Paul had consumed. Would he even eat dinner tonight?

"How come we don't watch TV?"

That had come up before. Joannicus didn't watch, but he didn't stop Paul. He could hardly remember the last time he sat in front of the television, even after the monastery bought a color set. Many monks watched shows–Brother Ambrose and Paul laughed together at cartoons on Saturday mornings.

Gracie continued, "Perhaps you can explain hell, fire, and damnation?"

Paul stood statue-like, grimacing. His hyperactivity drained Joannicus's energy like a hole in a bucket. Joannicus shook his head. He had not talked to Paul about salvation. The road to heaven began with good works. The threat of damnation didn't enter their conversations. All the bible stories he read to Paul spoke of love, forgiveness, and acts of kindness.

How much sugar had Gracie consumed?

Tobacco and Irish spring soap filled his nostrils.

"Oh, that's mostly nonsense," Ambrose said. "Hellfire and damnation, that's me. You wouldn't want me using those other words now, would you, ma'am?"

"What other words?" Paul asked, eyes filling with curiosity.

Joannicus wondered what words Ambrose would use.

"Paul is clever. The other day, he was asking about swamp monsters and wanted to know why Santa had more magic than Jesus. He claims he sat on Santa's lap and got his wishes granted faster than when he prayed. Paul also says he loves to eat cake and ice cream for breakfast."

The room whirled. Santa. Joannicus no longer felt on the spot.

Irritation, like an itchy rash, tickled his tongue. Joannicus had asked her specifically not to introduce the jolly man dressed in red. She had undermined him. He could hardly believe the audacity of the woman.

Paul tugged on Ambrose's sleeve and glanced at him with a guilty, beguiling look.

"Tell me the words. I won't repeat them. I just want to know them. Please, Brother Ambrose, please."

Gracie turned a little pink as she pursed her lips. Patrick grinned and cleared his throat.

"Must be getting to them chores," Ambrose said as Paul followed him, begging for words.

"Well, dear," Patrick said. "Shall we head home?"

Joannicus watched them leave, Paul begging Ambrose and Gracie in stunned silence. Joannicus headed back into the church. He stopped and then turned around. No, he was not dealing with Santa. Let that be Gracie's problem. She let the genie man into Paul's life. Let her explain why all wishes weren't granted.

CHAPTER 23
BROTHER MELLITUS

Psalm 104: 30
Their land was alive with frogs,
even in the halls of their kings.

Joannicus heard about the Vaseline on doorknobs long before he entered the monastery. When he saw Mellitus and Paul in the community room, he said, "I assume you cleaned every knob?"

"Why do you assume it was Paul? It might have been the novices," Mellitus said, peering over his spectacles at Joannicus.

The complaints had piled up. Joannicus felt forced to step between Paul and Mellitus.

"Seriously, our novices are more mature than that. Enjoy your time together because, after today, Paul's time with you is over."

Paul's mouth hung open, but Mellitus trailed after Joannicus, following him into the peaceful hallway. "What are you saying?"

Joannicus stopped, turned, and looked at the bent old monk. He couldn't be that dense.

"You cannot spend time with Paul except during recreation."

"You have no right. He's not a novice. Don't take away Paul's friends just because you don't have any."

"I gave you fair warning. I told you to stop with the jokes. Paul doesn't need lessons on how to misbehave."

Paul tried to pull Mellitus back to the community room as Joannicus walked away.

"Don't get mean. He won't change his mind if you get mean."

"We'll see about that."

The week began with gnats–clouds of them rising and descending around him. He didn't eat in the office.

Joannicus found the rotten peach in a withered plant, an apple core in the trash, and a half-filled wineglass. He opened the window and door to his office, hoping the breeze would send the insects out of his space. The day worsened with a failing, tearful student, and missing test scores required his attention. Now, his throat seemed scratchy and sore. Joannicus looked forward to a quiet evening, perhaps with a cup of hot tea and lemon. He pulled on the monastery's front door, but it would not open. He set down his briefcase and fished in his pockets for keys. The jingling keys were for the guesthouse. His key slipped into the lock, but nothing happened when he turned it. The March wind gusted, and he shivered. He would return to the monastery. Someone had to be inside. Joannicus walked around to the backyard of the monastery. Despite the wind, his head seemed on fire.

He pushed the iron gate, but it didn't open. He pulled, but the metal seemed welded to its hinges. As undignified as it was, he had no choice but to climb the wall. He tossed his briefcase over the rock wall, removed his habit, and placed it on the rocks above his head. He searched the wall for anything poisonous. Last week, he had cleaned out the flower vase to find that someone had added a branch of poison oak. He had to forgo being the principal celebrant for Mass because his hands were red and swollen.

His first attempt over the wall scraped his shin and left his toe throbbing, but determination brought success. He realized too late that he was too old to jump off walls. The ground was damp and cold. With elbows and knees scuffed, he limped to the patio.

"Well, if it isn't Abbot Joannicus," Ambrose said, his feet propped up on the table as he smoked. Paul hung upside down from the other end. In no mood to banter, Joannicus dressed in his habit and tried the glass doors to the community room, only to find them locked.

Joannicus scratched his head. His fingers were still tender from the wall. "Why is the monastery closed up like a sarcophagus?"

"I had to pee in the bushes," Paul said.

"Seriously," Joannicus said, looking through the window. He saw Mellitus sitting, his back to the doors and a warm fire glowing. He tapped on the window, but the old monk didn't move.

"No use. The old man has decided he is deaf today."

Joannicus slipped on his gloves and zipped up Paul's jacket. "I'm well aware of his selective hearing, but that doesn't stop him from walking."

"His cane is here. He's separated from his power source and growing weaker. You got to save him," Paul said while scratching his head.

Ambrose smiled. "I'm not sure separating Batman and Robin was a good idea. He seems to have a lot more vinegar than sugar in him."

"I had no choice. Mellitus would not listen. The community

was tiring of the practical jokes," Joannicus said, giving Paul a stern look. This was an attempt to intimidate them.

Ambrose lit another cigarette and sent Paul to gather sticks as he vigorously scratched his head. "I hope you aren't blaming him for the fuse fiasco. I can't believe he could plunge us into darkness like that. The whole hilltop?"

"Not without help," Joannicus said. He wondered if Paul had the key to the door. From the moment of separation, Mellitus had become unbearable, sending notes through anyone who would deliver them. Then, there were phone calls all day and night, asking, demanding, and begging him to set Paul free. Even Paul pleaded, promising not to let Mellitus be naughty. Had he finally convinced the stubborn monk that Paul was not a puppet for his manipulation?

Joannicus pulled his hood over his head as he observed Paul's layer of clothing and the woolen hat. Paul was a co-conspirator. They should wait this game out.

"The man's got fortitude," Ambrose said, striking a match. The twigs blazed on the barbecue.

They stood around the fire as their breaths grew white and the day dark. Soon, the community gathered. Thanks to Ambrose fixing the gate, rock climbing was unnecessary. The community marveled at how one monk could lock all the hilltop buildings.

Joannicus glanced at his watch. It would soon be time for Mass. Mellitus would let them into the church. Yet the hour came and went. Hooded monks circled the fire like pagans, trying to keep warm. When Barnabas, the cook, entered the yard, groans of dismay escaped the monks. Several of them headed down the hill to the student cafeteria for a meal and warmth.

"Let's go out for pizza," Paul said, unaffected by cold or events.

"Monks don't do that," Joannicus said, scratching his head. He wished the Abbot could kick Mellitus out or at least threaten him.

The man needed a wake-up call. *We should treat him like a child if he acts like a child.*

The sky grew dark as Abbot Gordon and Jacob entered the backyard.

"I had hoped that Brother Mellitus had reconsidered," Abbot Gordon said.

Jacob laughed. "He is Merlin. What can we do with him? He is old and mean. He thrives on chaos. We need to supply him with anarchy to control him."

Three monks scratched their heads as if pondering Jacob's wisdom.

Paul brought the worst and the best out in people—sometimes in the same person. Changes had occurred within the community, and Joannicus feared it would continue. Who would they be after Paul?

Shame caused Joannicus to look away and reconsider his former thoughts. Mellitus had been in the monastery for 50 years, his adult life. Where could he go? The words of Psalm 70: 18, 'Now that I am old and gray-headed, do not forsake me...,' haunted him.

"Why are you all scratching? Do you all have fleas?" Jacob said, taking a step away from the monks. "Was that not the fourth plague?"

Brother Ambrose frowned, and his wooly eyebrows became one.

"Little one, com'ere."

He set Paul's head in his lap and parted the curls. Ambrose placed his thumbnails together. There was a distinct crunch.

"Flies—not fleas or lice," Joannicus said, looking at the miniature insect on the ragged nail—the eleven plagues on Pharaoh. Mellitus was a jackass likening him to Pharaoh. He listened to God.

Tiny white balls fell and bounced on the patio. The monks pressed against the window in a solid black line. Hail.

"I know one plague was hail. I am impressed that our brother has God's ear. I suggest you break the window," Jacob said, going to the gate.

"There's an open window right there," Paul said, pointing to the third floor from under the tree's protective branches.

"Hey, that's your room, Jacob," Ambrose said. "Why don't you have head lice? Come back here, you traitor."

"Not on your soul on either account," Jacob called from the gate as the sun smiled on the now-white patio.

"I say the boy goes climbing," Ambrose said, examining his beard for bugs.

Joannicus shook his head. Paul's eyes lit up. Scaling the outside of the monastery was a dangerous idea.

"Seriously, it's too risky," Joannicus said, envisioning Paul falling. Contempt rose inside Joannicus. Such was the story of the Pharaoh. Was this a Mellitus attempt to kill the firstborn? He wouldn't dare, would he?

Someone placed a red woolen skein in his laundry, causing rivers of blood and his whites to turn pink. The tadpoles in the holy water fountain, frogs leaping in the atrium, fruit flies in his office. Were these all orchestrated by Mellitus? How many accomplices did he have? Then the flies came, invading everywhere, even in the church. However, Merlin could not control the weather. Or could he? Joannicus shook his head. He could not have summoned the hail.

"Do you have any other suggestions?" the Abbot asked, rubbing his chin.

Joannicus thought of wringing the man's neck. He watched the older monks suffer as they shivered in the cold.

"Paul is an excellent climber," Ambrose said.

"No, fine, send Paul."

Joannicus bowed his head and prayed. The lice caused a prickly sensation on his scalp, and he could sense them having races around the shafts of his hair. Joannicus focused on the statue of Saint Gertrude the Great. His eyes locked on the chip of paint missing from the cat in her arms. Looking up required more faith than he could muster. He placed his hands in his pockets to keep from clenching his fists in worry. There was the note from Mellitus, one of many designed to soften his stony heart.

A cheer rose once Paul disappeared through the open window.

A few minutes later, Paul appeared in the community room.

"No, Little One, no," Ambrose moaned, his nose pressed against the glass.

Joannicus opened his eyes and saw Paul mesmerized halfway between the sliding doors and Mellitus. The old monk had moved to a chair between the inside and outside doors. Paul took a step toward the sliders.

"Don't listen to the voice of temptation," Ambrose shouted. "Come on, this way."

Paul turned and took two steps toward Mellitus.

"Oh no," Ambrose said as he slumped and pressed against the glass.

Joannicus watched with fascination. Paul's face was knotted in turmoil and confusion. Whatever the old monk said caused Paul to pause. The man's stronghold was visibly present. Paul's lower lip quivered. He stomped his foot. Then his head fell to his chest, and he flung himself onto the old monk.

"We're doomed," Ambrose sighed, turning away from the glass. "We put all our hope into the hands of a child, foolish, foolish."

Murmuring and alarm rose in those gathered as the Abbot tried to provide hope.

"I could get in and help Paul," a novice offered.

"Why are we playing this game? Just break a window."

"Paul will unlock the door," Abbot Gordon said.

Ambrose looked at the Abbot in disbelief, mirroring Joannicus's reaction. Maybe he should stand by the window and encourage Paul to open the door.

Cheeks burning, matching the burn on his scalp, Joe stood by the door, knowing he had little influence. A painful grimace pinched the boy's face. Minutes passed, and a red-eyed Paul walked to the door and pushed the latch up.

"Thank you," Joannicus said as he opened the door.

"You're welcome," Paul said, his chin drooping to his chest.

"Good boy," Abbot Gordon said. "Brother Mellitus, a word in my office, please. I suggest anyone with an itchy scalp stop by the infirmary and change linens."

"Don't beat him," Paul wailed, following the old monk.

"Seems easier just to burn the place to the ground," Ambrose muttered.

The bells rang for prayers, and Father Joannicus entered Paul's room, rather than the church, for the third consecutive day.

"Are you sure? Father," Brother Augustine asked.

"Absolutely," Joannicus said, moving a chair closer to the bed and allowing Brother Augustine to attend prayers with the community rather than sit with Paul. "We will be fine."

The monk dashed off to the church. Joannicus switched on the lamp next to Paul's bed. Unknown to all, Paul was allergic to the medication used to treat head lice, and his hair had fallen out in chunks. Most of the community members had opted to shave their heads, Joannicus included. The medicine to treat the allergic reaction had left Paul lethargic.

Joannicus pulled his hood up and prayed aloud, "Oh God, come to my assistance..."

"Oh Lord, make haste to help me," Mellitus said.

"I'll second that," Joannicus said, looking up to see Mellitus in the doorway.

"How is he?"

"He will survive," Joannicus said, lips tight, wanting to say more. With the concern on the old man's face, he stopped. Was Mellitus to blame for the infestation of head lice? Paul was in school with other children. Barb had mentioned the illnesses children bring home.

"Ah, so God doesn't answer all your prayers."

Whatever compassion Joannicus had a second ago evaporated like water on a hot skillet. He didn't want Paul to stay but never wished the child to die. "God always answers my prayers. Sometimes I don't want to listen."

The old monk smiled, and the wrinkles cut grooves into his face. "Yeah, so what do you do?"

Joannicus sat taller in his chair, "I do as he asks, accept what is. Remember, I am chosen."

The words echoed in the silence.

"Picked by a child. I wouldn't brag about that." Mellitus leaned heavily on his cane as he stood next to the bed. "You don't love him."

"Nothing is instant. I could say the same to you. Seriously, you have mistreated him, and love doesn't hurt," Joannicus said as the old man's words burned holes in his soul.

"Oh, ask your good buddy Jacob if that is true?" Mellitus ran a ghostly hand over Paul's cheek. "I didn't know he was allergic. I love him. When will you?"

Joannicus drew in a sharp breath. He hadn't seen Jacob since

Paul fell ill. He knew Jacob had a challenging time dealing with sick children. The deaths of one's children will affect a man.

Mellitus was correct. He didn't love Paul, but he cared for him.

"That's not the point. What you did hurt Paul. Those actions that intended to punish me have hurt others. Father Wolfgang broke his arm when he fell during your blackout. Fabian is still recovering from that day you made us sit outside in the cold while you sat roasting your toes by the fire. What if Paul had fallen before getting to the window you left open?"

"I didn't send him up there," Mellitus said, crossing his arms. "What you don't do hurts him as well."

Joannicus swallowed hard. "You need to stop. I'm not playing Exodus with you."

Mellitus tugged the blanket up around Paul's shoulders. It was such a kind gesture from a man who enjoyed teasing people. He was not sure he could trust Mellitus.

"Then let him go. Let him be with me."

"Give me one good reason."

"I need him," Mellitus said.

Had he heard the old man correctly? The man had a need, a weakness. Joannicus now had an advantage.

"Fine, but promise to be Benedictine," Joannicus said, hoping the Rule would guide them when he wasn't around.

Mellitus nodded, turned, and walked away with agility reserved for one-half his age.

"Out of my way, ogre," he said as he passed Brother Ambrose.

Joannicus shivered, sure he had just made a deal with the devil.

CHAPTER 24
MOTHERS' DAY

Psalm 67: 6
Father of the orphan, defender of the widow.
Such is God in his holy place.

T he first of May arrived, and with it, sunny days. Father Joannicus looked forward to the summer's heat, although Mother Nature had surprised them with a few sweltering spring afternoons. He hurried to the community room to check his mailbox. A white envelope gleamed in the dark slot. With trembling fingers, he opened it and unfolded the letterhead from Saint Vincent's Arch-Abbey–*approved*. Joannicus tucked the letter into his pocket, delighted that he would be in Pennsylvania for the summer.

"Come on, Little One, drop your stuff off, and let's get our chores done," Ambrose said as he stood in the doorway. "Chop, chop."

Paul walked slower than one of the old monks, his backpack dragging behind him.

"What's wrong, Paul?" he asked, scolding himself for inquiring.

"It's stupid Mother's Day. I don't like Mother's Day," Paul said, releasing his pack inside the door. He pulled out a tissue paper-wrapped object, handing it to Joannicus.

Joannicus unwrapped a small plaster of Paris handprint with the date on it.

"You could give the gift to Gracie," Ambrose said.

"No, Mrs. P made us put 'Happy Mother's Day' on it. I tried to put happy day, but she added mother to it. That wasn't nice." Paul stared at Joannicus with hopeful eyes.

"She was trying to be helpful," Joannicus said.

"I knew what I was doing. Now it's ruined."

"I don't like that Mrs. Pee," Ambrose said. "She crushes the spirit."

Father Joannicus shook his head. Those comments were better off expressed outside Paul's hearing. Joe made many visits to discuss Paul and his offenses, from holding prayer circles during recess to refusing to print.

"Have you seen the notes she writes?" Brother Ambrose asked. "Paul corrected me in class. This behavior is unacceptable. If she's wrong, then she's wrong. And she calls herself a teacher."

"Paul needs to learn to deal with the Mrs. P's of the world," Joannicus said. He ignored most of the woman's remarks and had long ago given up on reading her notes.

Paul came to prayers late the following day, dressed in his

bathrobe and elephant slippers. After prayers, Joannicus approached him with dread.

He wasn't able to take off today. He had finals to administer and grades to turn in before the registrar's office closed.

"I feel sick," Paul said as Joannicus touched Paul's cool forehead.

"What hurts?"

Paul frowned. "My head, my stomach, and my big toe. I think I caught the grout. I need to stay home today."

"Poor boy," Ambrose said, ruffling the curls on Paul's head. "Guess it's to bed with no raisin nut bread for you."

"Well, maybe I'm just weak from hunger," Paul said, changing course and heading towards the refectory.

Ambrose and Joannicus followed.

"What's that all about?" Joannicus asked.

"They are singing at school today," Moses said, placing Paul's backpack and fresh clothing on the bench outside the doors to the refectory. "He probably doesn't enjoy singing." The farm crew always escorted Paul to the bus stop and picked him up in the afternoon. Joannicus was grateful for their help.

"He doesn't like tea," Ambrose said, holding his massive hand on an invisible cup. His pinky pointed out with grace.

Paul loved singing and often watched the Schola practice. Something was amiss.

Brother Ambrose handed Joannicus a wadded piece of baby blue paper.

"Found it in the sheep's stall. He should have given it to the goat."

A Mother's Day Tea? Paul's class this afternoon? The crumpled note smelled like the farm. If he had known earlier, he could have scheduled someone. Gracie would have gone. She loved those sentimental moments.

Father Joannicus graded the papers at the oaken desk in the classroom as they appeared before him. Between classes, he raced up and down the stairs to the registrar's office with recorded grades and made phone calls.

The search for a substitute mother had failed. Even Barb was no help. Her words had not consoled him, informing him it was a short, sweet celebration.

Joannicus looked at the lady in the registrar's office as he handed in his grades, which weren't due until four o'clock. She was a stranger to Paul. He chided himself as he headed to the monastery parking lot. Arriving at Chet Huntley Elementary School, he felt ill. An hour with children and women made him lean against the car, take several deep breaths, and smooth the wrinkles out of his habit.

He hadn't changed into secular clothing. His jeans and tee shirt were not for this tea and crumpets event. As he approached the classroom, the air radiated excitement. There were females everywhere–high heels, perfumes mixed with cinnamon, gingerbread, and the burping of the urn in the corner on a lace-covered table. *I shouldn't be here*, he thought.

Joannicus slipped in, hoping to stay unnoticed in the tumult. Heads turned, plain and makeup-caked faces, tinted and braided hair, thirty feminine eyes focused on him as he sat in a chair designed for baby bear. The skirt of his habit billowed out as he seated himself at Paul's isolated desk. He wondered what Paul had done. Then he noticed Paul had rewritten his name in cursive, right over the printed name tag. Joannicus glanced at the desks stuffed with paper and pencils, threatening to erupt at the slightest disturbance. There were no broken crayons or crumpled papers in Paul's place.

Children wiggling in a mass before them, eyes riveted on Mrs. Piasano as she rang a tiny bell. The children stood tall as if reveille had sounded. They sang. Joannicus watched. Three or four sang as if they were performing at Carnegie Hall. Others exaggerated the gestures that went with the songs. The girls wore pigtails, and the boys sported untucked shirts, their faces filled with pride. He spotted Paul standing in the front row, mouth barely open, arms to his side like a wooden doll. The songs were sentimental, heralding the virtues of motherhood. Joannicus rubbed his eyes, pretending that they itched.

Sadness washed over Joannicus. He should have allowed Paul to stay home, for this seemed like torture, an orphaned boy having to sing with joy about something denied him. The relief filled Paul's face at the last song.

Mrs. Piasano requested the mothers to remain seated so their children could serve them. The room grew noisy, with eager children moving about. Joannicus searched for Paul but couldn't find him in the chaos. He approached the teacher.

"Reverend Brookes, how nice to see you. Did you come to pick up Paul? He's here somewhere. He didn't tell me he was leaving early," Mrs. Piasano said.

"Early would have been a blessing," Joannicus said under his breath.

"I told him he could bring a pretend mother, but he said no, his mother was dead, and he liked it that way."

Ouch. Joannicus considered the harshness of the words spoken out of sadness. That was untrue, and Mrs. Piasano was an insensitive oaf for accepting that. He knew Paul missed his mother more this year than last, and he could pinpoint the change to this celebration. The photo of Sarah Warner had moved from the shelf to the nightstand and currently lay tucked under Paul's pillow.

Joannicus refrained from using the colorful words that Ambrose used to describe the woman, but he had to agree with the crusty monk. She lacked compassion.

"Hi, Father," Charlie called, breaking the tension-filled moment. Charlie wore a three-piece light blue suit with a lavender vest and tie. This was Paul's best friend. The attraction baffled Joannicus. They spent many Saturdays together until he discovered that Charlie was a girl. Once he knew, he shifted the visits to Gracie's house. A little guilt crept up inside of Joe. He had not disclosed Charlie's gender to the monks for fear of repercussions.

"Hi, Charlie. Have you seen Paul?"

Charlie pointed to open cubbies that lined the back of the classroom. Joannicus made his way, weaving around kid-sized furniture and moving children. The room grew warm. Joannicus endured the staring. He saw the nudges and smirks. He ignored the snippets of conversations about the little orphan boy and his odd familial arrangement mixed with various perfumes. His face burned.

Paul sat wedged into the box. Joannicus crouched down.

"Hey," Joannicus said. Paul's eyes brimmed with tears. "You okay?"

Paul's bottom lip quivered as Joannicus helped him out of the tight space.

"Want to go home?"

The answer didn't match the look on Paul's face. He had seen compliance before.

"Or we could stay. I saw Charlie's mom and should say hi, hospitality being important and all."

"Okay, do you want tea?" Paul said, a smile growing on his face.

"Sure," Joannicus said, hoping his voice didn't betray him. He moved Paul's chair and desk closer to the end of the grouped desks.

A little girl with red ribbons in her brown hair stopped Paul as he carried the floral printed teacup to the table.

"You said you didn't have a mother," she said.

"I don't. I have a father," Paul said.

"This is a Mother's Day tea. He's a man," the girl said as she eyed Joannicus suspiciously.

"My, what an observant little girl you are," Joannicus said, rescuing Paul from the awkward social moment.

"You're not supposed to move the desks. Paul's place is over there," the girl said, pointing to the space between the bookshelves and coat closet.

Mrs. Piasano smiled awkwardly, announcing, "It's okay, Susan. Today is special."

Susan frowned disapprovingly, and her mother grumbled loudly enough for Joannicus to hear: "I understand he's a troublemaker. Seems the apple doesn't fall far."

Joannicus could not believe what he heard–adults relying on information reported by children. His association with Paul had taught him that children's observations were less than accurate.

Charlie's mother, Mrs. Winters, cleared her throat. An apologetic smile appeared on her lips before turning towards the woman.

"Lois, you know Paul's an orphan, and this isn't his biological father. Paul isn't trouble, he's just smarter than most."

The woman glared. Mrs. Winters was one of the regular room mothers and knew the children and their women. "Paul's reading at a second-grade level and doing division. Most of our kids are struggling with telling time."

Joannicus hid his smile behind his paper napkin.

The room cleared of mothers and youngsters, growing quieter with each exit.

"How wonderful of you to come," Mrs. Piasano said.

Joannicus perceived the insincerity of her compliment.

"It's important to include children in celebrations."

The little girl with the red ribbons pulled Paul's chair back to the corner space. Then she tried to move the desk, but Joannicus placed his foot in the way, making her efforts futile. Paul and Charlie played tug of war with his backpack.

Father Joannicus hadn't planned to make a scene, but the unfairness rankled him. *How early do we teach others to be exclusive?*

"Why is Paul excluded?" Joannicus asked.

Mrs. Piasano blinked several times and redirected the little girl to her mother. "Paul, put your chair by your desk," Mrs. Piasano said.

The children stopped their play. Confusion clouded Paul's face.

"Am I sitting here?"

"Yes," Mrs. Piasano said, her voice clipped.

"You're sitting next to me," Charlie crowed as she and Paul bumped into each other.

"That won't be a problem, will it?" Mrs. Piasano asked.

The two children shook their heads.

"I'm sorry, I thought you knew," Charlie's mother said as they exited the classroom. The two children playing tag raced in front of them.

"You're forgiven. Children tend to accept things as they are. They don't place judgments on events. I don't think Paul realized he was ostracized."

Paul circled Joannicus with Charlie in hot pursuit.

"I'm not an ostrich. We are panthers," Paul explained, referring to the school mascot.

Charlie head-butted Paul. They toppled to the ground, giggling.

"I think you both are mistaken. I see two baby goats," Charlie's mother said with a laugh.

CHAPTER 25
BARB

Psalm 76: 3
In the day of my distress, I sought the Lord.

A month had passed since Barb's last visit. Joannicus looked at the calendar, wondering when she would return.

"I have books for her," he said aloud in his office, glancing at his open door to see if anyone was there.

They discussed everything from parenting to the Pope. He enjoyed those discussions. She was interested in his life, too interested, some warned.

Joe's mind wandered too often to the secular world. So much so that he missed his intimate moments with God. He longed to sit in the garden with the Creator, thanking him for the surrounding beauty. Lately, if he sat there, the worries of Paul came crashing in. Other times, he wished he could share an insight with Barb.

Guilt washed over him like a flash flood. These thoughts were unacceptable. *God comes first, the community second, and people last.*

It was time to pray. Joannicus rose and left his office, passing a group of students. A tall, willowy blonde coed in a short skirt flashed a smile at him as he passed by. Barb wouldn't dress like that.

He moved down the hall, mumbling greetings as he hurried to the hilltop. Inside the church, he blessed himself with holy water and paused. The sun shone through the stained glass, making a cheery pattern on the carpet. He genuflected and blessed himself again before fishing in his pocket for his rosary. Cool, heavy obsidian beads caressed his fingertips as he began the mantra prayer, "Hail Mary full of grace..."

Mary didn't appear in Joe's mind. Barb did. He frowned and sighed, refocusing on the sorrowful mysteries of the rosary. He whispered the prayers aloud to keep himself focused. Somewhere between the third and fourth mystery, Joannicus lost himself in meditation.

The smell of sweetness mixed with the odor of incense, and Joannicus found his heart beating faster. He inhaled deeply as if waking from a restful slumber. Alertness slapped his mind. He was not alone. Barb had arrived. A glow, like that of moonlight, softened her silhouette as she stood in the sun-drenched atrium.

A year ago, she would have spoken or interrupted his praying.

Even a pagan can understand and respect, given proper instruction.

The bells rang in a thunderous gong. Noon prayer would begin soon.

Barb smiled when Joannicus entered the atrium of the church.

The hours of praying fortified him, his heart united with his spirit, and he discovered solace in God. He guided her to the prayer books and found the page for noonday prayers.

After praying, they walked silently to the refectory and joined the community in eating. They were in ordinary times, liturgically, so there was a wide selection of leftovers. Joannicus selected what looked like yesterday's potato breakfast mixed with last night's vegetables coated with cheese. The label read Barnabas's ratatouille. Barb helped herself to salad and fruit.

After a hearty lunch, Joannicus attempted to dismiss himself.

"Would it be possible to sit in on one of your lectures?" Barb asked.

"Sure, why not? It's an upper-division class. Don't be disheartened if you can't follow it all," Joannicus explained. They walked down the hill to the Grand Quad. The school building was four stories high, with an inner space where students could eat and meet. The ground level held the administration and business offices and the library. The second and third floors were the high-ceilinged classrooms. On the fourth floor was the professor's office—long and narrow, with a large window that beckoned one to enter and traverse the room.

As they entered the classroom, Joannicus heard Paul's voice. Why wasn't the child in school? Then he remembered strawberry-picking day.

"It's really an Iroquois ceremony. But we all get to pick. I'm surprised you don't know this, being in college and all," Paul said as he sat crossed-legged on the big wooden desk.

"We're not Iroquois," a greasy-haired boy in the corner exclaimed.

"Mexicans observe the Fourth of July, so you can celebrate. My new teacher said it's the gift of spring. We got to squish the berries and make strawberry juice. Brother Barnabas is making some for dinner tonight. It's so yummy."

"New teacher?" Barb asked.

"Yes. I moved him to a native-taught school, less of a bus ride and smaller classes," Joannicus said, hoping she wouldn't question his decision. After hearing Joe's concerns about how Mrs. Piasano treated Paul, Jacob recommended the new school.

"It's so late in the year. How did he react?" Barb asked. Concern was etched on her face.

"He's happy with Mrs. White Dove and enjoys the hands-on aspects."

Barb nodded. "Thank goodness, she understands what Paul is into doing."

Joannicus entered the room, and Paul jumped off the desk.

"How come they don't know about other religious holidays?" Paul asked.

"Strawberry-picking day is not a religious holiday," Joannicus said.

"Well, it should be," Paul's voice trailed off as he noticed Barb. "I'll be quiet and write on my side of the board."

"Very well," Joannicus said as he faced his class. "Good afternoon. Thank you for being here." He caught Barb's confused look. She obviously hadn't heard that Father Joannicus always started with a 'thank you.'

Before Paul attended school, he often was in the classroom with Joannicus. Paul would doodle on the blackboard, but Joannicus never paid attention to the scribbles of Paul. One day, Paul had scrawled, 'Paul loves Father Jonah.' The message made its way through the halls to him. He'd been too eager to teach hungry minds that he dismissed the child's wisdom. He realized his error and added a question to a quiz, 'What doesn't Father Jonah know, and why?' The insights of his students fascinated him for weeks. That started the dialogue part of his classes. He had Paul to thank for that. He had never allowed the students to ask the questions. Now, he could not teach without their input.

Class began, and Father Joannicus became oblivious to time

and space. The blackboard was thumped with white chalk words, underlined for emphasis. The once pristine scapular became dotted with chalk dust as Joannicus moved from board to desk. Students sat alert and erect as they listened. Father Joannicus could tell a parable.

With class dismissed, Joannicus paused before erasing the board. Today's message was more of a pictorial version of the stories Joannicus told. Paul's depiction of Satan looked more like a dragon snake without feet. Were dragons linked to evil? Were there friendly dragons, or did they all devour people?

Barb cleared her throat. He remembered his company. The hour-long class left Paul restless, so Joannicus sent him to the monastery to warn Brother Barnabas that they would eat in the monastic dining room rather than the guest dining room.

"Wow, what a class," Barb said as they made their way up the hill. "I understand what drew the crowds to Jesus."

"What do you mean?"

"I'm not a bible reader, but if he taught the same way you tell the stories, I get his popularity. I even understood the lesson you were giving."

Joe's face flushed, knowing he wasn't Jesus and wondering if it was a backhanded compliment.

"Thank you."

An awkward silence walked with them as they approached the church.

"I have to set up for Mass."

"Can I watch?" Barb asked.

The request was odd, but he was now used to Paul's appeals to watch or help. Joannicus explained the various items, a little history, and clarification as he set up for Mass.

"I need to select some wine from the cellar."

"You have a wine cellar," Barb said. "I thought all wine was the same."

Joannicus opened the door to a stairwell that twisted and turned its way downward.

"Seriously, the wine must be pure, made from grapes, not mixed or deluded. We use a variety depending on the significance of the celebration. We have even used port."

When he reached the cellar floor, he switched on the bare bulb, which sent a bright glow to the small room. Barb's heels clattered on the metal stairs as she followed him down. The cellar's musty odor contrasted with Barb's floral scent.

"I need a bottle from that shelf behind you," Joannicus said. Barb was too close. Joe glanced at the light above him. Barb handed him a bottle. The room grew warm. He clutched it tight in his sweaty palms.

"Thanks, after you," he said, hoping to exit the enclosed space.

She wiggled past him, her chest brushing up against his arm. Joannicus gripped the banister, blocking her way. Barb turned, and he found himself level with her. Then, without thought or intention, he kissed her.

CHAPTER 26
SIN

Psalm 140: 8-9
To you, Lord God, my eyes are turned.
In you I take refuge; spare my soul!
From the trap they have laid for me, keep me safe.
keep me from the snares of those who do evil.

There was no resistance as their breaths mingled. The room exploded and imploded. Joannicus heard footsteps over his head.

"Father Jonah?" Paul called. His body blocked the light. "There you are. Brother Barnabas wants to know how many guests are eating with us."

Barb took a few steps up the winding staircase. Her bottom and shapely legs passed by Joannicus like a delectable on a silver tray.

He tried to speak but found his mouth dry, and his voice muted. The room spun. His logical mind scrambled for a foothold as he ascended the stairs into the light.

He needed to get out of there.

He placed the unopened bottle of wine on the counter and headed out the door, the voices of Barb and Paul trailing after him.

The depictions of the Way of the Cross in the hallway to the monastery glared at him accusingly as he hurried to his cell. He leaned against the door and slid to the floor.

What had he done? Is temptation that easy? How does one fight it when it sneaks up and consumes? Every prayer of penance flooded his mind.

He was a sinful monk, offering something that was not his to give.

The bells for Mass rang, and Joannicus stood up. But he could not stop shaking. He stumbled to his desk, sending folders cascading to the floor like the dominoes Paul and Ambrose set up in the community room.

He must leave. She must go. Stop. Joannicus tried to harness the panic.

One bite of an apple, a kiss on the cheek, four small words. I don't know him. All had changed the path of history in mere moments.

What had he done?

Joannicus prayed and wept. Did Peter suffer this way when he denied Christ? He heard Paul humming a hymn and slid into his closet, holding the door shut as a hanger poked him in the back. He could not face Paul now. The entrance to this cell opened and, seconds later, closed.

Twilight crept in around him. He listened to the voices as they drifted through his open window. Barb's laughter floated toward him, and he prayed harder. There would be no sleep tonight.

Life was over. He couldn't even think. Forgiveness is every-thing. If he believed that, he must trust that the Lord will forgive him. He would return wiser and resolved.

Like a morning glory vine, fear twisted itself around Joe's mind. *Are you stronger? How many confessions had he heard the penitent repeat the sin?*

He continued to pray. The answer came in the psalmist's words, "To you, Lord God, my eyes are turned. In you, I take refuge; spare my soul! From the trap they have laid for me, keep me safe. Keep me from the snares of those who do evil."

The bells rang for evening prayer. Paul ran up to him.

"Where were you? You missed dinner and strawberry juice. I saved some for you."

"Thank you," Joannicus said, his throat raw. "I felt ill."

"Are you sick?" Paul asked.

"No, seriously, I'm better," Joannicus said as he gathered his books. "Sit with Ms. Carr and be her helper tonight, okay?"

Paul's face lit up, and he ran to be with Barb.

He took his place in the choir, glancing to see Jacob staring at him.

His heart thumped faster. Normally, he would spend hours in prayer and review before partaking in the sacrament of Reconciliation, but his despair was so great, his burden so heavy. He wanted to grab Jacob during prayers and confess his sin.

He had to do this tonight.

Prayers ended, and Joannicus hurried out of the church before Barb exited the atrium.

"Paul," Joannicus said, "Could you please see that Ms. Carr has all she needs as a guest tonight?"

"Me? Really?"

Joannicus nodded. Paul let out a whoop and raced to the guesthouse.

Jacob headed in the same direction. Joannicus made haste to stop him.

"Father Jacob, I need to talk to you."

"Sure thing. What is up?"

"Not here," Joannicus whispered. "Your cell, five minutes?"

Joannicus turned and hurried into the monastery. The look of alarm on Jacob's face lingered. Joe rarely entered another monk's chamber for a visit. To Joannicus, a cell was like a sanctuary, the Holy of Holies.

Shame filled Joannicus, and he avoided his confreres, making his way up the rear stairwell from the first to the third floor. He knocked on Jacob's door. There was no answer.

He couldn't just stand here in the hall. Someone would notice, so he opened the door and slipped in.

The room smelled of sweet grass. Joannicus fumbled for the light switch. One bulb glowed, leaving the room in a shadowy darkness.

He hesitated. Maybe he should prepare more. Words of judgment rattled his ears. He was not ready. He turned to leave and jumped back, for Jacob stood there watching him.

"What is wrong?" Jacob asked as he pushed a discarded chair from the corner toward Joannicus.

Joannicus sat. The room faded, and he imagined himself in the center of an arena, the church fathers staring at him from their lofty heights.

"Jacob, I need to go to confession."

"You have a regular confessor. I am your friend. This might not be a good thing."

"I'm aware of that, but I can't continue unless my soul is clean. What if I should die tonight? I'm scared. I don't know what to do."

Joannicus pulled an alb from this pocket. A scowl painted Jacob's face as he placed the alb around his shoulders and lifted his cassock skirts to straddle the chair, leaning his chin on the back.

As soon as the blessing was uttered, Joannicus began. A flood of words tumbled out.

"I told you I thought Paul had replaced God. I was wrong. I'm surrounded by temptation. I can't be the Guest Master anymore."

Jacob shook his head. "The guesthouse and guests are a temptation to you? What is going on there? Too much talking, gambling, and eating snacks between meals? You cannot be serious."

"God has eluded me for a while. I'm empty, and just today, I filled the emptiness with a different passion," Joannicus said. His voice squeaked, a sound he didn't recognize.

"What desire in the guesthouse? Or should I ask who?"

"Barb, Ms. Carr. She, I've succumbed to the temptations of the flesh."

Jacob shifted in his chair. Father Joannicus glanced up into the blue eyes. He saw no judgment, just concern and confusion.

"Seriously, she's not to blame. She's hungry for knowledge, so eager and innocent."

"She is far from harmless. How do you handle the female college students? Surely, they come on to you?"

The chair creaked as Jacob shifted his weight.

The students were mere children, far from a temptation. He didn't need female friends, even if they added a unique perspective to life. Sister Clarence was a female friend. He had been her confessor. She had written weekly for years, asking questions about the church, theology, and God. Had he missed something? Her seeking was not unlike Barb's quest for knowledge. She was a nun. Barb was not a nun. She didn't get seeking God above all else.

Joannicus waved his hands in frustration.

Jacob leaned forward. "So, what can we do to keep your soul from descending into debauchery?"

"I thought I was careful, talking in public places where others were. We talked about theology and Paul. I don't understand how this happened. This was far too easy. One second, I'm educating, and the next..."

Joannicus paused. His tongue stuck in his mouth, and his heart beat louder than drums during a native Mass.

"Jacob, I kissed her."

Silence hung in the air like frozen breaths.

Jacob unbraided his hair and ran his fingers through it. "Oh. Well, what kind of kiss?"

Joannicus jumped up from his chair as if it were on fire.

"Seriously, does that even matter? My vocation is doomed. I'm not even sure how it happened, but I'm clear I don't want it, and it can't happen again," Joannicus said. He took the end of his scapular and dusted the empty bookshelf.

"Kissing is not a sin. You have not ruined your vocation."

Joannicus stopped his pacing. Truthfully, that was correct. Benedictines didn't take a vow of celibacy. Monks took a vow of conversion. Priests were to be celibate.

He spoke, his voice an octave higher, squeaking as he said, "It is for me."

"Fine, I absolve you. Mistakes happen. I am certain it will not happen again. How will you make this true?"

"You believe that?" Joannicus said, blinking.

"Yes."

Joannicus wiped a tear. Jacob told him repeatedly that he had no faith. Yet he was showing the most fundamental trust in another human being. That was faith. He couldn't avoid her.

"I'm just going to set things straight with her. Apologize and move on. She will understand. If she can't forgive me, so be it. But she will understand. We talked a lot about sin and reconciliation."

A shadow of sadness clouded Jacob's face. Joannicus assumed it was a moment of disappointment in his failure. He now had another reason to try harder. He never wanted to see that again.

"You need a backup plan. She seeks you out to chat. She likes you. There is nothing wrong with that. I like you. You need stronger parameters."

Joannicus resumed pacing as panic filled him, and he gripped his rosary beads.

"I'm a monk. God comes first in my life. I can't allow myself to be distracted."

"If you say that to her, she will not believe you. You let others in your life, Paul, community, teaching. Try honesty. Say I do not want to pursue an intimate relationship with you. That is not for me. Keep the friendship door open."

"I don't want a friendship, not if it leads to this."

"But she does."

"Seriously, she can't be my friend."

Joannicus stopped pacing and stared out the window at the pastoral view.

Jacob rose and stood next to him.

"Your penance is to pray for guidance. Be open to listening. Watch how others balance friends and family."

One doesn't argue with penance, Joannicus sighed. His life had been stable. How did it become so easy to be swayed? He was unsure if his relationship with God was enough.

The bells for morning prayers rang, and Joannicus recognized Barb's footsteps as she entered the church. There would be no way to avoid her, so he steeled himself.

"Why are you avoiding me?"

Joannicus looked around. "Seriously, we can't talk here."

They walked to the guesthouse in silence. Inside the parlor, Joannicus sat in a chair as far from her as possible.

"I'm sorry," Joannicus blurted out before she even sat. "I've avoided you because I don't know what else to do. I'm not leaving the monastery. I'm a monk. I made a mistake if I led you to believe otherwise."

Joannicus worried his words would hurt her. She shook her head. The look on her face told him she didn't understand.

"I don't want to marry. I prefer being a monk."

"I see," Barb said, moving a chair closer to him before sitting. "I'm not asking you for marriage."

Don't sit so close.

Her perfume, pleasing, licked his nose.

"This has nothing to do with you. You are nice and smart; anyone would like to be your friend. But we can't be friends, or lovers, or whatever. I made a mistake in the wine cellar, and it ends here."

Joannicus folded his hands. This wasn't going well.

"I think what I hear is that I'm a temptation to you, and you don't want to be around me?" Barb said, smoothing her skirt over her lap.

"Exactly," Joannicus said, jumping from his chair and walking to the window.

"I was joking," Barb said, her voice laden with anger.

"Oh. Seriously, I cannot continue to be alone with you."

She rose from the sofa and crossed her arms.

"You're crazy. I know you made a mistake, Father Joannicus," Barb said as she turned her head away. Pink colored her cheeks. "I'm not here to mess you up from your pursuit to heaven, Abbotship, or popehood."

Such defensiveness–it was his sin, not hers. She was behaving as if scorned. Was it true? Was Jacob's assessment correct? Did she have feelings for him?

"I'm sorry," Joannicus said. "You're a pleasant, caring person. I don't mean to hurt you. It is me, all me."

"Yes, I see it is you. You can't face the fact that you are human," Barb said. Her eyes darted at him like an electrical shock.

"That's not fair. I'm a man. I have feelings."

"But you're afraid of them," she countered, hurt cracking through the anger.

"Yes, I'm fearful. I don't want to be in an intimate relationship with anyone but God. I don't expect you to understand. Just accept it. I've enjoyed our talks, so we can continue discussing theological matters as long as others are around."

He looked at her. She wiped her cheeks with the back of her hand. He fought the urge to move toward her.

The door to the guesthouse opened, and a shadow darkened the doorway. Barb's soft features suddenly seemed hardened.

Barb laughed, "You're kidding me. *Chaperoned?* You're in denial. If it's so hard to be alone with me, why bother?"

She stood inches from him. Temptation and frustration collided with logic and desire.

"It's a choice I've made, and I intend to stick with it."

"Even if it's a mistake?" Barb said more softly.

Joannicus stepped away from her, bumping into the cabinet. The cups rattled, and his resolve wavered. The faint odor of sweet-grass floated in the air–Jacob.

"It isn't the wrong choice. It's my choice. I need your help. Please respect my wishes. You wouldn't put alcohol in front of a drunk, would you? I'm not that strong. I'm asking for your help."

"You're insane, and you're a hypocrite, preaching 'love one another' but not being able to do so yourself," Barb said. "I'm still coming to check on Paul."

She turned and walked out, causing Jacob to jump to one side.

Joannicus smiled uneasily, hoping she would forgive him someday for his choice of God over her.

CHAPTER 27
JESUS IS COMING

Psalm 123: 2-3
If the Lord had not been on our side,
When men rose against us,
Then would they have swallowed us alive,
When their anger was kindled.

The wind blew the dried leaves across the patio, and the blinds fluttered at the open sliding glass door. Father Joannicus placed a hand on the papers he was correcting as Ambrose and Moses stopped by the bulletin board in the community room.

"You see that Abbot Gordon has put this notice on the prayer request side. That means he's worried," Brother Moses said.

Paul popped up from behind the kitchenette counter. "What's he worried about?"

"You," Ambrose said. "So, you best start minding us. Funny, I thought Abbot Gordon had received a blessing for this brief experiment."

"Oh, please," Mellitus said, his head popping up next to Paul's. "The Abbot has been playing the patience prayer card. I bet he never got approval. He waited. The word trickled out. Perhaps he hoped that the idea was too preposterous for anyone to believe. But now he's caught. The Federation big boys are coming. I look forward to seeing holy butts spanked by the powers that be. Maybe he'll resign or be reassigned." Mellitus shot a glance at Joannicus. "We could use a change."

Because they were members of the Federation of the American Cassinese Monks, regular visits were made to ensure harmony and adherence to the rules. Joannicus sensed this one was not that kind of visit. The rumors of what St. Alberic had done reached the ears of the wise and powerful.

"Maybe they won't be so harsh if someone confesses," Ambrose said. A crooked smile filled his furry face. "We could play 'guess who is the father.'"

"Sometimes you still get a spanking if you confess," Paul said, pointing at Jacob as he walked into the room.

"This is out of our hands. If it's God's will, then it all stays the same," Moses said.

Joannicus gathered his work and marveled at the man's faith.

"God's will," Mellitus scoffed. "Man's choice, God's tolerance."

"Is that a bible quote?" Paul asked.

Joannicus agreed with Mellitus. He prayed God would intervene.

The visiting Abbots arrived. The doors to Abbot Gordon's office remained closed on the first day. Joannicus watched the efficient hustling of men with mounting curiosity as they kept Abbots from Paul and Paul from Abbots. This was a dangerous game to play.

Everyone appeared jittery. Even Jacob seemed caught up in the drama of impressions. Joannicus found them watching Paul rather than participating in Mass.

Paul sat quietly in Ambrose's lap, as any cradle Catholic, picking barley from the man's massive beard. At the end of Mass, Joannicus cringed as he watched Paul skipping out of the church behind the monks.

"Oh, for the love of Mary, Joannicus, lighten up. Do you not recognize joy when you see it?" Ambrose snapped as he entered the hallway.

"Skipping is not proper church etiquette," Father Joannicus said, glancing around for the Abbots.

Ambrose's calloused hand snatched the child and redirected him toward the outside doors, away from the blockade of lingering monks. "Why are we so stressed? We all said 'yes.' It's too late to return him to the sender."

Paul was not a package.

"Wait, you mean we could do that?" Jacob asked with a laugh as he skipped up to them.

"So, when do I get to meet Jesus?" Paul asked, stopping at the bubbling holy water fount. "I'm so excited."

Ambrose laughed.

"What made you think Jesus was coming?" Jacob asked, flicking holy water at Paul.

"All the whispering tells me that someone important will visit, and who is more important than Jesus?" Paul said, trying to splash Jacob back.

"Who indeed?" Mellitus said, pushing the door open with his cane.

"Little One, Jesus is not coming. The Abbots are the important visitors," Ambrose said, extracting Paul's hands from the font as he tried to splash Jacob.

Paul stomped his way out of the church, arms dripping holy water. "Darn."

"I'm with you, Paul. We should wait for Jesus. To hell with that hoity-toity Abbot Willy," Mellitus said.

Joannicus shuddered. He could hear Paul using Mellitus's words, knowing that would not improve the situation.

"They are a little late to stop us. Paul is here. What can they do?" Jacob asked, heading to the community room.

Disband us. Close us down, scatter us to different monasteries. Isn't that why you want to change your stability? Ambrose's accusing voice bounced in his mind.

If only Abbot Gordon had consulted them. If only the visit had occurred before they had adjusted to Paul. They had changed. Patience and tolerance shown to Paul slipped over into kindness to each other. Laughter seemed to abound, brought on by Paul and his endless questions and explanations of how he perceived the world around him.

If Paul were a man, he would make final vows. Joannicus wondered what the real reason for the visit was. *Had someone complained? Who?*

Father Joannicus stopped at his cell and wiped the sweat from his brow. What would he say to these men? The truth. What was the truth? This is about him, not Paul. Christian up. Could he really blame Paul for his vocation's challenge?

He marched to the community room, determined to talk with Paul about visiting Abbots.

Jacob stood in the doorway.

"Go away," Mellitus said, stepping in front of Jacob.

"I love you too," Jacob said as Joannicus ducked between them into the room.

"Oh, Mellitus, what have you done?" Joannicus stood watching Abbot William with Paul.

"This monk is in Lent forever, only because I used a permanent marker to ash him. But it's okay cuz Father Jonah said we all need a monk who can pray constantly for us. He's on his way to sainthood. As soon as I get a cannon, he will be one. Merlin said his mark would fade and that every Abbot makes a mistake. I get to be Abbot of my monastery. I'm Abbot Jonah cuz you get to change your name, and I like that name," Paul said, holding up a Ken doll dressed in a black monastic habit with a giant black dot on his forehead.

"They had to meet sometime," Mellitus said, stepping aside and letting Jacob enter the room.

"All Abbots make mistakes. You really are a heretic," Jacob said. "That kind of talk will not endear the child to an Abbot."

"You either love him, or you don't," Mellitus said. "Where do you stand?"

Merlin's eyes moved to Father Joannicus, and he felt naked. This was not a contest. Paul was not the prize. Merlin was the monk of colorful truths.

"Chief, what is the plan? How shall we defeat the enemy?" Mellitus said, pointing an arthritic finger at Jacob.

"Which one is the enemy? Is it Paul or the Abbots?" Jacob asked before changing the subject. "I heard Ambrose is learning husbandry skills from Gracie."

Merlin laughed. "The big oaf couldn't tell Paul that women were penis-less. I'm sure Gracie will be down at the farm with charts. She used that word at least six times in one sentence. I'm seeing the merit in a woman's touch. Get me some beer."

"That isn't true," Father Joannicus said, turning as if to leave the room. "Paul wanted to know what women had. Ambrose was just trying to put it in discrete terms."

"Rose should know better. Speak the truth in four words. Go ask the Abbot," Jacob said, handing Mellitus the beer he had ordered.

Brother Mellitus laughed again. "Good one, Chief."

Joannicus backed out of the room when he realized that Abbot William was the Abbot of Saint Vincent's Arch Abbey, where he had summer plans to teach. Were they here to shut them down? Where would everyone go?

Joannicus trembled as he leaned against the wall to steady himself. *This is a two-fold disaster.*

What was William looking to do? Abbot William was here to scrutinize him.

"What do you think they want?" Jacob asked, causing Joannicus to jump.

"Seriously, I don't know," Joannicus said, opening the door, letting in the blossom-scented air.

"Are they here to see a miracle or condemn us for our stupidity? Mellitus is right. They are a little late for disapproval," Jacob said.

"There is nothing to disapprove. We are educating a child according to his mother's wishes," Joannicus said. Anger tinted his statement as the gravel crunched under his steps.

"Yeah, as long as nobody mentions the money, it will look good."

Money was not the reason Paul was with them. And no amount of wealth could bring back his prayer life and solitude.

"Which Abbot is here to vet you?"

Joannicus forced his face to remain passive and his fingers not to fuss with his rosary.

Jacob's blue eyes pierced him. He would confess.

"You're right. I asked to teach at Saint Vincent's this summer."

Father Joannicus stopped in front of the pink cherry tree. "It's not general knowledge."

"Just for the summer?"

"Yes, should I stay longer?" Joannicus said. "I'm not taking Paul."

He knew it was a poor ploy to deflect Jacob's questions before he felt compelled to confess his secret desire to change stability.

Unspoken emotions swam between them. Joannicus's cheeks flushed. The wind gusted, tangling scapulars. He felt the pain of his decision. The question rang like the church bells. *Why are you leaving us? Who needed him more, Jacob or Paul?*

"Seriously, just for the summer," Joannicus said, voice cracking, as little pink petals floated down, dotting his black habit.

He had not fully committed to more.

Stability, the word stuck in his stomach like an anchor. The issue is prayer and reconnecting with God. Paul was like a heavy fog keeping him from God. Joannicus walked on the path that forked and paused as the monastery loomed behind him, where Jacob stood with his hands in his pockets.

"What will you tell them?" Jacob asked softly.

"The truth. I will speak the truth," Joannicus said.

He didn't like children, yet Paul wasn't so bad. They had adjusted. Paul was not the enemy.

They continued walking until they stood at the iron gates to the cemetery. Joannicus turned and froze as he saw the Abbots William and Martin approaching them.

"Damn, you go left. I will go right. I am sure we can outrun them," Jacob said.

"Gentlemen," Abbot Martin said. "It's Fathers Jacob and Jonah, right?"

"I'm Father Joannicus. Only Paul calls me Jonah," Joannicus explained.

Abbot William's expression changed to a keen interest. The microscope was on him.

"I'm hoping to have an honest conversation," Abbot Martin said, his voice like the snake in the Garden of Eden. "This community is extremely loyal and closed-mouth. I ask about the boy, and I get smiles and nonsense. This is not sitting well."

Joannicus swore he could feel the earth spinning, and he held his breath.

"Perhaps you need to ask different questions," Jacob said. Sarcasm painted the tips of his words.

"No, I need answers, not biblical quotes. And silence."

"Sometimes an observation is the best answer," Joannicus said, meeting the Abbot's glare.

The wind blew, and yellow leaves floated to the earth.

"Surely, you see the difficulty this presents," Abbot William said in the tone of an over-educated theologian. "How is this conducive to monastic life?"

"It isn't," Joannicus said before Jacob could answer.

"But we are adjusting," Jacob added.

Some of us, thought Joannicus. Several dried branches littered the ground, causing them to step over them. The wind gusted. Father Joe's scapular danced, and he grabbed it, tying it around his waist.

"I have heard minor complaints," Abbot Martin said as Abbot William stood silent.

Joannicus felt like a caged canary being watched by a cat.

"We all prayed, discussed, and voted. The Abbot approved. I took a vow of obedience. It has been three years. Where have you been?"

"Ah, yes, obedience," William said, looking at Joannicus. "Are you aware that Abbot Gordon is being less than that?"

Joannicus exhaled slowly. That didn't surprise him.

Father Jacob shrugged his shoulders. "He is the Abbot, bound by different parts of the Rule. My life is plain, and my vows are simple."

"A child is anything but simple," Martin said, his face soured. "In the last three days, I have seen countless interruptions, excessive noise, not to mention lack of control."

Abbot William fingered his pectoral cross. "Father Jacob, are you deaf to the scandals that the church endures? Some people would harm a child."

Jacob's eyes opened wide, and he raised his hand to his heart. "Really? Here at Saint Alberics? Profiled pedophiles?"

Abbot Martin stopped walking, and Joannicus considered continuing to the monastery, but he stopped. The air prickled around them. Jacob had named the evil in the hearts of men.

"So, are you here to weed out the alleged or confirmed ones?" Joannicus asked, wishing to hold on to the potential goodness of humanity.

"I'm here as God's emissary to help," Martin spoke, his lips thin against his white teeth.

"More like an avenger, using God's name to murder and expel the demons. Oh, please, spare me. You are not God-sent. This is human interference. I have a question for you. How can you presume to know how God works? Are you that holy? Paul is not the enemy. We have united. He is one of us," Jacob said.

Father Joannicus scraped the ground with his foot.

"We all experience the will of God, Father," Martin said. The sweetness of his words sickened Joannicus. "It's my job to ensure we're not all brought down by one man's indiscretions."

Jacob kicked a stray rock, and it bounced down the path in front of them. "One man? You do not know who that is. You cannot undo inaction. The public is outraged when you claim higher ideals and fall short. You must pay the consequences when you turn a blind eye."

"Exactly," William said, his voice taking on a softer tone. "Saint Alberic's will fall short."

The wind blew hard, and the sun ducked behind a white cloud, casting a shadow on the small group.

"Thanks for the vote of confidence. You are mistaken. Unlike the church, we are not blind. If one is doing wrong, we will confront him, not transfer him to some remote parish in a foreign country," Jacob said with a confident loyalty that made Joannicus proud.

He has talked to others to stand firm in their vote and to trust God's plan.

Abbot William chuckled sinisterly. An evil smile graced his face. "Your faith in humanity is commendable but short-sighted. Some men don't live up to the vow of conversion. You cannot go back after we have released the devil. We could avoid this, should avoid this."

"Then they will pay for their actions," Jacob said, trembling and clenching and unclenching his fists.

"Seriously, you're talking as if the evil has happened," Joannicus said, wishing he knew God's plan.

"Statistically, don't you think he's safer in the outside world?" Abbot William asked.

Jacob snorted, stepped away from the group, and headed to the monastery.

"We are men of God," Joannicus said, turning and following Jacob.

"Are you that naïve, Father?" Abbot William asked.

CHAPTER 28
RETURN TO SENDER

Psalm 14:4
He who keeps his pledge come what may.

Father Joannicus entered the church. The sound of his sandals echoed. His chair felt hard as he sat watching the candle in the chapel flicker and sputter, threatening to go out. A slight breeze moved through the open window as voices floated by. Two birds argued over the inch of water in the birdbath. The stained-glass patterns on the rug no longer delighted him. The four walls felt like a prison.

Abbot William had made himself clear. Obedience and stability were the vows he took seriously. The two Joannicus now toyed with. Soon, he would leave under false pretenses. Approved to teach at Saint Vincent's this summer, he planned not to return to Saint Alberic's in the fall. He believed his sin of disobedience would shock others. He suspected Jacob knew of his plans to stay beyond the season. He would miss that smiling face and practical advice. "Follow your heart," was all Jacob said this time.

Father Joannicus rose and walked out of the church into the corridor toward the monastery. He watched his sandaled feet move until Father Pius cleared his throat. A startled glance found him nose-to-nose with the man.

"Sorry," Joannicus mumbled, stepping back.

"No problem. There are many distracted monks today. Jacob came through here ranting about the stupidity of humanity, disclosure, and secrets."

"He views life differently," Joannicus said, suspecting there was more to Jacob's anger. "I'm not sure I understand this visit, either."

They stood at the window, looking at the fallen spring petals dancing in swirls like miniature hurricanes.

"The world is big, our corner limited," Father Pius said.

"Seriously, that doesn't mean we aren't aware of the world. I'm well aware of the church and its mistakes, just as I'm conscious of the history of the state of Montana. I don't assume we are all doomed to continual repetition. What happened to forgiveness, repentance, and conversion?"

"What is your point, and how does it pertain to Paul and the Abbots? I thought they were here on a visit," Pius said, his pleasant face pinched with concern.

"No, I think they came with predetermination."

Rain fell, and the wind forced the droplets against the windowpane. This was not how Joannicus had imagined his separation from Paul.

Father Pius frowned. "He doesn't belong here, even with our monastic history of taking in youth. He's far too young, and this isn't a balanced environment. Where are his peers? Has anyone asked about his other parent?"

Drops raced each other to the bottom of the window frame.

Joannicus shook his head. Paul had school friends, and not every child had siblings. As for a biological father, Joannicus assumed the man was dead.

"He goes to school. There are children and temptations there."

"Joe, you can't have it both ways."

They walked in silence to the community room. Pius was right. Paul didn't belong there. But after all this time, why now? Joannicus had listened to all the reasons Paul must go. He had seen the change in his confreres since Paul's arrival. The evil the Abbots alluded to seemed inconceivable, yet he understood the lurking potential. However, to disrupt Paul's life again struck him as cruel. How many times could a child suffer the whims of adults and be undamaged?

Joannicus felt the tension as heavy as stale incense as they entered the community room. Jacob stood in the corner, arms crossed with the stern look of an Apsáalooke warrior ready for battle. The two Abbots sat together, looking like kings on thrones, and Paul stood before them. The scene had a biblical quality. Only Paul was not Jesus.

"Why do you want me gone?" Paul said, standing with his arms crossed.

"Who told you that?" Abbot William asked. The monks stared into space as if seeing an apparition of Mary.

"Nobody. I'm very smart. I figured it out. Someone important was coming, and I knew it. I thought it was Jesus. But he is not coming this week. Are you sad because you don't have a little boy at your monastery?"

"No," Abbot Martin said emphatically. The shades on the open windows rattled with the breeze.

"Have I done something bad?" Paul asked, moving away from the men toward Joannicus.

"No, you have done nothing wrong," Abbot Martin said. His voice reeked of some vague lie.

Paul said in an exhale of frustration. "Then why are you upsetting my monks?" Joannicus almost laughed aloud at the possessive adjective.

The little Abbot had spoken. A silence deeper than a Good Friday meditation filled the room. The coffee urn moaned. Movement slowed, games stopped, papers lay unread, books bobbed in hands with pages left unturned. Joannicus heard Jacob's teeth grinding. Paul pressed up against him.

Abbot William spoke, chewing each word. "You don't belong here. You need a family."

"This is my family. I have lots of mothers and fathers now. I like it here."

Father Joannicus felt an ache in his heart. This is so wrong—arrangements first and disclosure second.

"No, this is not your family. Not the kind you need. We'll find you a new family," Abbot William said.

"No, thank you," Paul said politely. Pride surged. Paul was learning from them.

"No, child..." Abbot Martin stood towering over Paul.

Darkness clouded Paul's eyes, and his chin quivered as he glanced up at Joannicus. "Father Jonah said this was my home forever."

It was like a nuclear test gone wrong–a picture of the future. He was a child sentenced to an endless life in foster care. Joannicus looked around for Abbot Gordon. The man was absent.

"Father Joannicus was mistaken. This is a monastery for men."

Was he mistaken? No, this was Paul's home.

"I'm a boy," Paul said firmly. "I have a penis."

Ambrose harrumphed, and it sounded like thunder in the quiet room.

Paul heaved a sigh.

"Well, I do," Paul muttered.

"That's fine, but you're a child, not a religious man. We'll find you a nice family with two parents and children to play with," Abbot Martin said, sounding like a dirty old man offering candy.

"Damn it. Damn it all to hell," Ambrose said as he stood, bumping the table and scattering checkers onto the floor. "Enough, this is nonsense. We voted you will not remove this boy."

"It's not advisable to make unrealistic promises. In fact, it's cruel," Abbot Martin said, stepping toward and appearing dwarfed by Brother Ambrose's massive body.

"We made a promise, and we shall keep it," Ambrose said, fists clenching and unclenching by his side. Abbot Martin shook his head. The bells for prayers clanged, and Paul headed towards the door, tugging on Joe's sleeve.

Father Joannicus headed to the church as Ambrose's voice reverberated. "Maybe what we did was wrong, but what you're doing is worse. Benedict asks us to be converted, and I believe we've all adjusted."

"Brother, your compassion is appreciated, but children don't belong in a monastery. We've already decided he's leaving."

The bells for prayers clanged, cold and loud.

"I don't like that man. I wish Jesus had come instead," Paul said as they headed to the church.

"I agree," Joannicus said.

"He can't take me away, can he? I don't want to live with him. I want to live here."

The halls were empty, with no rush of feet or swish of skirts that sometimes filled the walk from the monastery to prayers.

"Well, that is one way to clean house," Jacob said, standing in the atrium. Amusement tinted his scowl. "I will bet you a rosary decade that the self-righteous Abbots do not make it to prayers."

"Good. I didn't want them there," Paul said.

"Why wouldn't they come to prayers?" Joannicus asked, putting his arm around Paul. He hoped the Abbots were not in the hall to hear this rudeness.

"Abbot William said 'No.' Ambrose said, 'So long,' and the community followed him out the door," Jacob said.

"Out the door. Do you mean they left? What about Abbot Gordon?"

"He's granting the leaves," Pius said as he approached them. "The few pennies they give you to start again have left the coffers empty. If you're leaving, hurry, or you will have to rely on the kindness of friends and family."

"Where did they go?" Paul asked. "Are we going too?"

Good question, thought Joannicus, since most of his brethren were not from Montana. Most didn't socialize with the local lay folks. When did Ambrose become so popular that others would follow him?

They turned to head into the church. In the atrium, a man dressed in tails and a top hat, his cane reminiscent of the stage, black with a gold tip, stood before them. Joannicus realized it was Brother Mellitus.

"You, Chief, fetch my suitcase," Mellitus said as he pointed to the large black satchel by the door. "I approve of your unifying plan. A walk out."

"Was not my plan," Jacob said.

"Where are you going?" Paul asked, breaking the spell Mellitus's clothing had cast

Mellitus smiled, tipping his hat. "To hell if I don't change my ways."

PATRICIA MCCLURE

"Can I go with you?" Jacob asked.

Paul gasped, running to the window as a white limousine pulled up to the church.

"You don't sin enough," Mellitus said, walking quickly to his ride. "But here, if you want to improve." Mellitus pressed a folded piece of paper into Jacob's free hand. The driver aided Mellitus into the back. Joannicus saw legs with heels stretched out as the doors opened and closed.

"Is he coming back?" Paul asked as he waved to the smiling old man.

"I don't know," Joannicus said.

"Was there a lady in there?" Father Pius asked. "How did he afford a limo?"

"Yep, two," Jacob said. "I did not realize there was a limo service in this part of Montana." Jacob opened the paper and shook his head. "He is going to hell. That is an escort service called Den of Iniquity."

"Perhaps he saved his allowance," Paul said.

They stood watching the shiny car head down the hill.

Joannicus turned and headed inside to his place in the church. Prayers should have started ten minutes ago, but the place remained silent. Novices entered like frightened sheep. Paul moved from behind the monks to the empty chair next to Joannicus.

"This is scary," Paul whispered.

Joannicus counted ten monks, ten out of a community of forty, and not one of them was the Abbot. Disappointment coated with a deepening sense of sadness enveloped Joannicus. Paul sniffled. Joannicus pulled Paul to his lap.

"It will be all right. Don't fret. They will all return."

They sat surrounded by empty seats. Pius nodded to Joannicus. Tonight, he was the most senior monk present. He would need to lead them in prayer. He allowed Paul to stay beside him as he stood and said, "Oh Lord, come to my assistance." His voice sounded hollow, yet this was the sincerest prayer he had ever prayed.

CHAPTER 29
DOING THE RIGHT THING

Psalm 119:121
I have done what is right and just.
Let me not be oppressed.

Father Joannicus sat in the glow of the desk lamp. He didn't even try to make Paul go to his cell tonight. Instead, after a few tears and a heartfelt blessing of protection for the missing monks, Paul fell asleep on the unmade bed.

Sleep eluded Joannicus. His desperate decision to seek God above all else had caused the community to split, deserting each other and abandoning Paul.

He wondered if he was to blame. Secrets didn't stay secret in a monastery. He had told no one he wanted to move, but he had Abbot Gordon's permission to teach at St. Vincent's for the summer. Had the Abbots talked? The bits of argument spun in his head like dust devils. Everyone chooses. His confreres had left of their own accord. He didn't send them away.

In the stillness, Joannicus searched for his briefcase. He thumbed through his files, selecting what he would need to continue his research for the book he planned to write.

Joannicus unzipped his suitcase and held his breath as Paul moaned in his sleep. Paul would be unhappy to wake up and see him packing. The mass exodus had upset Paul.

He'll bounce back. They will return.

When had God's will become unclear? He recognized what needed to happen but was not joyous with the choice.

Would the community return if Paul left? He looked at the sleeping boy, and a heaviness filled his heart.

If they take Paul, the problem is resolved. He caught his reflection in the night window. The words of Moses came back to him, "Even if he doesn't remember me, I will remember him." Paul would recall him. He tucked the blanket around Paul's shoulders. What did Paul see in him? There was irony in that–God redeeming all humanity–not just his chosen.

Joe had heard others asking the same question: "Why him? He is so stuffy and haughty?"

Jacob's explanation was simple, "You like who you like."

Turning to the large crucifix on the wall, Joannicus sighed.

He didn't dislike the child. He didn't know how to care for the boy.

The others will return. The community was making a statement, a show of loyalty, a protest. They would return, wouldn't they? He looked again at the crucifix as if it would answer him. Joannicus stared at his half-empty suitcase and added his rosary and prayer book.

The sound of the phone startled him. He pushed the suitcase under his desk. Paul groaned and sat up.

"You have a phone?" Paul asked, rubbing his eyes.

Joannicus hunted for the handset. Nobody called his cell because he never gave out the number. This room was his refuge. Messages could reach him through the front desk. Under a pile of books, Joannicus found the object of his disruption. He glanced at the clock; it was time to pray. The bells remained silent.

Paul slipped from the bed and headed out the door.

"Brush your teeth and change your underwear," Joannicus said, picking up the receiver and realizing he sounded more like a parent than a monk.

"Where the hell are you?" shouted the piercing soprano as Joannicus held the receiver away from his ear. She was calling. Did that mean she had forgiven him for his choice?

"Good morning, Barb," Joannicus said.

"What is going on?"

"What do you mean?" Joannicus cradled the headpiece with his shoulder and tried to move the suitcase to his closet.

"Everyone wants a piece of Paul. Why? I'm assuming these people who want to raise Paul are relatives. I haven't heard from those greedy lawyers. They should be on your doorstep. Do I need to remind you of the contract you signed?"

The lawyers. He had forgotten about them. Contracts, like vows, could dissolve. The visiting Abbot did not mention the money. They didn't know about the generous expense account the monastery received for caring for Paul. Perhaps Joannicus could persuade them by greed. What was he thinking? Their abbeys did not need money, yet they did not answer Saint Alberic's plea for help three years ago. Tethered by the phone line, he pushed the suitcase into the closet with his foot.

"I have to go to prayers," Joannicus said, yawning. "I'll call you back."

He hung up, shook out his habit, and pulled it on. Walking to the church, he heard the tap, tap, tapping of heels on the floor—a quick, agitated pace.

Rounding the corner, he smelled the floral scent of Barb's perfume. Joannicus glanced into the darkened interior.

"Nobody is there," Barb said, running her fingers through her messy hair.

"How did you get here so fast?"

She ran her hand through the soft strands of her hair. "Are you that dense? I came for prayers and called from the phone in the sacristy. I saw Paul. He said everyone left, and a mean Abbot wants to send him away."

"It's a mistake," Joannicus said, his voice harsher than intended. "The Abbots from the Confederation are sending Paul away. In protest, most of the community left. The monks will be back."

"Those men have no authority. Paul is staying here. He's happy and doing well. Where are they?"

Joannicus admired her conviction, yet he was not sure Abbot Martin would agree. Martin liked his position and power. She would get nowhere challenging him in that arena.

Morning prayers were empty of voices. Three novices without the sense to join the protest and leave filled the void.

"I need coffee," Joannicus said after prayers. His head felt fuzzy as they walked from the church to the refectory together. The sunlight glared, and birds twittered in the nearby bush. The smell of burned toast greeted them as they entered the kitchen area.

Paul's protests echoed around them.

"No," Paul said. "I'm not going."

"You will go to school," Jacob said. His voice sounded calm, and Joannicus wondered why he had not left.

"What if everyone leaves while I'm gone?"

"Someone will be here."

The doors creaked as they entered the space. Paul and Jacob looked up from where they were sitting. Paul's eyes widened, and his face paled.

"No, don't let her take me."

"She won't do that," Joannicus said, getting coffee and offering some to Barb.

"I'm here to fix things," Barb said, kissing the top of Paul's head.

"Will you bring the monks home? I want them back. They shouldn't have left," Paul said with conviction.

"I'll do my best," Barb said, glaring at Jacob as if this was his doing.

"I want to stay home with you. Do I have to go?" begged Paul as he clung like a blackberry bush to Joannicus.

"The novices will walk you to the bus," Joannicus said, untangling himself from the child.

"Sweetie," Barb said, ruffling the curls on Paul's head. "Everything will be fine."

Paul pushed his plate away. "Everyone better be back when I get home, or there's gonna be trouble."

"Yes, little Abbot," Jacob said as the novices chuckled.

Paul continued with a stomp of his foot, "I don't want to be an Abbot. Abbots are stupid."

"Shush, or you will have to say Hail Marys until you are thirty," Jacob scolded.

"I don't care. They're stupid."

Joannicus cleared his throat, and Paul looked at him. Maybe

the Abbots were acting ridiculous, but the language had now crossed the line.

The novices led the protesting child away. Joannicus helped himself to the odd mixture of bread, cheese, and fruit that Jacob had set out as a meal.

"Not sure it is wise to lie to Paul," Jacob said, looking at Barb.

"I'm not lying," Barb said, helping herself to the blackened toast. "Those stupid Abbots are not removing Paul. There is no cause. If the others don't return, Joe will be here."

Jacob choked on his coffee and looked away.

Barb's head snapped toward Joannicus. Her eyes were ablaze.

"You're leaving?"

Damn Jacob.

"Yes, I'm checking out Saint Vincent's in Pennsylvania."

Barb's voice reverberated. "What's wrong with you? A man so full of passion, don't you see Paul needs you, especially right now?"

"The monks are coming back," Joannicus said. The words hung hollow in the room.

"I recommended this place because of you. Paul loves you. Why, I don't know, but you had me convinced. I had my doubts. A house full of men hell-bent on God. But the Rule, your faith, and kindness have shown me otherwise. I thought you were different– the instructions, our discussions, all the time we have spent together. I thought you cared. Was that bullshit?"

"Cared?" Joannicus said, his voice squeaked.

The room spun. Joannicus placed his head in his hands and rubbed his temples. A wave of nausea washed over him, and the coffee percolated in his stomach.

"Barb, if I misled you, I'm sorry. I was only feeding your hunger for knowledge. You have been helpful when it comes to Paul."

"And to think I liked you."

"You can like me," Joannicus said, sounding too eager.

"I don't think I do."

"Seriously, why not?" Joannicus asked.

"You can't love me or Paul, only your God," she said as she concentrated on scraping butter across the charred surface of the bread. "Have you told Paul that you are leaving?"

"Well, no, I didn't want to upset him. Saint Vincent's is a suitable place where my talents will be welcomed."

The knife in her hand waved, slicing the air between them.

"Your talents? What about your obligation? There is something wrong with you."

How dare she make this about him?

Anger bubbled.

"No, I'm a monk, and you've lied. I thought your interest was genuine, but you were here to judge."

Jacob leaned back in his chair, smiling.

"You're damn right that I was judging you. I was too hasty. You're not what you appear to be. If you were a monk, you would not leave Paul," Barb said with venom.

"This is not about me," Joannicus said, knowing it was untrue. He had to save his soul. That was more important than one child's feelings.

"Yes, it is," Jacob and Barb said in unison. They glanced at each other, shocked at their agreement.

"I have to pursue God," Joannicus said, feeling betrayed by Jacob's truth.

Jacob didn't understand. He knew God had never been Jacob's reason for entering or staying. He was in a crisis of faith. This crisis was his dark night of the soul, his St. John of the Cross moment.

"And you call yourselves fathers. Men," Barb said, her speech quivered with indignation. "Paul deserves better than this. I should've known."

Barb's knife clattered to the plate, and she rose. Her heels thundered as she marched with determination out of the building.

Jacob stood. "Do me one small favor and at least admit to yourself the real reason you are leaving."

"Which is?" Joannicus asked, feeling anger rising.

"You are afraid. Plain afraid."

Jacob's blue eyes bore into him. Joannicus rose, pushing aside the trickle of truth.

"Where does she think she's going?"

"What do you care? You are leaving." Jacob's words ripped into Joe's soul.

Joe's shoulders slumped. He was leaving. The monastery would continue. He planned to leave Paul with the community. Only they were gone. The monks were coming back. He was about to leave. Would Barb do as the visiting Abbots asked and removed Paul? Confusion clouded his thinking, and he hurried across the courtyard to the monastery. The door to Abbot Gordon's office stood open. Joannicus stepped in to see the three Abbots with Barb.

"You've yet to tell me who you are?" Martin said.

"I'm the social worker with the authority of the State and a court order that placed Paul here. You have no power here."

He has authority. Joannicus looked at his worn-out loafers.

"I care nothing for your laws," Martin said. "This is a church matter, not a civil matter." His chin raised high as if smelling the air for the scent of fear. "But now that you're here, you may take the child with you."

Barb's lips became two parallel lines. Joannicus prayed for lightning to strike as he looked from Abbot Martin to his superior. Abbot Gordon sat silently behind his desk.

Barb crossed her arms. "We made a contract. Paul is staying."

"You'd keep him in a place where he's not wanted?" Martin asked, his words dripped with malice.

"Paul belongs here," Barb said. "They voted yes. Paul is loved and cared for here. I'd be a fool to risk this because you don't like this. You've not been here observing–I have. This has been good, right?"

Barb turned from Abbot Gordon to Joannicus. She was directing the question at him. Joannicus swallowed. All the eyes focused on him.

Abbot Gordon was silent.

"Paul is a blessing, a challenge, and an opportunity. We're united in the cause of raising Paul," Joannicus said. He had seen changes. Jacob smiled more and talked about his children, something he hadn't done since their deaths.

Martin fussed with his sleeve. He didn't care. This was not the status quo. The right thing to do was clear. This man would not sacrifice his principles.

"If you somehow displace Paul, it will be on your soul. I'll make this front-page news," Barb said, pointing a finger toward Martin.

"I think not," Martin said, a deep purple rising into his face.

Abbot William shook his head.

For once, Joannicus saw the vast distance between his world and hers. The built-in respect and acceptance did not exist beyond the hilltop.

"Try me. I have placed hundreds of children. Paul stays. You proclaim you're Christian, prove it or face the consequences, and believe me, you won't like them."

Morality. *Good, come back.*

He shifted to see Martin's reaction and instead caught a look of disdain from William.

Contempt for doing what is right didn't seem Abbot-like. But then, he'd never been an Abbot.

Barb pointed to Joannicus, and her polished finger poked him in the chest. "As for you, mister, I should have gone with my first instinct. You might fool God with all your praying, but you haven't fooled me. Higher standards. Don't you think you must live up to those to preach them?"

The room became hot. Joannicus knew his face glowed. Barb walked out of the office, muttering.

"Father Joannicus," Abbot William said, shattering the sudden silence. "We are leaving within the hour."

Joannicus exited and went to his cell. *My cell.* Tomorrow, this space would be empty. Twenty-two years of monastic life would be erased. Would they see him as a saint or as a devil? He guessed that depended on one's version. *Merlin... Mellitus...* he corrected, would spin the devilish view. The weight of his wretchedness felt like a chain around his waist as he grabbed his suitcase.

A novice arrived with a car.

Thank you, God.

He feared Jacob would volunteer to drive Abbots Martin and William to the airport.

"I'm so glad to be going home. You're fortunate, Father Joannicus, that Abbot William is allowing you to join his community," Abbot Martin said as the car suddenly swerved.

"Father Joannicus is not like the others. His faith is solid," Abbot William said. "He knows a child in a monastery is a preposterous idea."

Joannicus watched the novice's ears turning red.

You're the reason he stays here.

Barb's words whipped around in Joe's conscience. She let Paul stay because of him. He was not a good monk. If she only knew.

The second-guessing and the failure to heed God's voice glared at him like the shiny medal dangled from the car mirror.

There was nothing wrong with Saint Alberic's monastery. Joannicus had many teaching assignments and spent months with other communities. Each had a way about them. A peaceful joyousness he had never tried to explain. It seemed right. Every place had issues. Monks who drank too much. Ones who complained. Those who imagined they were humble and saintly. *Even Saint Vincent's had its vices,* thought Joannicus as he closed his eyes, feeling exhausted.

"I wonder if any of them will return," Abbot William said.

"They're not welcomed at my Abbey, such disrespect for all we stand for," Martin said.

"They will return. They are loyal monks," Joannicus said as he opened his eyes and watched the plains roll by. "And human."

"We are men of God. He comes first," Martin said, and it sounded like blasphemy to Joannicus.

"Yes, in all things, may God be glorified," Joannicus said. Only this event did not glorify God. Maybe they were foolish. But they had a blessing. Many older members had become alive and active, like Mellitus. A new patience and listening had crept in because of Paul's presence. That positive change had to be visible to others.

"I, for one, think they need a serious wake-up call," Martin said.

"Even misguided." The word stuck in Joe's throat. "The endeavor is noble. Bad press is not good for anyone. Do we want the public scrutinizing us again?"

William nodded, and Joannicus wondered what was hiding at Saint Vincent's Abbey.

"Seriously, you want to be seen as compassionate," Joannicus said. "You should support them so they will succeed. Then count it with our triumphs."

"Are you suggesting we walk away?" Abbot Martin asked.

"Sort of. I would wait. Time will tell."

"They bear watching," Martin said.

He has such little faith in us.

The sun had set. Joannicus watched the orange disc disappear behind the school building, along with his hope for a summer teaching position at Saint Vincent's or any abbey. He had returned, leaving the Abbots at the airport. The power they wielded worried and frightened him. They seemed resolved to let Paul sit among wolves, but he wasn't sure they wouldn't bring formal proceedings against Saint Alberic's.

Stop worrying about tomorrow. His own words came back to him.

He walked to the monastery and paused outside of the community room. Laughter spilled into the hall. He listened to his brothers discussing the recent events of where they had been and what they had done. Some debate floated over the mirth. Would the confederation take their disobedience to the next level and disband them? They had all come home. They had not abandoned Paul or the Benedictine way.

He was guilty. He'd betrayed them.

They had returned because they had faith. He came back because he could. Eyes turned when he entered.

"Told you he'd return, pay up," Ambrose said to Jacob, sticking his hand out for payment.

"Fine, you have more faith than me," Jacob said.

"Where's Paul?" Joannicus said, missing the child's expected greeting.

Jacob and Ambrose exchanged an uncomfortable glance.

Joannicus trembled. Had Barb taken Paul away? Turning, he

left the room, walked to his cell, and pulled his suitcase behind him.

He should have felt good.

But sadness elbowed through him as if he had lost something important. He entered, pushed the bag to the side, and leaned against the closed door.

"Why do you have a suitcase?" Paul asked as he popped up from under the desk.

"It needed a home. My closet was empty."

The child didn't seem to know what had nearly happened. They had taken a risk for the greater good–for a child.

"Everyone came home. We had a party. I even got presents." He held up a shot glass with a horseshoe on it. "This was better than Christmas. Can we do this next year? I saved some treats for you," Paul said, producing a napkin and placing the wrinkled cloth on the desk. Several cookies, one with a bite, making it a moon shape, and some crumbled barbecue potato chips lay in a pattern of color on the white napkin.

"Thank you," Joannicus said. "Seriously, I think it is bedtime. Don't forget to brush your teeth."

Paul ran out of the room, and Joannicus placed his suitcase in the closet. He had missed the evening prayers. Joannicus knelt, bowed his head, and whispered, "Jacob is right. I'm afraid, afraid of losing You."

CHAPTER 30
MERLIN

Psalm 143:3-4
Lord, what is man that you care for him,
mortal man, that you keep him in mind.
Man, who is merely a breath?
Whose life fades like a shadow?

Father Joannicus walked towards the guesthouse after prayers. The words of Psalm 143 followed him. The heat from the black asphalt pressed at him, slowing his walk. The exodus was a distant memory, and the monastic routine softened the event.

Paul had not attended prayers, but Father Joannicus knew where to find the child. Paul sat in front of the iron gate. The protective eyes of the metal angels, Michael and Gabriel, looked down at him.

"You were not at praise."

Wet, puffy eyes greeted him. "I want to see Merlin."

Joe's resolve grew thin. "Brother Mellitus is ill. He needs his rest."

"Nobody needs that much rest. He needs me."

He doubted that since he knew Paul had much to learn about silent companionship.

"He does," Paul said, with less confidence. "I miss him and need to see him before he dies."

This was just what he feared. Paul had figured out that Brother Mellitus Hearne was dying.

Paul stood, and his face showed a slight bit of contempt. "I'm not stupid. We only pray for the sick and dying."

Trepidation crept into Joannicus. Praying for the sick didn't mean they were dying. Yet Joannicus feared the endless nights of sorrow and grief that came with death.

Paul's brown eyes and wet lashes flashed up at him. "I want to say goodbye this time."

Joannicus took in a painful breath. The senior council decided Paul shouldn't see his friend dying. Joe's conscience stirred at sparing one from death. Sorrow needed closure, as did the living. These two buddies–Joannicus admitted—had balanced each other. Paul was the cautious one, and Mellitus was the playful, adventurous one. Paul nicknamed the man Merlin. Others picked it up, and Mellitus became more Merlin-like, playing the myth for all it was worth. He wove his off-brand of Benedictine spirituality with the Arthurian legend. Mellitus lingered, and Joannicus wondered if he was waiting for Paul.

Joannicus took Paul's hand, and they headed upstairs to the infirmary. The small space had three beds.

The infirmarian, a monk with nursing skills, rose upon seeing them at the door.

"Father, I thought we had agreed."

"We have changed our mind. We would like a quick visit."

The nurse entered the small office, leaving them alone with Merlin.

Merlin lay still, his arms folded across his chest as if already in a coffin. As the door to the room closed, Mellitus opened one eye.

"Grew a heart, did you, Father?" Mellitus rasped.

"Merlin," Paul scolded. "I figured out the words to open the chest."

Joannicus bristled at the reference to himself as being a closed trunk. The old man reached a shaky hand to Paul as color filled his pale, gaunt face. Paul climbed onto the bed next to his old friend and talked about the entire week, informing Mellitus of every detail he had missed. Mellitus closed his eyes, holding Paul's hand, his comments faint and few. Finally, with the news reported, the room grew silent.

Paul sighed. "Merlin, I don't want this."

Mellitus opened his eyes and gazed at the child. "I know, but it's okay. I'm ready."

"I'm not. I don't know what to do."

"There is nothing to do. It's like the weather. Complaining is all we can do. Never forget to complain to make them listen."

Joannicus felt like he was in a Dickens novel, complete with the sweet floral smells wafting through the open window. He wondered if he should leave.

Soft light spilled in as the Abbot entered with a familiar black box that held the items for the last rites.

Was it time?

Mellitus opened his eyes and focused on Joannicus. "Thank you."

An unfamiliar lump caught in Joe's throat.

"Now go away. I'm having my last confession."

Joannicus frowned. Brother Mellitus was a jokester to the end. Paul couldn't hear his last confession. At this moment, did it matter? There was no backing out. The twilight engulfed the room. With shaking hands, Joannicus set the simple wooden crucifix between two beeswax candles. After assembling the small vials of oils for anointing, he struck the match, and it sounded like an explosion crashing over the whispering voices.

Paul leaned close. Tears filled his large brown eyes. Both drew ragged breaths, and Joannicus made the sign of the cross upon Mellitus's forehead.

Paul squeaked, "Merlin, I love you. I will miss you."

Merlin reached out and touched Paul's cheek.

"And I, you."

Then his hand fell away. Paul crumbled into the man.

Joannicus turned. Someone started the litany, and the room became crowded with the community. Nobody tried to remove the sobbing child.

The tolling bell rang a slow ninety-two peals.

Brother Mellitus Hearne lay in state for three days in the church. Each monk, wrapped in his dark thoughts and black habits, sat with the silent Mellitus until his burial. Paul seemed to manage the death with bravery. He followed Joannicus like a lost puppy.

The month-long ritual of remembrance, of keeping Merlin's places vacant—his place in the choir and his seat at the table—had once seemed comforting. Now, the empty places appeared as a daily reminder to Paul of his loss.

Joannicus paced the length of the church as he prayed. The quiet felt creepy, and the darkness threatened to overpower the sputtering candlelight. A familiar, adolescent feeling washed over him; he recognized it as loneliness. Although he had turned that feeling into solitude, there remained a great emptiness, and it echoed when he prayed, "Oh God, come to my assistance."

Father Joannicus sat for an hour, yet no one came looking for him. He glanced at his watch. It was well past Paul's bedtime. Paul never put himself to bed. Curiosity overtook him. Joannicus went to Paul's cell and then his own, but only his rumpled blanket lay on the bed. Puzzled, he stood in the silent hall. He listened for sobs as the soft glow of lights caught his attention. He found Paul in his pajamas with Jacob and Ambrose in the community room.

"God does not have a hit list," Jacob said as he poured sugar into his coffee.

Joannicus hoped that wasn't a cup for Paul.

"Everything I love dies," Paul said in a voice firm with truths.

"That's not true. Father Joannicus is still around," Brother Ambrose said, taking the sugar away from Jacob.

Joannicus stood in the shadows. The great visitation marked him as a traitor, and he found the brand uncomfortably correct.

"I don't like this God. He's mean. I'm going to believe in Father Jacob's God."

"Ah, if ever a man needed his own God," Ambrose said, patting Jacob's arm.

"There is only one God," Joannicus said, making his presence known. "We all worship that one God."

"No, Father Jonah," Paul said in his know-it-all tone. "Father Jacob's God is more powerful than our God. Perhaps he won't take my family away if I pray to him."

"No, no, Little One, there is only one God," Ambrose said, licking something sticky from his fingers.

Paul clicked his tongue and shook his head. Reminiscent of Mellitus. "Don't you even listen to the Psalms?"

The Psalms of the daily office once had comforted and inspired life in Joannicus. A quake of revelation shook him now.

Had he become Mellitus, bitter, and resigned to his monasticism? Psalm 45 echoed in Joe's head. *The Lord of hosts is with us. The God of Jacob is our stronghold.*

"Psalm 145 says, 'He's happy who is helped by Jacob's God,'" Paul said.

"Impressive," Ambrose said, scratching his beard. "Let me try. 'May the name of Jacob's God protect you.'"

"Shout in triumph to the God of Jacob," Paul said.

"I like it," Jacob said. "My favorite is, 'These are the ones who seek the face of the God of Jacob.'"

"That's us," Paul said. "Merlin said you will be warrior chief and a horse thief."

Jacob shook his head. "To be a warrior chief, you must perform four tasks. Be the first in battle to touch an enemy, snatch a weapon in hand-to-hand combat, steal a horse from the enemy camp, and lead a successful war party. We are not at war. So, I cannot become a warrior chief."

"We don't have horses, but you have ermine hides. I saw them."

Ambrose laughed.

"If anything, I am a vegetable and fruit thief."

"That is the truth. So, ermine is for horse thieving?" Ambrose asked.

"Back in the day. And I do not think you were the enemy camp," Jacob reaching for a cookie. "Mellitus gave them to me when I took my vows."

Joannicus walked to the table holding Brother Mellitus's last possessions.

When a monk died, the community reclaimed his belongings. Joannicus looked over the books on theology and Aramaic translations.

"Did you know 18 of 150 psalms have Jacob's name in them?"

Paul turned to Joannicus. "Why does Father Jacob have his own God, and we all have to share one God?"

Ambrose grinned. "He needs extra help."

Jacob slapped at Ambrose as the large man ducked out of reach.

"They wrote the Psalms a long time ago about a man named Jacob, God's favorite," Jacob said. "Certainly not me, but I like your interpretation. I enjoy having my own God."

Brother Ambrose returned with another cup of coffee for himself and one for Jacob.

Paul pouted, visibly disappointed by the news. Joannicus fingered the leather casing of a book, its gold leafing worn thin in places. It was the story of Merlin. He opened it and smiled as he stroked the picture of the white-bearded wizard with a mischievous twinkle in his eye.

"Paul, there's one God, all powerful. We're all stuck with Him. Now it's bedtime," Joannicus said as he picked up the series of leather-bound books. "I have a special story for us to start tonight."

"Is it another saint's story?" Paul asked.

"Nope, God isn't mentioned this time," Joannicus said, leaving the community room.

Paul ran to catch up.

The adventure had not ended. This was only the beginning. The words of Saint Benedict reverberated in Joe's mind: "Always we begin again."

Joannicus moved a chair next to Paul's bed, opened a book, and read, "It was in Warwick Castle that I came across the curious stranger whom I am going to talk about."

ACKNOWLEDGMENTS

This story could not have happened if it weren't for the enriching experiences I had going to St. Martin's College. It was there I learned about Benedictine life. I want to thank the Benedictine monks of St. Martin's Abbey who shared their insights and life with me. Their faith, joy, dedication, perception, and wisdom shine in this series. I was also fortunate to be welcomed as a visitor into many male and female Benedictine communities absorbing the rhythms of their lives and listening to their hopes. Particular thanks to the religious community and Oblates of St. Placid's Priory for allowing me to absorb their values and truths.

I am eternally grateful to St. Martin's Abbey in Lacey, Washington for introducing me to the Benedictine way of life through the program of Benedictine Oblates. I wish to thank Benedictine Fathers Jude Anderson, Alfred Hulscher, Benedict Auer, and Gerard Garrigan for their patience and kindness in answering my many questions about how a monastery works and how one lives the life of a monk.

At Saint Martin's College, I majored in Psychology because at that time Theology was not an option for women there. I have always been interested in why people do what they do, believe what they believe, and what events influence them. During my time at Saint Martin's, I studied and learned about the Rule of Saint Benedict and became an Oblate. In doing so, I learned how to apply the spirit of the Rule of Saint Benedict in my day-to-day living. This philosophy has been a wonderful guide to my ability to weather the changes in life. If you are interested in Benedictine Oblate life find your nearest Benedictine monastery and check out the lifestyle.

When I first started writing this series, it was in the middle of a personal crisis and writing was a way of healing. The theme that men can raise children also weighed heavily on my heart. Books do not impact lives unless they are read and talked about. You will note that if it weren't for my belief in families, this unlikely family of monks raising a child could not have blossomed into the novels that are forthcoming. I have been so blessed to have found my first audience. Thank you to the many friends at the organizations who help children. My husband attends many conferences professionally and I often travel with him. I would spend the days in our hotel room writing my story and socialize with the attendees in the evenings. The dedicated folks in these organizations work diligently for children and families. They took an interest in my creative endeavors, and their curiosity, enthusiasm, and friendship has kept me focused. I wouldn't be writing still if it wasn't for you all. Among those dedicated professionals is Kathy Sokolik, who introduced me to my magnificent editor, Maggie Sokolik.

Endless thanks to Maggie, and all those at Wayzgoose Press, who saw the value of my stories, polished them to the tales you enjoy in these pages and the books to come. Heartfelt thanks to the cover designers. They are awesome.

Thanks to Puget Sound Writers' Guild (PSWG) for their participation, patience, and pride, and all the hours they spent listening to and helping me enhance my story. You have made me a better writer.

None of this would be possible if it weren't for the loving support and patience of my daughter and husband, who made sure I had time to write.

THE SERIES: THE BENEDICTION OF PAUL

Thank you for reading Book 1 of *The Benediction of Paul*. Books 2 - 4 will be published in 2024/2025.

Book 2: *Less Thunder, More Lightning*

Book 3: *All for One Child*

Book 4: *Counting Coup: The Making of an Abbot* (prequel to the series)

www.ingramcontent.com/pod-product-compliance
Lightning Source LLC
Chambersburg PA
CBHW020417260626
47156CB00007B/2427